Atlantic LoveSong

A NOVEL

G. J. SUPERNOVICH

Atlantic LoveSong

A NOVEL

G. J. Supernovich

Published by

RED BARN BOOKS of vermont

Shelburne, VT 05482

This is a work of fiction. The characters, incidents, and dialogues are products of the author's imagination and are not to be construed as real. Any resemblance to actual events or persons, living or dead, is entirely coincidental.

Atlantic LoveSong

ISBN: 978-1-935922-44-5
Cover design by Lindsay Graham

Published by Red Barn Books of Vermont, an imprint of Wind Ridge Books of VT
P.O. Box 636, 233 Falls Road
Shelburne, Vermont 05482
www.windridgebooksofvt.com

Printed in the United States of America

for Patricia, Isaac and Jonah

Acknowledgments

I want to give my heartfelt thanks to all those who have encouraged and supported me in one way or another in the writing of this novel: my mother, Simonne Jeannie Forman; my in-laws, Anthony and Mary D'Andrea; my colleagues, Joyce Thomas, Nancy Means Wright and Michael Kasum; my friends, Sam Fogel, Marianne Brown, Nina Baker, Marc Sherson, Pakamas Suwannipa, Sanga Simanjuntak and Pam Potter; and Massachusetts State Wildlife Photographer, Jack Swedberg, who taught me about the majesty of the eagles.

Also, I want to express my gratitude to those who offered me their professional assistance: the Vermont Studio Center for its invaluable residencies; Castleton State College for generously sustaining my writing development; Lin Stone and the team at Red Barn Books for their fine publishing expertise; Ross Browne at the Editorial Department for his help as a writing coach; and the Seacoast Writers Association for kindly awarding me its Doris Ricker Marston Grant. And, I offer my most sincere and humble thanks to the many gifted novelists, including, Marilynne Robinson, Rick Moody, Howard Norman, Kim Barnes, Larry Brown, Monica Wood and Mary Robison, who over the years taught me fiction writing one-on-one at various courses, conferences and residencies.

One

Why should I care what others think? Yet, here I was, a little nervous, noticing the rumblings in my stomach, not sure what to wear. *Stop, Julia. You're a capable and interesting woman.* I stepped into the walk-in closet and pulled the string of the overhead bulb.

After I pushed aside my khaki park uniforms, business suits, blazers and skirts, I unexpectedly came to my beige wedding dress in a zippered plastic bag. I took the dress from the closet pole and set it on the floor. Yes, it was time to give it away to the local thrift shop.

From among a pile of sports clothes on one shelf, I pulled off my red Boston University sweatshirt, and then hastily put it back. Too co-ed. Besides, it was springtime. I needed something pastel, so I slipped into my lavender blouse and put on a pair of light, summer jeans. A quick glance in the full-length mirror. *Would he notice me? I hoped so, but if he didn't, oh well, it was his loss.*

Back in the bedroom, a second-story room with antique-white walls and a low, angled ceiling, I sat at my dresser. Lavender lipstick to match my blouse. A decorative feather in my hair. Silver earrings. Suddenly, I heard the horn of the ferry headed out of Northeast Harbor. It was the

5 p.m. boat. Time to get going, or I would be late. I buckled my sandals and hurried down the stairs.

The light on the answering machine was blinking. I paused and listened to the message. It was from my brother, Sal. "Hey, Julia. Don't forget the lasagna. *Ciao.*"

My brother was a friendly guy, always had a big crowd at his gatherings, but he was also a jerk sometimes, like not letting me talk about our father, even though our Dad was probably the reason we were so screwed up. At least he let me talk about our Mom. I needed that badly, needed to remember her.

I ran out the door and started my compact station wagon. Soon I was driving north along Somes Sound. Sheer cliffs towered on the right. My mind, like the mind of the naturalist, drifted back in geologic time, and I pictured the slow grinding of the glacier as it carved the deep sound that now divided Mount Desert Island into two. Those in the know called the sound a fiord. I liked the sound of that word. Fiord. Conjured up images of Norway.

Five minutes later, I passed over the bridge at Somesville. The tide was out, and the mud flats were exposed. A white egret with its long neck stood in a shallow tidal pool, poking for food. There were more and more egrets now along the Maine coast. They were making a comeback, like my eagles.

Ah, my eaglets, my babies. It was easy for me to transfer my feelings to them, to call them babies, because I believed that humans and animals were part of a similar family. And, after all, people had been doing the baby-thing forever, treating animals like they were their children, especially dogs and cats. Now, eagles, though, were a bit of a different story. They weren't exactly the affectionate type.

I had last seen my eagles that morning on top of the Park Service's fifteen-foot tower above Seal Cove. There, I had taken deer meat (road kill, not my kill) from my backpack, and had spread it on the catwalk, cutting it up with my pearl-handle knife. When I was done, I opened the trap door of the large cage and tossed it in. From behind a plywood wall with a one-way glass window, I watched the two eaglets. They were young birds, about eight weeks old and two-feet tall. They jumped at the meat at same time, but the larger bird, Maria, jabbed the smaller male, Ismael, with her beak, pushing him away with her flapping wings; then, she seized the meat with her talons and began eating. Ismael found another slice and dragged it off into the corner. They were tough birds. Wild. Free. I loved them.

I let out a laugh, suddenly thinking of David. Would he be interested in my eagles? Probably not. Oh well, I guess that most guys would think that my job wasn't very feminine. *Careful, girl,* I reminded myself. *Don't expect too much from David.* I had only met him once. He ran Zuckerman's Outfitters, a store that carried quality clothes, camping equipment, and sporting goods, exactly the kind of business to do well in a trendy, vacation place like Bar Harbor. The one time I was in his store, I was standing at a mirror, holding one sweater after another up in front of myself, when he walked over with another armful. "Here, try these."

"Thanks," I said. "I guess you saw I was having a hard time choosing."

He watched as I held up the next one, and the next, and he flashed his brilliant smile over my shoulder in the mirror each time, saying, "Gorgeous." Then he left me to help someone in the camping section. Later, I went to the cash register and bought two sweaters, one which he had suggested and one I'd picked out on my own.

So when Sal mentioned that one of his buddies had invited David to the picnic at Pretty Marsh Harbor, I felt a rush thinking he and I might get to know one another better. It was a silly wish, but hey, a divorced woman needed to have some hope in her life.

When I arrived at Pretty Marsh, a dozen of Sal's friends had already settled in at picnic tables. Here too, the tide was out, and platoons of gulls patrolled the seaweedy shore, hunting mussels and crabs. At the far end of the beach a pair of diminished figures hovered, clam diggers, bent over, raking the muddy sand. Bartlett Island wavered jade in the distance.

I looked for a tall, fit man with black, curly hair, and so easily spotted David, who was standing in the food line. I took a place near him and behind Clifton McFarland, an archaeologist from the Park Service. I talked briefly with Clifton about my work with the eagles, but kept an eye on David, who definitely seemed to be showing some interest in me with quick, fleeting glances.

You're David, right?" I said. "From the outfitting store downtown?"

He finished spooning some potato salad onto his plate and nodded gratefully. "That's right. I thought I recognized you. The woman with a dozen sweaters." He let out a short, kind laugh. "Nice to see you again."

"Ah, so you remembered."

"And if you don't mind my saying, that lavender looks great on you. It's Julia, right?"

"Julia DeCarlo."

I put out my hand; he shook it. A good handshake, firm, warm.

"Nice to meet you. Officially, that is."

"What have you got there?" he said, pointing to the foil-covered, casserole pan of lasagna I had just put down on the serving table.

"See for yourself."

He lifted a corner, sniffed. "Mmm, smells wonderful."

We filled our plates and headed for a quiet table where no one else was sitting. I sat across from him, twisted the top off a bottle of beer, and nibbled my food casually while we talked about the campaign to save Maine's North Woods.

"The federal government should stay out of it," Clifton said from behind us before sitting down without waiting for an invitation. "You know, people around here are big believers in state control. Our local politicians and business leaders can handle this just fine."

"I wish I thought that would take care of it," David said, but it's not going to happen. Those guys are primarily concerned with making a quick buck. Now, look at White Mountains in New Hampshire. That's protection. And who did it? Uncle Sam."

"You really feel strongly about it, don't you?" I said.

David nodded. "It's the only world we have."

After a while Sal came to sit at our table. "Say, Julia, the lasagna was great."

"Was is right," David said. He smiled and rubbed his stomach, pointing to the empty plate. "Julia can really cook."

"Oh, Sal. This is David Zuckerman. David, my brother Sal. So Sal, did you really think it was good? Not too salty?"

"Perfect," Sal said, taking a chug on his beer. "Good as Grandma's."

"You really think so?"

"Julia, do you hear an echo?"

Something in Sal's tone seemed to make David uncomfortable because he stood up suddenly and picked up his plate. "Nice to meet you, Sal." He moved away to speak to somebody he seemed to know.

Sal put his arm around me. "So how are you doing?"

"It's been fun talking to David."

"Really? He doesn't seem like your type."

I squinted at him. "Who asked for your opinion?"

He rubbed his forehead for a moment, then let out a short laugh. "Sorry. You know me. I'm just mouthing off." He patted me on the back, stood up and moved near the volleyball net. He shouted, "Hey gang, let's get the game going before it gets dark."

I staked out a spot opposite Sal's team. David took a place next to me, gave me a smile. The game started slowly, relaxed, almost lackadaisical, but we soon started loosening up and hitting the ball harder.

Sal, shirtless, his skin tan from the summer sun, grunted as he leapt to the top of the net and slammed the ball down. His teammates shouted encouragement. He picked up his beer, raised it in salute, and took a long swallow.

We were really starting to get into it when I went for a sideline spike too aggressively. Somehow, my feet slid out from under me, and I fell awkwardly to the ground, scraping my knee along the rocky sand. There was a slight rip in my jeans. David immediately offered me a hand getting up, a bemused expression on his face.

"Thanks." I felt chagrined, my face hot.

"Nice save," he said as our eyes met. "You all right?"

"I'll be fine."

Later, after the game broke up. David took my hand, and ushered me away from the group. "So how's that knee?"

"Forgot all about it, actually. Until now."

"Sorry. I couldn't help but notice that you've got one heck of a serve."

"Played varsity at BU."

"Ah, I should have guessed."

We came to a rocky ledge and sat down, taking in the beauty of the scene. The whole seascape blazed with the orange glow of sunset. It was that intense burst of color so rich, it could only last for a moment before succumbing to dusk.

"Beautiful, isn't it?" David said in a reverent whisper.

"It really is incredible." We sat together for a little while, quiet, comfortable with each other. "Hey," I said. "How about a walk before it gets too dark?"

"Sure."

We crossed a sandbar that led out to a tidal flat where a legion of birds was pecking at shells and plants.

"Look at that one." I pointed to a gull hovering in the air. In a flash she dropped a muscle shell onto a large rock. It broke open, and the gull swooped down to eat it. "Birds are so interesting. You never know what they'll do next." I had my eye on two young gulls who weren't scavenging at all. Several gulls, and not just their parents, came to feed them. I pointed the oddity out to David.

"It's obvious why," he said. "They're relatives. Look. There's Aunt Ruth, there's Uncle Jacob."

I laughed, ran my fingers along his arm. He had solid biceps. Must work out. A good sign. I slid my hand into his. We were headed back along the sand bar when David leaned down for a clam shell, put it in his pocket. "For my daughter, Rachel."

I stiffened and pulled my hand away.

He gently grabbed it back. "Hey, it's not what you think. I'm a single parent."

"Oh…" I smiled uneasily.

"Divorced, not widowed."

"I'm sorry to hear that—no, wait, that sounds awful doesn't it?" Disappointment clung to my brain like thick fog. "What I mean is—"

"I know what you meant," he said, nodding slowly. "But I also know that look you're giving me."

"What look?"

"The *oh-shit* look."

I took a deep breath and tried to relax. The erotic charge I felt sitting close to him just moments ago was fizzling out of me faster than a leaking balloon. *His daughter.* "If you don't mind my asking," I said after a moment, "what happened to your wife?"

"Ah, Alice." He stretched, rubbed the back of his neck. "It's probably pretty crummy to answer that question with a criticism—"

"Oh, I can understand, believe me."

He smiled appreciatively. "She was nice to me at first. But after a year or so, she started telling me what to wear, what to think, even..." He looked down at the ground. "I guess I didn't listen to her very well because she eventually went and had an affair. Ended up moving to Boston with someone smarter and richer."

I squeezed his arm. "Maybe richer, but not smarter."

"Thanks for saying that, Julia." He ran his fingers through his black curly hair. "I could go on, but I'm sure I'm boring you."

"Oh no, I'm interested, otherwise I wouldn't have asked."

He put his hands in his pockets, lowered his eyes and pawed at the sand with his foot. "You know, at first, I was really angry with the guy she fell in love with, which was just absurd. It took me a while to realize that on some level, anyway, he'd actually done me a favor."

"So you're glad she left?" I asked, trying to keep the hopefulness out my voice.

David peered at me for a moment and then nodded hesitantly. "At the risk of sounding like a complete ass, what I really wish is that I had left her first."

"It's amazing what we'll put up with in the effort to pretend we're happy." I said.

He looked at me again, this time appearing rather surprised. "That's exactly it, Julia. Looking back now, I feel like a coward for not facing that and doing something about it."

"You did have a daughter to think about," I said.

"That's what I keep telling myself."

We looked at each other and smiled.

"So, the good news is I have the sweetest, most precious daughter a guy could ever ask for."

"I bet. How old is she?"

"Five. She's held up really well, though it can't be easy on her, losing her Mom for all practical purposes."

"Well you seem like a very patient guy. I bet you're a great father."

"I sure try, but sometimes..."

"Sometimes?"

"Well, a good dad is still a dad, not a mother. Sometimes I feel like I need an interpreter to understand her."

"Ah, an interpreter..."

"Something like that." He pretended to wipe the sweat from his forehead. "Whew, glad I got that off my chest. Haven't talked about it for awhile. Thanks for listening." He smiled mischievously. "Say, you're not married, are you?"

I laughed in spite of the unease the topic brought up. "Not anymore."

"Sorry to ask. I haven't dated since Alice left, so I'm not sure of the protocol, anymore, you know, like what I can ask and what I can't ask when I first meet someone."

I lifted my hair back off my face. "Don't worry about me. I'm not much of a protocol person."

He put his arm around me and pulled me closer, and we resumed walking. "You seem like such a nice person, Julia. So I'm guessing the divorce was all his fault."

I paused before answering. "It's funny you mention that. Because I've thought about the whole issue of blame a lot lately, or maybe culpability's a better word. And here I am one year later, and I honestly have no idea if it was my fault or his."

"If in doubt, I say always blame the other guy." David said. "Did you have kids?"

I shrugged. "Too busy with our careers, I guess."

"Maybe that's for the best."

"Maybe." I felt my stomach churn, knowing that I hadn't told him the complete truth.

The conversation took a less serious turn, and I felt myself relaxing again. David turned out to have a playful streak, and he had me laughing so hard my sides hurt. But then as the last hint of dusk faded from the sky, we stopped walking, and he turned and looked at me expectantly.

The moment seemed to blur, and next thing I knew our lips met in a brief, tender kiss. I drew back to study his face. He gently smoothed down my hair. I breathed in deeply, savoring the smell of the sea, the rhythmic sound of the surf, the erotic tingle that was again running through me.

He touched the feather that I had braided into my hair. "Crow?"

"That's right. Sometimes they call me bird brain, you know."

He laughed.

"But this one is very special. It's a Dumbo feather. When I was a girl, my mother told me I could fly if I just wished hard enough."

"Well, if that's the way it works," he said, pulling me closer as he looked deeply into my eyes, "then I'm going to wish for something very special one day soon."

"Don't tease me," I said.

It was completely dark when we got back to the picnic area, but several lanterns were burning as the others were gathering up their belongings and saying their goodbyes. Someone had to give Sal a ride home; he was apparently soused by the time things wrapped up.

Soon, David and I were the only ones left. We were standing together near my station wagon when David said, "Well, I better go...Rachel's sitter can only stay until eight, but please tell your brother it was a great picnic, okay?"

"He loves compliments."

"Just out of curiosity, does he always drink that much?"

"Oh, today was nothing. He's a terrific guy, but sometimes overdoes the whole party animal thing."

David shook his head knowingly. "He should cut back."

I stepped away, stared hard at David. I heard the irritated edge of my voice: "I'm not into 'shoulds'."

David started to say something, but stopped, his face showing first a twist of anger, then hurt. I certainly didn't want to push him away so soon. I took a step towards him, let my body bob a little like I was dancing to music, and I touched his hand. "You know, I really had a nice time."

He hesitated for a moment. "Me too, Julia." He looked at his watch. "Are you in the book?"

I nodded.

"Great, I'll give you a call, okay?" He looked at his watch again. "Time to go." He kissed me lightly on the lips, and then walked toward his van.

I followed. "Just a minute, David." He turned to me. I drew a finger along the side of his neck. I ran my hand through his hair, kissed his forehead, his eyelids, his lips. "I did have fun."

I slid my hand under his shirt and ran my fingernails up and down his back. "Are you sure you have to run off?" I kissed his ear.

He stiffened up and stepped back awkwardly to hold me at arm's length. "Sorry, but I'm afraid so. Responsibilities, you know."

"Oh." I slipped into my car, sat still, watched his taillights disappear into the night. I was too excited to drive, and too frustrated. There was a strange feeling in the space where he had just been standing. I reached out the window and waved my hand in it. Nothing. For a surreal moment, I wondered if he'd even been there at all.

Several days after the picnic, Deb Gianelli and I took a table near the window in Galyn's Galley in Bar Harbor. Deb was a good friend from the Park Service, also divorced, and someone whose friendship I always enjoyed. We ordered some red wine before dinner. I took a sip, glanced outside at Main Street. The lights on top of the black lampposts were starting to flicker on. I turned to Deb. "So break it to me gently. What's happening with the Coasties?"

She circled her hands around her neck and pretended to strangle herself. "One of the engineers changed his mind about the wharf. Said our dredging plans were confusing. So it's back to the drawing board, I guess."

"Sorry to hear that."

"Me too. But hey..." She paused to straighten the bra strap beneath her blouse. "Oh, by the way, I managed to get out of the office for a few hours yesterday and spent some time working on a trail project with your brother. He seems like a really nice guy."

"I'm glad to hear that."

"Is he dating anybody?"

I let out a short laugh. "Sorry, but I'd be the last to know. Besides, he doesn't..." I stopped myself. No loose lips from me, especially about my brother.

Deb sat upright, waved her hands in the air a little, her silver bracelets jingling. "Okay, so what about this guy Sal told me about. He said you disappeared with him at the picnic."

"You mean David?" I twirled my finger around the rim of the wine glass. "We took a walk is all, really had a good time together, but..."

"But what?"

"He has custody of his five-year-old daughter. It might sound heartless, but that's a big turnoff for me. I didn't tell him that, though. Who knows what'll happen? It's been five days, and he still hasn't called."

"David? Someone in town?"

"He owns Zuckerman's Outfitters."

Deb's face lit up with recognition. "I know exactly who you mean. Friendly guy. A hunk, too."

I picked up a menu. "What do you say? Shall we order?"

Soon the waitress brought us broiled haddock and salads. I set my napkin in my lap and relaxed. Deb was so easy to talk to. I didn't have to hold anything back. I leaned forward, whispered to her. "What do you think of the guy a few tables down in the tan blazer?"

She glanced around, and then faced me. "Not bad."

"Have you ever made love with someone like that?"

"Can't say that I have. Men like that usually want the perfect-looking babe, and I don't fit the package." She tapped her nose. "Kids used to call me Pinocchio."

"Stop Deb. You're a pretty woman."

She blushed. "You're sweet to say that."

I smiled, then took a long sip of wine. "This may sound a little weird, but do you ever feel really sexy, and want to do it with anyone, even a stranger?"

"Why, you want to do it with that guy?"

"And David too." I nodded, feeling a pounding in my head. "Guess I'm a little confused. It's that time of the month, you know. Raging hormones." I let out a short laugh. "Besides, I'm not too big on intimacy these days. Terence killed that dream. You know what intimacy is? It's some guy sucking the life out of you."

"I'm with you on that, honey." Deb said, and we clinked glasses.

Two

"It's okay little chicks. Uncle Sal's here to take care of you," Sal said with a laugh, as he climbed the ladder of the Park Service's fifteen-foot, eagle tower. I followed behind him. On his shoulder rested a five-gallon, plastic water jug. He held the jug with one hand, and used his other hand to pull himself up the rungs, letting out a few grunts as he ascended. Upon hearing Sal's voice, the eaglets started whistling in high tones, leaping and flapping against the cage.

Once on top, I opened a small wooden door in the plywood wall of the large cage, and I retrieved the eagle's water pan. After dumping out the old water and cleaning the pan, I poured in fresh water from the jug. Meanwhile, Sal tossed in deer meat; then, we watched Maria and Ismael eat and drink through the one-way glass window.

"That's a weird name, Ismael," Sal whispered.

I also spoke in a hushed voice. "Stuart Nudelman picked it. You know him, the state wildlife biologist. Named the eaglet after his grandfather."

Soon, Sal sliced up the rest of the meat, and we dropped it inside the cage. Sal nudged me. "So, Sis, how's the new boyfriend?"

"You mean David?"

"Yeah, Mr. Curly Hair."

I was used to his teasing, and I wasn't going to let him get to me. "I'm still waiting to hear from him."

"What a surprise."

"How's that?"

"He seems a little uptight, that's all. What's in AA, or something?"

"AA?"

"Yeah, he wasn't drinking at the picnic."

"How would you know?"

Sal let out a short laugh. "It means...yeah, what it means is...he doesn't know how to have a good time, and that's why..."

"Get off it, Sal. Would you? You're acting stupid. When he calls, I'll let you know. Okay? Besides, I got something else on my mind." I gave him a serious look.

His face tightened. "Please, don't tell me."

I hesitated for a moment. "I've been dreaming of Dad."

He clenched his teeth. "Sorry to hear that."

"I know you don't want...Oh, what the heck? I may as well just ask you. Do you ever think about him?"

"I try not to."

"Mom had told me he was in New York."

He shook his head. "I was hoping he was in hell."

I knew he would talk like this. "He had sent her a postcard."

"Oh, fuck."

"She gave me his address before she died."

Sal let out a groan.

I lowered my eyes. "This is going to sound strange, but she told me our life with him wasn't always bad, said there were some good years. Sometimes he was a lot of fun."

He turned his back to me. "You know, Mom wasn't herself near the end."

"Level with me, Sal. Can you honestly say you never loved him?"

He faced me, his voice growing steadily louder. "I was ten years old. What did I know then? A bag of chips cost fifty cents. I'm older now, and a lot fucking wiser."

The eaglets leapt from the floor to the perch, looking around with curious gestures.

"Whisper, Sal. Remember, we don't want them bonding with humans."

"I know, I know."

"Maybe we should go down to the campfire and talk."

"I'm done talking."

"Please, Sal." I climbed down and moved to a smoldering campfire near his tent. Soon, he joined me. "What I'm trying to do..." I touched the bun in the back of my hair, pushed the hawk feather back into place. "...is to figure out why Mom wanted us to get in touch with him."

He pawed his foot on the ground. "You really believe that?"

I fixed my eyes on the fire. "I've been thinking about this a lot, Sal. Maybe it's time to face him."

"Face him?" He choked on the words. "You'd have to be crazy to see that asshole. You know what's going to happen, don't you?"

I picked up a stick, stirred the coals of the fire. "It wasn't entirely his fault."

"Bull shit."

"He had a disease."

Sal squatted on the ground. "Poor Dad. Is that what I'm supposed to think?" Sal took out his knife and jabbed it in the ground several times. "I'll never forgive him."

I was trying to get him to come around a little, for his own sake. I paused, not sure what to say next. "What if he knocks on your door one day?"

He took in a deep breath, blew it out. "I hope he doesn't."

"Maybe he's changed."

Sal held out his hand, palm up. "You see this?" His hand was shaking. "And at this moment, all we're doing is talking, and he's far away from us. If I ever saw him...Christ, Julia, who knows what I might do?"

He smoothed down his black hair, straightened out his pony tail. “I can’t talk anymore.” He went to the tower and climbed up.

At first I busied myself straightening up the campsite. Later, when I went up to the top of the platform, Sal was observing the eaglets through the one-way window. He turned and faced me: “Don’t say—”

“I got the picture, Sal.”

“About time.” He turned back to watch the eaglets, and I stood next to him, looking through the glass. The birds were perched on a branch, preening their feathers. I smelled their feathery odor, a pungent fragrance, almost otherworldly. I dreamed about them often, dreamed I was flying with them.

Suddenly, a distant whistle came from the north, and they bolted upright. I heard the sound, but I saw nothing. I reached for my binoculars and focused. An immature bald eagle was flying our way.

As the bird came closer, Maria and Ismael watched it with great intensity; then, in a flash the bird dove towards the water, her wings pressed tight against her body. When she pierced the surface with her talons, she grabbed a fish and lifted into the air.

“Home run,” Sal whispered.

“And don’t forget the mustard.”

He raised his eyebrows, gave me his ‘you’re weird’ look.

“You know. Home run. Ballpark. Hot dogs. Mustard.”

“Oh, I guess I never learned eagle talk.” He knocked the top of his head with his knuckles.

The eagle flew off, disappeared in the pines of Moose Island; then all at once Marie and Ismael leapt at the bars, flapped against them, pulled at the wooden poles with their talons.

Sal tapped on the wall. “Hey, stop it.”

“They just want some friends.” I whistled to them in a high pitch, and they relaxed and fluffed out their feathers. “It won’t be long, my pretty birds.” Soon, they settled back on their perch. Sal grew restless, descended to the ground, and began gathering kindling. I remained behind, staring out at the sea.

Seal Cove shimmered emerald, one of hundreds of coves along the rocky shoreline of Acadia National Park. Beyond in rough water, a white lobster boat bobbed up and down, its captain turning a crank and pulling up a lobster trap. To the east the summit of Bernard Mountain vanished into the misty clouds. I closed my eyes, wrapped my arms around myself in an embrace. Tasted salt on my lips. Listened to the wind murmuring in nearby spruce and fir trees. Heard the waves pounding against the rocks.

Later that afternoon I drove home to my gray-weathered Cape cottage in Northeast Harbor. For supper I sat at the kitchen table, picking at leftovers and drinking wine; then, I poured myself another glass and went into the living room. Put on some music by Loreena McKennett. Sat in the rocker. Moved to the sofa, fidgeting, thinking. Sal was my brother, and I needed his help with our father. That's what brothers are for, right? And why hadn't David called? Problems. Too many problems. By the time I climbed the stairs to my bedroom, I had drunk three, maybe four glasses of wine. Who was counting, anyway?

In bed I twisted beneath the blankets, unable to fall asleep. Maybe an hour passed. I turned on the light, propped myself up and tried to read some poems by Emily Dickinson. After a few minutes, I set the book aside. I lit a candle and switched off the light. The flame swayed in the breeze that was blowing through the open, gable window. Candlelight flickered on the angled ceiling.

I took a wildflower, a Maiden Pink, from a vase on my night table. Pressed it close to my lips. Sweet. Delicate. I used to think I was that. Then Ter came along. That bastard. Sure, he was good-looking, and he knew it. Loved to stare at himself in the mirror. What a catch.

I closed my eyes, trying to drift away to a happier time. I remembered Luke, an old boyfriend, and I imagined that he and I were making love. He would glide over me, sweeping his long blond hair from the top of my head down to my toes. How I shivered when he did that. Now, as I thought about him, I eased my hand between my thighs and began to press, gently at first.

When I awoke in the morning, my head was pounding, and my mouth tasted like dry sand. *Damn, not again.* After taking two ibuprofen tablets, I sat at the kitchen table and nursed a cup of coffee; then, in a flurry I wiped the kitchen counters, mopped the floor and vacuumed the living room. I was following my mother's advice: "When you're down, get busy."

Three

David finally called. He had been busy. Still was, but we decided to meet for a quick lunch in the town park near the gazebo. He arrived with coffee and sandwiches from Whitmore's, sat down on a bench next to me. Below us Frenchman Bay stretched towards distant peninsulas. A schooner and a whale-watching boat were headed out to sea from the town wharf. Nearby in the park a mother pushed her two girls on swings. David touched the sleeve of my blouse. "You look nice, Julia."

"Thanks." I had taken care to choose a white cotton blouse that reflected light to my face, and I twisted two silver hairpins into my hair. I set my hand on his. "It's good to see you, again, but maybe we should find a table indoors." I pointed to the dark clouds in the sky. "Looks like we're in for a downpour."

He shrugged. "Not to worry." He unwrapped a tuna salad sandwich and gave it to me.

I took a bite. After a moment, I asked, "So David, I'm curious about your accent. You're not from Maine, are you?"

"Portsmouth, New Hampshire."

"I was thinking Boston."

"That's where you're from, right?"

"West of the city. Milford. Ever hear of it?"

He shook his head.

"So, we're both flatlanders."

"I've been called that. People on Mount Desert Island don't seem to mind if you're from 'away.' Besides, I'm happy here. And, business has been good." He took a bite of his chicken-on-rye. "My Dad had his doubts about the store. Felt it was too far from the Portsmouth operation. But I talked him into it."

"Operation?"

"We have four stores. My Dad runs the one in Portsmouth. My sisters take care of things in Portland and Brunswick."

"Wow, the American dream."

He let out a laugh. "We've been lucky...So Julia, what are you doing in Bar Harbor?"

"Got a good job offer. The Park Service agreed to let me raise and release eagles, something I did in Massachusetts. It's my passion, if you know what I mean?"

"Passion?"

I searched for a better way to explain it. "I guess you could say it's my purpose in life. I'm trying to save the eagles from extinction. We humans have been pretty tough on them."

"I've read something about that. What's the situation in Maine?"

I shook my head sadly. "Bad. Fifty years ago, there were thousands of eagles in Maine. Now they don't even nest here. The ones you see in Acadia are young migrants. They'll eventually nest in another state where they took their first flight."

He thought for a moment. "How are you going to get them back in Maine?"

"We're taking chicks from other states, then we raise and release them here. In maybe five years, when they're adults, they'll come back and nest."

"That's terrific. I can see it's important work. I'm impressed."

I glanced at him, wondering if he was sincere.

"Really, I mean it. You're so young, but so accomplished."

I blushed. I never was good at handling praise.

We ate our sandwiches in silence, then he said, "Maybe you'll think I'm being too personal, but I've been wondering about your age?"

I crossed my arms over my chest. "I'll tell you if you tell me."

"Twenty-six," he said without hesitation.

"I've changed my mind." I pretended to cover my eyes with my hands. "What the hell. Some women wouldn't tell you the truth. I'm twenty-nine. Is that too old?"

He touched my cheek, smiled. "You look twenty-one. Your face is..." he smiled, "so delicate...beautiful."

I kissed his hand and glanced up at him sheepishly. "Can you tell I'm feeling attracted to you? Attracted and scared."

"No surprise. The same for me, otherwise I wouldn't have called."

I rested my head on his shoulder, closed my eyes, felt warm inside. All at once the sky let loose in a torrent of dime-sized drops. David popped open his umbrella and pulled me close. The wind ripped in every direction and splashed us with water. We ran to the octagonal bandstand in the park, scrambled up the steps.

We were laughing, shaking the water off ourselves. David embraced me; our lips met, playfully. I nestled my chin in his neck, nibbled his skin. "Ummm," I murmured. We stood together like this; then, I drew apart.

I circled around the octagon with my hand outstretched into the rain, catching the water as it spilled off the roof into puddles on the ground. Mist from the downpour drifted into the gazebo like fog. Rivulets ran down the sidewalk. I went to David. "Rain makes me happy."

"Happy?"

"Reminds me of my mother. Rain was like gold to us. We'd sit on the porch and watch it falling, or we'd put on our raincoats and walk in it." I hesitated. My voice caught. "She died of stomach cancer last year..."

He stood up, took my hands. "I didn't know. You didn't tell me. I'm so sorry, Julia. Just last year? It must be hard."

He pulled me close. After a moment, I moved away and paced. "It's so unfair, losing her..." I brushed my knuckles at an errant tear.

He came to me, stroked my hair, eased me down on the bench. I avoided his eyes. "It's so sad. She was a wonderful woman. She was divorced with two young kids and no money. She found us a clean, cheap apartment in Worcester, took a job at a local factory. Worked the nightshift. Assembled circuit boards. Sal and I had to sleep alone. That was scary. I was only ten; he was eight."

David squeezed my hand. "You grew up fast."

"Didn't have a choice. We waited for her to come home from work in the morning. She made us breakfast, sent us off to school, then she slept a few hours. At noon she woke to mend clothes for extra money."

"Such a hard worker."

My eyes glowed with pride. "She sacrificed everything to raise us. In the evening, she cooked us supper, and after, helped us with our homework. At nine we went to sleep, but she was up at eleven to get to work by midnight."

He put his arm around me. "What a grind."

"They were rough years, but they were some of the best. Safe and happy."

"If you don't mind my asking, where was your father?"

It took a moment for his question to register. "It's a boring story. He was a jerk, and my mother left him." *Why scare David off so soon?* I stood up, needed a distraction. I did my best imitation of the waltz around the gazebo, and I began to sing: "I'm singing in the rain..." I took his hand, pulled him up and led him in the dance. He was laughing, and I was singing, and we were dancing. After a little while, he stopped me, held me at arm's length. "I won't be bored by your story, really."

I shook my head. "Why so many questions?" I tickled him. He retreated. I caught him. He was laughing, holding up his hands; then, he pulled me down on the bench and held me tightly, gave me a serious look.

"I'd be wasting your time" I said.

"But you've got me wondering."

I stood up, looking out at the bay and the rain. "Okay, here goes... When I was..." I put my finger to my lips, chewed on my nail.

He sat upright, his face attentive and caring.

"When I was girl, my father...He was schizophrenic...He was drinking heavy. Paranoid. Getting into fights at work. Beating my mother. Sometimes every day. Sal and I saw it all. One day he went to get his gun from the basement." I paused. "My mother got us out of there just in time."

"My God, Julia. It sounds like a story in the news. I always think these things happen to other people. I'm terribly sorry. Thank goodness you're mother got you guys out."

I folded my hands, held them under my chin, felt my shoulders stiffen. "She had to put him in a mental hospital. A place for veterans. It was awful. The police. The court hearings. He was in handcuffs, glaring at my mother. He got better. Then he got worse. Had to be committed again. That's when my mother left him for good. Later, when he was out, he just up and disappeared. I haven't seen him since. Just before my mother died, she gave me his address. He's in New York City." I paced more. I was standing with my back to David. "I wish I hadn't told you. I'm ashamed of that part of my life."

He came to me and pushed my hair to the sides of my face. "Then you don't know me very well. I would never judge you."

I lowered my eyes. "Thanks, David. I wasn't sure you'd understand."

He put his arms around me, and I burrowed into his embrace. It had been a long time since someone had held me. I felt the tears come to my eyes. I wiped them on my sleeve.

"Say, you're shaking." He touched my blouse. "No wonder. You're all wet. Let's get you home and changed before you catch a cold."

I was relieved we were leaving. I was afraid he might ask me more about my past, might ask about my scars.

Soon we arrived at my house. I was proud of it. I had worked hard to come up with the down payment for the mortgage. I gave David a tour. Downstairs: a kitchen with vintage Westinghouse appliances, and a living room with French windows and a fieldstone fireplace. Upstairs: one bathroom and one bedroom with white walls, a low, angled ceiling, and white lace curtains and lampshades. There was a black and white photo of my mother on the night table. David picked it up, sat in a recliner near the gable window and looked at it.

I went into the closet and took out a violet print dress. I tossed it on the bed and went to David, ran my fingers through his hair. He stared up at me with wide brown eyes. I wanted him at that moment; after all, he had listened without humiliating me.

I stooped down, wet his lips with my tongue; then we lost it and kissed wildly. I pulled away, stood up, and slowly began to unbutton my wet blouse. I took it off, looked for his reaction. He stared at me with disbelief, with longing. I took off my jeans, then opened my arms wide. Did he want me like I wanted him? I pressed against him, squeezed him tightly.

He ran his hands over my legs, my chest, my arms. Our mouths met in a rush. I felt free, giving. Then suddenly, he collapsed in the chair, hung his head low.

I lifted his chin with my fingers. "Is something wrong?"

He said nothing.

I knelt before him, rested my head in his lap. "What are you doing, David?"

He stood up, moved to the bed and sat down. He folded his hands, leaned forward. "Give me a second, okay." He closed his eyes, let out a deep breath, then looked at me. "I'm sorry." He reached out his hand. "I'm just as excited as you." He pointed to his pelvic area. "I know I'm acting weird, but I don't feel good about this."

"You're religious?"

"It's not that...I...I want to find the right word." He flopped backwards on the bed. A moment later he sat up. "I don't want to hurt you, and I don't want to sound like a jerk. It just feels...too soon."

I rose from the floor, covered my chest with my arms. I went to the closet, put on a red, terry-cloth bathrobe; then, I sat next to him on the bed. "No offense, David, but look what you're doing. I'm..." I threw my hands up in the air. "Frustrated as hell." I picked up my blouse and jeans off the floor and threw them into a wicker hamper. "Am I supposed to feel guilty?"

There was a long silence. He ran his fingers through his hair. "Look Julia, I like you. You're intelligent. And damn sexy." He took a pillow from the bed, put it in his lap and began fumbling it. "But what happens if I get serious? Are you into commitment? I just went through a bad divorce. And to tell you the truth, I'm afraid of getting hurt again."

I went to the dresser and brushed my hair in front of the mirror. I saw his reflection in the glass. He was rocking back and forth on the bed, his face confused, but honest. Was he for real? I faced him. "Okay, I'm sorry. I get cranky when I'm frustrated." I tapped the brush against my chin. "It must've been hard for you to tell me that." I sat next to him on the bed. "But still, David, this isn't a very good beginning."

He set his head on my shoulder. "Well, what should I do?"

A long pause.

He pulled back, and he stood up. "Let's go over to my place? I want you to meet Rachel."

My stomach tightened. "So soon?"

I saw Rachel for the first time from David's kitchen window as she bounced out of her babysitter's car. She was wearing a yellow T-shirt with a green turtle on the front. In a flash she burst through the kitchen door with a wide smile.

David stooped on the floor, held out his arms. She ran to him, kissed him on his lips.

"How's my sweetheart?" he asked.

"I missed you."

He hugged her, then took her by the hand and came to me. I was slicing cucumbers at the kitchen counter. "Rachel, this is my friend, Julia."

I bent down and reached out my hand to shake hers.

She hid behind her father's legs, peeked around once to glance at me.

He scooped her up. "Julia's going to have dinner with us."

Rachel said nothing and clung to him.

I held out a cucumber slice. "Would you like a bite?"

She shook her head.

I put it in my mouth. "Hmmm. It's good."

David took another slice, handed it to her, and she ate it. He stroked her hair, set her down. "Guess what? I bought you something today from Sherman's." He took a book off the top of the refrigerator and gave it to her. It was a *Winnie the Pooh* book.

She leafed through it quickly. "Thanks, Daddy."

He tapped her on the behind. "Now go wash your hands. Supper's almost ready."

Rachel darted upstairs.

"She's adorable." I touched David's hair. "I see she has your curly hair."

When we began eating at the dining room table, I placed my hand on Rachel's and was about to ask her a question. She jerked her hand away, almost as if she had touched by a hot iron. She looked at me with a bewildered expression. I said, "I just wanted to ask you about your day with Vanessa."

She faced her father, raised her eyebrows. "You tell her, Daddy, okay?"

"Since when can't you talk?"

Rachel said in a barely audible voice, "We went to the movies."

I was curious what they saw, but decided not to push it.

After dinner she took a box of horses from the closet and arranged them under the table near her father's feet. I moved my chair back a little and watched her.

She had a dozen plastic horses, all different colors, brown, black, white, tan. The big ones stood a foot tall. She pretended the lower cross-pieces of the table were a corral. She went to the kitchen and returned with a bowl of water for her horses. "Be a good little horsy and take a drink." She laid them in a corner and covered them with silk scarves. "Go to sleep now."

I sat on the floor next to her and picked up a large brown horse. "What's his name?"

Rachel puckered her lips, squinted her eyes, but didn't answer.

I put the brown horse back in the corral. I made him paw at the ground, then raised him over the fence. "Oh no, the horse has escaped. Help me catch him."

She hesitated for a moment, then took a small black one, pranced her around the corral. The horse whinnied and reared on her hind legs; then crawled under the cross piece of the table and ran to the brown horse. I lowered my horse, had him muzzle the black one with his snout. I lifted him to Rachel's cheek, had him muzzle Rachel.

Suddenly, Rachel withdrew to her father, burying her head in his lap.

Disappointment weighed me down like a lead coat. I returned to my chair, pushed my salad around with my fork, glanced at David and Rachel. Maybe Ter was right about me and kids.

David stroked Rachel's hair. "Why are you acting so shy?"

She sat up, put her arms around his neck. Soon I started to clean up the table, and Rachel began whispering into his ear. When she finished, David said, "Oh, I see." He lifted her up. "Julia, if you don't mind, I'm going to put Rachel to bed. We're going to read a bit. We always do. Will you be all right?"

"Sure," I lied, putting on an upbeat face.

They started towards the stairs.

"Good night, Rachel," I said.

She didn't respond.

They climbed the stairs, and I went into the kitchen, putting things away and washing the dishes.

Later David found me in the living room in a rocker looking at a clothing catalog I had found on the coffee table. He said, "She's asleep. Sorry about the way she acted. She's not usually like that. You okay?"

"I thought that..." I pushed my hair to the sides of my face. "I guess I'm feeling rejected."

He came behind me, rubbed my shoulders for a moment. "See what I mean about an interpreter?" He moved towards the kitchen. "Say, can I get you something to drink? Wine? Tea?"

"Tea sounds good."

When the tea was ready, we sat on the front porch in a wicker sofa, sipping from our mugs, not talking. It was dark, and our faces shone yellow from the streetlights. A branch of lavender lilacs stretched over the porch railing and waved gently in the wind. I pulled the branch towards me, smelled it. I was a child again, smelling the lilacs alongside my sandbox in Milford. Once, I had overheard my father boasting to his cousin about the shrubs: "Didn't pay a penny for those lilacs. You know that Jewish cemetery in Framingham? Got them there. Free." As I thought about his actions, I was ashamed, and I wondered where my father's mental illness ended and his anti-Semitism began.

"Something wrong?" David asked.

I rubbed my eyes. "Just tired."

"Dinner was stressful." He breathed in the warm vapors from his tea. "You know, I never brought anyone home before. Maybe I jumped the gun? I should've thought of Rachel's feelings."

"She seemed upset."

"She was afraid."

"Afraid?"

"Remember when she was whispering to me?" He paused, twisted his neck around, then back the other way. "She told me her mother said if another woman ever came into the house, she would never visit Rachel here again."

"That's awful. You think she really said that?"

"I hope not."

I picked up my tea, sipped it for a moment. "Why don't you ask your ex?"

He raised his eyebrows. "Wish it was that easy. Alice would turn it into a shouting match."

"That's not fair to you, or to Rachel."

He nodded. "Well, maybe I'll catch her in good mood."

"How often does she see Rachel?"

"About once a month. One month she comes to Bar Harbor for the weekend. The next month I take Rachel to Boston."

"She stays here, in your house?"

"Oh no. In a hotel. We're divorced, you know."

I straightened the silver pins in my hair. "I've never dated a guy with a child before." I rested my head on his shoulder. "I don't really know what to say to Rachel."

"You were very nice."

I looked up into his eyes. "Maybe I tried to hard?"

He stroked my hair. "It wasn't your fault." He stood up, sat on the porch railing. "Hey, it wasn't a total disaster. Maybe now you see how my life is different than yours?"

"Because you're a parent?"

"With a lot of responsibility." He shook his head, let out a knowing laugh. "But Rachel's given me a lot of joy, too. There's a word in Yiddish that explains it perfectly. English doesn't have a word that works. *Naches.* The joy a child brings a parent. Like, some nights she doesn't want to go to sleep. So we sit on her bed, and I hold her in my lap. She snuggles against my chest." He pretended she was there and stroked her hair. "I sing a lullaby: 'I've a Pair of Poodles.' It's the same lullaby my mother sang to me. Pretty soon, she begins to snore, a little gurgle in her throat. I take her hand and kiss her fingers. That's *naches.* Do you know what I mean?"

"That's so sweet." I took a sip of tea. "Say, this chamomile is perfect."

He sat next to me on the wicker sofa, put an arm around my shoulders. "You know, I like your name. Kind of like Romeo and Juliet. It's all those vowels, you know. Julia DeCarlo. So, you're Italian."

"Irish," I joked.

He laughed. "And Sal is short for..."

"Salvatore."

"He's okay with that?"

"Once a guy in high school made fun of his name. They had to pull Sal off the guy before he pounded him into a pulp."

David gritted his teeth, pretending to be afraid. "I better be careful."

I laughed.

He paused. "So, you were raised Catholic?"

I nodded.

He tapped my hand. "You know I'm Jewish?"

"With a name like Zuckerman?"

He let out a quick laugh. "I dated a Catholic woman once in college. Fell in love with her. Then she wanted to convert me. It ended very badly."

I tugged on his hair. "You and I are so serious today, David. Family. Religion. What next?"

He smiled. "Serious is okay, sometimes. Better we should talk about these things."

I took his hand and kissed it. "You're right. Let's put our cards on the table. Here's my queen." I pretended to put the card on his thigh. "You don't have to worry about me. I'm not the missionary type. Not even a practicing Catholic. So, are you religious?"

"I go to temple on holidays."

"I went to Shabbat services a few times at BU. I was dating a Jewish guy."

"You don't say?"

"Have you ever been to Mass?"

"My mother would kill me."

I pulled back a little "She's Orthodox?"

He stood up, stretched his arms upward. "Reform. But that's my Dad's choice, not hers."

"And when she finds out I'm Catholic?"

He hesitated. "I like you. That's what matters."

I believed him. It was foolish of me. Little did I know at the time how much trouble his mother would cause.

David traced my nose and lips. "I've got something I want to say. Contrary to the way I've been acting, I am a sensual guy. Really."

I gently pulled on his ear. "Just no sex before marriage, right?"

"You know what I'm talking about."

"So, you want me to take cold showers?"

He laughed. "*Oy*, Julia. The trouble you make for me."

I licked his lips with my tongue. "Consider yourself lucky."

Back at home that evening, I filled the tub, taking the advice of an article I had read recently which said a hot bath helps to relax the mind and the body. I stepped into the water. Too hot. A little more cold water, then I eased myself down. All my muscles relaxed, even my bones felt soft. I closed my eyes and lay still for a long time; then, I slipped forward and let my head sink down under. My hair floated like seaweed. All I heard was my beating heart. Up I came for air. Down again. I was inside my mother's body.

Afterwards, I changed the sheets on my bed; then, snuggled underneath. Everything smelled fresh, even my silk nightgown. I felt at peace for a little while, but soon my desire rose up again. I tried to push it away. "Why was David moving so slow?" I whispered; then, I thought, well, at least he showed some interest in the eagles.

Four

A month passed, and the eaglets were another foot taller and their wings were stretched six-feet across. It was almost time to free them into the wild. The day before their release, which was to be a big news event, Sal called me at the office, his voice frantic: "Maria's missing. She must've squeezed through a loose bar."

Like a madwoman, I drove to the head of the trail, parked the car and ran through the woods to the eagle tower. Ismael was pacing inside the cage, pecking at the bars, crying out in a high-pitched sound.

Sal and I hiked along the forested ridges near the tower, searching for Maria. I whistled to her. I prayed. Later, we rowed out in a dory and scouted the coves, but we didn't find her. Before I returned home, I put two fish for her outside the cage on the edge of the platform.

That evening I phoned David to tell him about the mishap. He and I had dated a few times in the past month. The movies. Dinner at MaMa DiMatteo's. Nothing earth-shaking. He wanted to take things slow. So, slow it was. I wasn't that happy about it, but he was a good listener. That evening over the phone, he sounded concerned and caring. "She'll turn up. Try not to worry. Get a good night's sleep."

It was fine advice, but it didn't help. I was only able to sleep a few hours. The next morning I was nervous as hell. Today was the big media event, the day I was to release the eaglets. Without eating any breakfast, I hurried to the tower. Maria hadn't touched the fish I had left outside the cage. I tramped up and down the shoreline of Seal Cove, checking the sea and sky with my binoculars. Not only did I dread the embarrassment of explaining things to the media, but I was worried for Maria. Was she able to find food? Had something happened to her? Why hadn't she come back to Ismael?

A few hours before the reporters arrived, Nudelman and I attached a tiny radio transmitter to Ismael's tail feather, so that once he was released, we could follow his feeding range and movements, and find him if he was injured. Maria wouldn't have such protection, but at least we had tagged her earlier with an orange wing marker and a leg band.

Just before the news conference I scurried into the tent and changed into a red T-shirt with the photo of an eagle and the inscription, "Acadia National Park. Bringing Back the Bald Eagle." Then I quickly braided my hair and tied a brown eagle feather to each strand.

David showed up with binoculars around his neck just as I was stepping out of the tent. I said, "No luck. She's still missing."

He gave me a big hug. "I'm sorry, Julia. I'm rooting for you."

I rubbed my forehead. "Hey, I'll think of something."

He hugged me again. "I'm sure you're busy, so I'll try to stay out of the way."

Soon Sal and I were handing out press packets to a dozen reporters and photographers. Several park and state officials were also on hand for the event. I gathered everyone near the tower, and I immediately told them about Maria. "I'm sorry, but sometimes these things happen. We're talking about wild birds here, not caged parakeets." I answered the reporters' questions as best as I could. "No, we haven't seen Maria since she escaped...Yes, it's true, she's never hunted before, but she has seen other eagles catch fish...No, we think she's still in the area."

I had done several news conferences over the years, and I had learned that above all, I wanted to be authentic, not slick. So I said, "I'm going to be honest with you. I'm a little worried about her, but I have this gut feeling she's okay. She's a tough bird. Fiercely independent. It's just like her to jump ship. But Ismael's still here, and soon you'll get to see him fly for the first time."

I put on a wide smile. "Today's a great day for the citizens of Maine." I gestured with my arms, said in a loud voice: "We're doing it, guys. We're bringing the bald eagle back to the Maine coast." David, Sal and several officials clapped. "Now, before we free Ismael, I'd like to give you just a brief history of the eagles. Please, bear with me." I paused. "About fifty years ago, we had thousands of eagles here, but we nearly drove them to extinction with development, high-voltage lines, illegal hunting, pesticides and chemicals. We've fixed a lot of those problems, and now we're beginning to reintroduce the eagles. If things go well, we should have nesting eagles in the next decade."

Sal let out a whoop.

I opened my hands to the reporters. "So, if you have any questions..."

The reporter from the *Bangor Daily* stepped forward. "I don't get it. I've seen eagles in Acadia before."

I nodded. "You're right, but they're summer migrants from Canada and the south. They won't nest here. Eagles only nest where they take their first flight."

I flipped my braids backwards, cleared my throat. "That's why we've brought young birds here. They've never flown before. When they do, they'll become imprinted on the area, and someday they'll return to mate and nest." I motioned with my hands. "The two eagles we have here are from different nests in Nova Scotia, so they may mate with each other, or they may link up with a migrant in about four or five years. When they do mate, it's usually for life."

"Too bad people ain't as moral," quipped an elderly reporter from the *Bar Harbor Weekly*.

Everyone laughed.

A TV reporter came near me, held a microphone near his mouth as his cameraman filmed us. "Ms. DeCarlo. Money's tight these days. It's hard enough paying for our schools and roads. Why should we spend tax money on a couple of birds?" He moved the microphone to me.

"Good question." I took out a dollar bill and pointed to the eagle. "Try to think of it this way. Eagles are our national symbol. They represent the American spirit. So do we want the next generation to only know them through a picture on a dollar bill, or through some stuffed bird in a museum?"

"Heck, no," David shouted. I gave him a thumbs-up. It was good to have a friend in the crowd.

I faced the reporters, again. "And let me ask you this. Can you put a dollar figure on the beauty of a soaring eagle? Can we afford to lose that part of God's creation? Can we ignore our responsibility to be..."

I saw Sal running his finger across his neck, and I let out a short laugh. "Sorry, guys. Guess I'm getting a little carried away. My brother over there..." I pointed to him. "...is giving me the signal to cut the talking and get to the action." I raised my arms into the air. "Okay, Sal. Set him free."

Sal climbed up the tower, clung to the front of the cage. The cameras whirled and clicked as he removed two bars and retreated to the back of the platform. Ismael waddled out to the edge, looked at the emerald water below, glanced at the reporters and scampered back into the cage. He stayed inside for a long time. The reporters started to fidget. One said, "Why don't you just push him off?"

I shook my head. "No way. That bird has talons like a knife. Ain't nobody going to tell him what to do."

A little later Ismael crept to the edge. He didn't budge for awhile, just stared down at the water, up at the sky. Then suddenly he plunged towards the water. There was only one problem. He wasn't flapping his wings. I whispered, "Oh God, fly Ismael, fly."

He fell fast, head first.

At the last moment he stretched out his wings and stroked, lifted up, and glided along the water. He pumped his wings, landed on the branch of a fir tree along the shore, teetered; then, regained his balance.

The reporters applauded.

I thought I saw Ismael bow. Impossible.

Then he jumped off the branch and climbed up into the sky. He made a rapid sharp chipping sound that echoed across the sea and against the mountains. He circled and dove. Climbed and called. Again and again, he did this.

All at once I spotted a bird in the west sailing towards him. Up went my binoculars. I recognized Maria.

Ismael climbed higher. Chipped, circled and dove with greater excitement. Within a minute Maria joined him in the air. They tumbled and rolled. Fell to the ocean. Climbed up into the azure sky on spirals of wind. Again they swooped down to the sea. Then, in an instant, they disappeared over a ridge of spruce trees.

At first the reporters hung around, as if they expected a repeat performance, but soon they felt the pressure of their deadlines, and almost at once they left.

David had stayed until the end and came up to me. "You handled the media marvelously, Julia. And the eagles were magnificent, just like you said. Thanks for inviting me." He kissed me on the lips. "Got to run. Have a big clothing order to place this afternoon. I'll call you, soon."

Later, Sal and I began picking up the campsite: paper coffee cups, cigarette butts and film canisters. He patted me on the back. "Congratulations, Sis. You did it."

I took a long, deep breath. "No, we did it, and the eaglets did it."

He let out a shout, threw his fist in the air, talked fast. "What a day. Can you believe Maria showing up like that, stealing the show?" He tugged the sleeve of my T-shirt. "So, how are you feeling?"

I could hear the weariness in my voice. "Great."

"Really?"

"Yeah."

"Come on Julia. Get with it."

I leapt in the air and let out a cheer, just like I used to at high school football games. "There. Convinced?"

He laughed, his deep belly laugh. "No."

"Okay, Sal, I fess up. I didn't sleep well last night, and I'm just plain pooped."

"You could be pooped and excited. I can tell something's wrong."

"God, Sal, what are you, my therapist?" I went to him and gave him a hug. "Don't worry. I'm okay."

He squirmed free and smirked at me, spoke in a consoling, but sarcastic voice. "I just wanted to let you know that if you ever need someone to talk to, I'm here."

I let out a short laugh. "*Touche.*"

Five

It was a three-hour ride to Portland, Maine, and as usual, I was a little late, so I was speeding across the causeway from Mount Desert Island to the mainland, and I was thinking: *What if I'm making a mistake? I could turn around, and he'd never know the difference.* No, I was sick of wavering. I knew, if I was ever going to build a lasting love with someone, whether it was David or someone else, I had to face my father. He was like a poison in my heart.

Hours later, I drove over Back Cove Bridge, and I saw Portland's silver cityscape loom before me. I exited onto Forest Street and looked up at the electronic billboard on top of the Time and Temperature Building. Time: 8:54 a.m. Temperature: 67 F. I drove down Congress Street past the eighteenth century home of the poet, Henry Wadsworth Longfellow. The street was a mix of historic buildings, high-rise offices and storefronts. I vaguely knew the city. Had visited a few times years ago when I was a student in Boston.

After a short drive, I parked at the corner of Washington and Cumberland in front of a three-decker house. It was his place, the one Father McBride had told me about, and I kept my eyes locked on the basement apartment. An hour passed. He didn't come out. Should I knock? No, I was too afraid.

Across the street I saw a young family come out of Stella's Diner. The father took his son's hand, and the mother held her daughter's. The boy looked like Sal at five with his curly, black hair and Red Sox cap. I hoped they were happier than my family had been. Suddenly, I felt hungry, so I went to the diner and ordered a coffee and bagel to go. While I was waiting, I kept looking out the window and checking my father's apartment to see if he was coming out.

As I paid my bill and turned to leave, my eyes suddenly fell on an elderly man sitting in a booth at the end of the diner. He was reading a newspaper, and his face seemed familiar with its square jaw and long nose. And like Father McBride said, he was bald.

My legs began to shake. I asked the waitress, "Excuse me, by any chance do you know the man in that booth?" I pointed to him.

She put her hands on her hips. "Who wants to know?"

I could hardly speak. "I...I think he's my father."

"Well, in that case, his name is Frank DeCarlo."

"Oh my God." I dropped the bagel on the floor.

She came around, picked it up and handed it to me. "I bet you're Julia. He talks about you kids all the time." She gave me a gentle push. "Go on. He won't bite."

I walked slowly past several vinyl booths, nervously counting my steps. "One, two, three..." I counted fourteen. When I came to the end, I knew it was him by the thick, inch-long scar just above his right eye, a shrapnel wound from the war. I stopped just before his booth. He looked up; then, he straightened his black eyeglasses and looked again.

"It's me, Dad."

In a barely audible voice, he asked, "Julia?" He squeezed my hand as if he was trying to make sure I wasn't a ghost. "Sorry...I never thought...I can't...Oh what the hell am I saying? Sit down. It's nice to see you."

I slid into the seat opposite him. His speech was slow and flat. Tranquillizers, I guessed. I put my hands on the table, and they were shaking. *Did I need tranquillizers, too?* I placed my hands on my lap where he couldn't see them, and all at once I felt self-conscious about the way I looked. I straightened my hair and rose-colored blouse. I had worn it and a black skirt because I wanted to look nice, to look sophisticated.

He reached out. "*Come stai*?"

"*Bene.*"

He shook his head in disbelief. "Jesus, what are you doing here?"

"I was looking for you."

He smiled. "Julia, the detective, right?"

I let out a quick laugh. "Got the old run-around. You know, the New York cops told me to call the Veteran's Administration, and they told me to call the detox center, and they—"

"Ah, so it was Father McBride."

"You don't have a phone?"

"No, they're a pain in the neck." My father stared at me for a moment. "My goodness, Julia. You're all grown up. Last time I saw you, Jesus, you only came up to here." He touched his chest.

I spoke softly. "Eighteen years, Dad. A lifetime ago."

The waitress came to the booth with a coffee pot and filled my father's cup. He beamed at her. "Hey, Kit. This here is my daughter, Julia."

She put her hand on my shoulder. "I know, Frank. We just met. I should've guessed you'd have such a pretty girl." She poured my coffee, handed us lunch menus and left.

My father tapped my hand. "She's right. *Che bella.* You have your mother's looks. I thought it was her for a moment."

I pulled on a strand of my hair. "Except for the nose, hey?" It wasn't as big and long as Deb's, but I was a little self-conscious about it. What Italian girl wasn't? This was America, right? Home of the Anglo-Saxon nose.

My father moved his head left and right, examining my face. "No, you're beautiful like her."

"It's too long, isn't it?" I turned to the side so he could see my profile.

"It's an Italian nose, Julia. What do you want? It's...What's the word?... It's noble. That's it. You look noble."

He had said just the right thing. Made me feel good about myself.

He tapped my coffee. "That'll perk you up. Go on, have a sip. The waitresses treat me royal here."

I sipped my coffee, looked at the menu for a moment, then glanced at him. The wrinkles in his face ran deep like sidewalk cracks; his sagging shoulders folded forward like a book about to be closed. He looked much older than his mid-sixties. He saw me staring at him, and he gave me a disapproving look. He pointed to the menu. "Better decide what you want. She'll be back in a minute."

I began to unwrap my bagel. "I'm all set. Ordered it to go. Was going to eat it in the car. You know, I was sitting outside your apartment, waiting for you to come out."

"That was you?" He gestured to the station wagon across the street.

I nodded.

"I thought somebody was casing out the building." He laughed loudly, too loudly.

I looked around a little embarrassed. I tried to make myself small, leaned over the bagel, took a bite.

He squinted his eyes. "Ain't that Jewish food?"

"It's a bagel."

"You Jewish, now?"

"I like bagels, cream cheese. Want a bite?"

He waved me off, turned back to the menu.

Should I tell him about David? No way. I had plenty of other things to confront him about without talking about my Jewish boyfriend and having to deal with his racist shit. The waitress returned, and he ordered fish chowder and strawberry-rhubarb pie. *Where to begin? How to get up the courage?*

He fumbled with his silverware.

"So, Dad, I wanted to..."

Suddenly, he stood up. "Sorry, got to use the john. Too much coffee. Be back in a minute."

When he returned, he sat down and said, "So, I should remember how old you are, but my memory ain't what it used to be."

"Twenty-nine."

"Jesus, you're a woman now. Ain't that something? Married?"

"Divorced."

"Sorry. The guy must've been an idiot."

"He was."

"Any kids?"

I shook my head. "I thought about it, but not with him."

"Too bad."

That was it, apparently the end of his questions, and he picked up his coffee and took a long sip.

I cleared my throat. "So Dad, I have a lot on my mind, like—"

He held up his hands. "I don't want to talk about it. The past is the past. It's great to see you. That's all that counts."

My mouth dropped open. "I can't do that, Dad. I need some answers. I need to know why you left us like that."

He said nothing.

"Dad, I was waiting all these years. Why didn't you contact us?"

He stared out the window, his voice monotone. "So, Julia, you still like dogs?"

I tugged on his shirt sleeve. "You hurt us a lot."

He turned to me, his face suddenly suspicious. "Is that why you're here? Your mother sent you? What does she want? Money?"

I paused. "She's dead." I saw the pain in his face and heard him groan. I found a weapon to hurt him. "She's dead. Isn't that what you always wanted?"

"No." His voice was choked with emotion. "I loved her." He put his head in his hands and sobbed quietly for a few moments; then, he took out a handkerchief, wiped his eyes, and blew his nose. "Sometimes I lose it. Happens a lot when an old guy like me gets sober. That's what the doc said anyway."

"Crying's good."

"Not for me."

Silence.

He stared out the window, turned his face away from me, and asked softly, "When did she die?"

"Last...last year."

A long pause. "How?"

"Stomach cancer."

"*Mi dispiace,*" he said.

"You have a lot to be sorry for."

His voice was meek. "May she rest in peace."

I closed my eyes, thought of my mother at the Dana Farber Cancer Institute in Boston in a hospital bed, her head bald except for a dozen scattered hairs. I hated looking at those hairs, and finally I cut them off. My mother was so exhausted she could barely finish a sentence. I was so angry. Angry at God. Angry at life. She had suffered and sacrificed so much, and then to die in her fifties and in such pain. But her love for Sal and I was unshakeable, even the last week when she had to struggle to hold our hands. Now, a few tears came to my eyes, and I wiped them away. My father was still staring out the window, and I tried to keep my anger at him out of my voice. "I know it's not easy for you to talk, Dad, but I have to know what you were doing all those years."

He said nothing.

I felt the heat rise to my face, my heart quicken. "You can be a bastard, you know that?"

"Such a big girl, cursing at her father."

"I thought you wanted to get better. That's what Father McBride told me."

He sounded repentant. "What can I say?" He covered his chin and mouth with his hand. "I can't talk anymore."

"Look at me, Dad."

He wouldn't look at me. I tapped the table with my fingernails. "I'm your daughter. And I'm giving you a chance to start over. But family comes with responsibilities, and one of them is to talk with each other."

He faced me, but his eyes were closed. "I've only been on the wagon a few months. Never made it much longer before."

"I'm willing to take the risk, Dad."

He shook his head.

"I need you to talk, please."

Silence.

He opened his eyes. "I'm too ashamed."

I stood. "Then I'm wasting my time." I picked up my handbag and turned to leave.

"Don't. I'll try."

I sat back down and waited.

A minute passed.

"I was getting by."

"And..."

"How does a father tell his kid this kind of stuff? You think that's easy." He spoke without meeting my eyes. "Okay, so, I was living in New York City, doing odd jobs. Cleaning, painting, fixing things. Nothing steady. I was homeless sometimes. Had to steal to eat, to buy booze. They busted me. Put me in the slammer. Three months one time. Six months another."

"That's terrible, Dad."

"I ain't proud of it, Julia. I sure hope I don't ever have to go back. There are some mean sonofabitches in jail. The only good thing about it was I had to sober up. But then, when I got out, I went straight for a drink." He covered his face with his hands. "This talking is hard."

"You have to, Dad."

He hesitated. "I had drinking buddies, but, you know, when I was down on my luck, they'd disappear. The booze was killing me, I knew it. What the hell. I was bitter. Your mother cut me deep."

I wanted to smack the table. My therapist, Odette, who I had started seeing in Bar Harbor, had warned me he might say something that would hurt me. I took a breath and tried to relax; then, I said as calmly as I could, "Blaming Mom is absurd."

He raised his jittery hands. "Amen, let bygones by bygones."

All at once it came back to me, the "amen" and "bygones," words he had often used when I was a child; yet, he could never keep his promises. His anger fed on itself, boiled up like a volcano. Had he changed now? I picked up my coffee, took a sip, looked at him over the rim of the cup. "So Dad, how did you get sober?"

He hunched forward, his arms on the table. "Like I said before, I've never been dry very long. So I can't predict nothing. One day at a time. That's what the program says." He fumbled nervously with the pens and cigars in the pocket of his flannel shirt. "Maybe I'll make it this time. Father McBride thinks so. He was *molto benevolo.* Never tried to tell me what to do. Just kept asking me about my kids. Maybe that's why I'm sober today, I don't know."

Suddenly the waitress brought the food and refilled our cups. He ate silently, and I glanced at him. He dipped his bread into the soup just like his father, my grandfather. I looked closely at my father's face. He had been handsome when he was young, and I was terrified of him. Now, he looked old and beaten, and I felt sorry for him.

He wiped a little soup from his lips. "How come Sal didn't come?"

I lied. "He was busy."

"What's the matter? He wishes I was some big-shot lawyer, some rich banker?"

"He's still angry."

"He should..." He raised his arms in surrender. "Hey, I wasn't always a bum, you know." He paused. "How about those games at Fenway? Remember them hawkers?" He cupped his hands around his mouth. "Hot dooggggs. Peanuuuuts." He let out a laugh. "We stuffed ourselves. Those were good times. Don't they count for nothing?"

"Maybe he'll change his mind. Give him time."

My father shrugged.

The waitress brought us strawberry-rhubarb pie and more coffee. I was eating the pie, savoring it, but I was also waiting, hoping my father would ask me about my life. Who was I kidding? Things hadn't changed;

he never was able to give us any attention. Finally, I said, "Say, Dad, I have this great job at Acadia National Park. I raise and release eagles. I'm a naturalist, and—"

"A nat-tur-rist?

What an opening. "You know, nudists. I run the nudist camp on a lake at the park."

He shook his head, his throat rattled. "Not my daughter. Don't tell me that."

I laughed. "Naturalist, Dad. Naturalist as in nature. I study plants and animals. And I take care of wildlife, like eagles, beavers—"

"Oh." He laughed, a deep laugh. "My silly Lilly."

"Lilly?"

"That's what I called you when you were a little girl. The name had a lot *L's* in it. Made me think of you. My lovely, laughing, little Lilly. *Mia bambina. Che bella.*"

"How sweet."

"You were very funny." He slurped his coffee. "And smart too. I bet you went to college."

I told him about my degrees from Boston University and the University of Massachusetts. "It was worth it. I make a decent salary. Can pay my own way."

"Ain't that something. And Sal?"

"He hated school. He's a carpenter. A good one. And he helps me with the eagles."

"I'm proud of him, too. You tell him I said so." He pulled a cigar from his pocket. "Hey, I could use a smoke. Can't smoke in here. Let's head out." He stood, picked up the check and left a generous tip on the table.

We went east along Cumberland Avenue, a street busy with cars and people, walled in on each side with three-story wooden houses, some with storefronts. My father lit a cigar and puffed on it as we walked, and the conversation turned to pleasant chit-chat. I felt myself relaxing. I was thinking: *Maybe I hadn't made a mistake; maybe he was going to make it this time.*

A half hour later, we came to the Eastern Promenade, a large hillside park overlooking Casco Bay; I grabbed the camera from my handbag and zoomed in on the distant islands in the bay. They looked like a school of migrating, gray whales. White cumulus clouds with flat bases floated over them. I shot off a few pictures, and I breathed in the ocean air for a few moments. Breathing it was like taking a drink of something cool, crystal and salty. It energized me. Then, I took my father's hand and positioned him for a picture with the bay in the background.

He frowned. "Do I have to?"

"For Sal." I focused my camera. "Mozzarella."

He smiled, and I clicked.

We walked to the end of the park and sat on a bench. An island ferry was heading out, sounding its horn as it left the dock. My father re-lit his cigar. "Say Julia, before I forget. Where's your mother buried?"

I told him.

He pulled a pen and paper from his shirt pocket. "Tell me again."

"St. John's in Worcester. On Lake Quinsigamond."

He wrote it down. "Say, before I forget. Do me a favor. Send me a photo of Maria. I lost a lot my pictures. Moving around, you know."

"Sure."

We sat quietly for a time. I looked at him. He was staring off at the sea. "Christ, Julia. I can't believe Maria's dead. I should be dead too. I don't know how I made it through the war."

He coughed hard three times, his smoker's cough. "Sicily. Did I tell you? You were probably too young to remember."

"Of course I remember, Dad."

He didn't seem to hear me. "There was a thousand of us on the deck. We were sitting perfectly still, could barely move. Had our M-1s in our laps. Explosions everywhere. Our big guns shelling the island. Enemy planes overhead. They sank three of our ships. I could hear the men screaming in the water."

He puffed on his cigar and blew the smoke off to the side. There was a strong wind coming off the bay, and it whisked the smoke away. "The landing crafts were pieces of shit. Couldn't handle the waves. Some capsized. We made it to the beach. Machine guns, grenades, mortars, everywhere. Many of my buddies died that day."

"Were you afraid?"

He nodded.

"Did you kill anybody?"

He straightened up. "A soldier doesn't talk about that." He stretched his neck and grimaced. "I was happy it was foggy. Couldn't see their faces. Bodies everywhere. Italian soldiers." His voice choked up. "*Fratelli miei sangue.*"

"What does that mean?"

"My blood brothers." A pause, then he said, "My only thought was for Maria. She was a young woman then. *Amore mio.* I told myself if I lived, I'd marry her." He put his head in his hands and let out a muffled sob.

There was a long silence. I didn't know what to say; it was hard to hear him talking about love and my mother in the same breath; yet, I could see he was sincere. What good things could I ever learn from him about marriage? I knew that kids looked to their parents as role models, learned things from them. That was the problem. I felt everything I had learned from my father was negative and mean and angry. I stood up, stretched my arms upward. "Sorry to cut things short, Dad, but I've got to head back to Acadia, okay? I promised a friend I'd go biking later."

"Got a new guy?"

"Yeah, he's very nice." And I thought, sadly, if David ever met you he'd run away from me faster than a deer.

Was my father disappointed I was leaving? It was hard to tell; his face was blank. We walked back to the diner. When we reached my car, I touched his arm. "I really enjoyed seeing you, Dad. I've missed you. Let's get together again." I handed him my phone number.

He hesitated and didn't take it. "Maybe that's...I don't want to hurt you, Julia...but maybe that's not a good idea."

I struggled to speak. "You don't want to see me?"

"I'll never forget today."

"I want to help you, Dad."

He looked away. "The program says I've got to help myself."

"Without family?"

He rubbed his forehead. "You want the truth, right? I knew you and Sal was living in Bar Harbor. Father McBride told me. But I didn't call you, did I?"

I held back my tears.

He lowered his head.

"Dad—"

He mumbled, "I'm sorry."

I reached out. "I don't understand."

He stepped back. "That's just it...Jesus, Julia." He pawed at the ground. "I'm not...You're asking me to explain it, and I don't know how to." He started to walk away.

I stopped him, kissed him quickly on the cheek, and my voice broke. "Maybe you'll change your mind." I put my phone number in his shirt pocket; then, I drove off and didn't look back.

Six

Upward, we climbed on a two-foot wide trail that must have been carved into the mountain with jackhammers. To our right, there was just empty space that fell downward one hundred feet along the face of the cliff. To my left, there was an iron handrail fastened into a rocky wall. I gripped the handrail and looked dizzily down the cliff, then I turned to David. "We should've taken the cable car."

He laughed. He knew there wasn't one. Unlike Sal, David got my jokes. Not many people did. No wonder I liked him.

We started up again on Precipice Trail. The name described it perfectly, a dangerous trail that snaked one thousand feet up to the summit of Champlain Mountain. We wove around several large boulders and climbed to the next ledge. Soon we came to another cliff. Embedded in its side was a thirty-foot steel ladder. I went up first. When we reached the top, the trail was still very steep, and we grabbed onto roots and shrubs to pull ourselves up.

It was hard going. I felt the strain on my legs, the aching muscles, but I pushed on. David had stopped for water, and I noticed he was a few minutes behind me on a lower portion of the winding trail about twenty feet directly below me. I moved forward, when suddenly, the area of my path gave out, and loose gravel and baseball-size rocks crashed downward. "Look out, David," I shouted.

He pulled backwards against the cliff. There was a moment of silence, then he said, "Hey, I'm not good to you dead."

I laughed, relieved.

He brushed the dirt off his cap. "Maybe we should turn back?"

I stared at the birch and aspen forest seven hundred feet below, then glanced up at the summit. "We're almost there, but let's take the easier trail down."

We trekked upwards, and twenty minutes later we reached the rocky, treeless summit where a wooden sign on a post read: "Champlain Mountain. 1,058 Feet." I looked through my binoculars across the waters of Frenchman Bay to Egg Rock Island and its lighthouse, and in the far distance saw Schoodic Point. The misty blue sea looked grand and godly from this height, as if it were a mother holding the land in her lap. Silver-white bulging clouds galloped toward us, almost touching the summit. The wind was strong and cool, September cool. I lifted my arms like wings. "Look, David, I'm flying." I circled around him, flapping and jumping.

He smiled, took off his backpack, found a spot on some rocks to sit down. "We made good time, but I'm tired." I sat between his legs, nestled my head below his chin. He circled me with his arms, kissed the top of my head.

My body relaxed. I felt safe and cozy and cared-for. It's crazy, but the first thought that entered my mind was I wanted to tell him I had seen my father, and then I wanted him to say that it was a good thing to do and that I was a good daughter. But I was afraid to tell him, afraid to scare him away with stories of my father's problems. I knew from experience that guys weren't interested in a woman with a mentally ill father. They think you might have a bad gene pool. I had two guys admit it.

So I tried not to think, to bring myself back to the moment, to bliss. I told myself: *Feel his arms. Breathe in the cool air. Smell the ocean.* I drifted away, lost track of time. A little later I heard David talking to me: "You know, I heard a biologist give a talk last year at Rachel's school. He teaches kids to look at the sky every day to see what's happening. What a great job. How does he ever make a living doing that?"

"Probably gets grants."

"Maybe he needs an apprentice?"

I laughed.

David playfully rapped me on the head. "You think I'm kidding. Retail is a damn, insecure business. We're only as good as the next season."

I bent my head back, looked up at him. "I thought...Didn't you tell me you've been doing business here for six years?"

He nodded.

"And it's been good every year, right?"

"Yeah, but you never know about the next season."

"That doesn't make any sense, David."

He shook his head. "Of course it...What I'm trying..." He stroked his chin, let out a quick laugh. "You're right. I think I heard someone say that at a sales exhibition." He laughed at himself again. "I guess I'm just repeating what I heard, like a parrot. It makes me sound important, though, doesn't it?"

I knocked his cap off, scrambled the hair on his head. I tickled him. We rolled over each other, wrestling, tickling, grabbing.

I was laughing, feeling young and free. He was on top of me, pinning my arms to the ground, and in an instant we were kissing with abandon. He slipped his hands under my purple cotton shirt, moved his fingers in circles around my stomach. "Hmmm, that feels good," I said. He burrowed his head underneath my shirt, kissed my navel, moved upwards. He lifted my bra aside, kissed me with his wet lips. I was growing excited, and I wrapped my legs around him.

Suddenly, out of the corner of my eye, I saw a middle-aged couple approaching the summit about thirty feet away. I whispered in his ear, "We have company."

He looked around, and I heard him sigh. We stood up, gathered our backpacks as discreetly as possible, and began heading down a trail away from the summit. Soon we wandered off the path and found a rocky enclosure. David put his arm around me, drew me close.

We kissed wildly, then ever so gently. We lay on the ground side by side, and he wedged his thigh between my legs, pressing, then releasing. I closed my eyes, rocked to his rhythm. We kissed deeply, lingering. I was flushed. I looked into his brown eyes, "I've been patient, haven't I?"

He took my hand, kissed my palm. "You've been very good." All at once I felt a wave of panic. *Did he see it?* I tried to pull my hand away. He held on tight. He nudged the cuff of my shirt upwards with his chin, then kissed the inside of my wrist. In an instant, I knew he had found the scars.

He drew back a little, lifted my wrist into the light, glanced at it. "What happened?"

I tried to laugh. "Oh that, just an accident. I think I was seven."

"Accident?"

I tried to keep my hands from shaking, but I felt the tremors inside. I sat up, and he pulled himself up, too. "I was carrying milk bottles to the car. Empty ones. I tripped and fell. There was glass everywhere. My Mom had to pull that piece out." I pointed to the scar on my wrist.

"It must've hurt."

"I cried a lot."

"Did you need stitches?"

"My Mom just put a big band aid on it."

He took my hand again, looked closely at the scar. "Healed up nice." He traced it with his finger. "Looks like there are two cuts, side by side."

"I never noticed."

"They're almost perfectly straight."

I let out a nervous laugh. "That's me. Everything has to be perfect."

His face grew serious, but he said nothing.

I took a brush from my backpack, began fussing with my hair. "How about you, David? Any scars?"

He locked onto my eyes. "You're lying, Julia."

I sat motionless, speechless for a moment. "Do I know everything about you, David?"

"Everything that's important."

I pointed to my wrist. "This isn't important."

He touched my hand. "Then why is it shaking?"

I stood up with a start, moved away, continued brushing my hair. "You're making me very uncomfortable, you know that?"

He threw his hands in the air.

I pulled my hair into a pony tail and clipped it with a coral hairpin. It was happening just as it always did: first peace, then a crisis. "How many times have we dated, David? Five, maybe six."

He nodded.

"We barely know one another, but you expect me to be an open book?"

"I want us to be honest with one another."

"Works both ways."

"Fine."

"And you won't use this against me?"

"Why would I?"

"Okay." I paced away from him, took a few deep breaths. "Last year...I tried to kill myself."

His face was blank.

"I was working at a wildlife sanctuary in Massachusetts. Near the Quabbin Reservoir. It happened at a place called Rattlesnake Cliff. I often walked there from the sanctuary." I folded my hands, put them to my lips. "On that day, I wanted to die, and I wanted to live. I was pitiful. Hard to believe now."

I sat down on the rock, dug the toes of my boots into the dirt. "Sal showed up just in time. Somehow he knew I was in trouble. Thank God. I think my Mom sent him, you know, her spirit. I think she was watching over me."

David leaned forward, rubbed his forehead, his face confused.

"I was drinking wine. It was winter. Snow on the ground. Had a fire going. I was heating up the blade of my pearl handle knife in the fire. I had that fuck-the-world attitude. But the blade hurt too much, I couldn't cut deep enough. Even toyed with the idea of jumping off the cliff. Something held me back. When Sal arrived, he was really freaked out. There was a lot of blood on my clothes, on the snow."

David stood up, circled around the rocky enclosure, then he came and sat in front of me on the ground. He touched my knee. "But why, Julia?"

I covered my face with my hands. I was whimpering. "I was under a lot of stress at work. I was trying to get over my divorce. I was trying to cope with my Mom's death. Then some bastard shot one of my eagles. Seemed like the whole world was falling apart."

He moved away, leaned against a rocky wall.

I went and stood next to him. "I'm a lot better, David. I'm seeing a therapist in Bar Harbor. She's a big help."

He said nothing; his face looked pale.

"You okay?" I asked.

He didn't seem to hear me. His voice trailed off, "A big help?"

"Her name is Odette Bouchard." That seemed to bring him back.

"Sixtyish? African-American?"

I nodded.

"I've seen her in my store a few times. Always pleasant, friendly." David shuffled his foot over the gravel. "People say she's very good."

I put my hands around his waist. "How about you, David? Ever done therapy?"

He hesitated for a moment, his face vulnerable. "Had to after Alice left me. I was devastated, humiliated. Went for two months. Saw Dr. Silverstein in town. It was okay, but I had trouble finding things to talk about. I'm not planning on going back."

I tried to reconnect with him. "Guess you were lucky not to have all the childhood shit to deal with."

"I can't imagine."

I pulled him close. "You know, David. I care about you. I really do."

He squirmed out of my hug.

The wind changed direction, blew on us through the open side of the rock enclosure. It was a northwest wind, blustery, raw. I took a parka out of my backpack, put it on.

He picked up a rock, fumbled it in his hands. "It's a lot to..." He tossed the stone aside. "What can I say? It seems there's a lot of craziness in your life."

I grimaced.

He noticed. "Maybe craziness is the wrong word. Dysfunctional. That's better, yes? My family seems tame in comparison. I like tame. Guess you can see, I'm feeling a little mixed up." He adjusted his cap. "Well, we should start back down."

I held onto his arm, felt the tears coming to my eyes. "David, I thought you said you wouldn't use it against me."

He looked at me, saw the tears, and wiped them away with his hands. "I'm not trying to, Julia. After what you just told me, that's the last thing in the world I want to do. But I'm concerned about how our relationship might affect Rachel. You do seem to have a lot of problems...I really hope things work out."

I tightened my lips. "You mean...without you, right?"

"I didn't say that."

"I can feel you pulling away, and I'm afraid. I don't want to lose you."

He stepped back a little. "I hear what you're saying, but I don't know what to think right now. Give me a few days to try to sort it out, okay?"

He didn't wait for my answer, but turned away and began descending. I followed. The hike down Champlain Mountain had never seemed so long and lonely.

Should I have been angry at him? I was disappointed, of course, but I guess I expected his response. How many guys want to get involved with a crazy lady?

A week later I still hadn't heard from him. I was kneeling on the kitchen floor in front of the oven. The door was open and the light was on. I took the racks out and sprayed cleaner on the metal walls; then, I wiped them with a rag. I was thinking about him as I cleaned. Would he call?

I put my head into the oven and looked around for any dirty spots I missed. The metal box seemed a strange place, but comforting, too. Gray and black. A small, contained little world. I thought for a moment how easy it would be to turn on the gas. Breathe in and out. In and out—

Suddenly, the doorbell rang. I yanked myself out and hit my head against the top of the oven. I tried to think. It was Saturday morning; I wasn't expecting anyone. When I came into the living room, I saw David beyond the six, small window panes set in the upper half of the front door. His face looked expressionless.

"Come in," I said, wiping my hands on my pants, trying to straighten my hair.

He took a step inside, and the storm door slammed behind him. He was dressed in a black overcoat and a black cap.

"Let me take your coat, David. I thought...It's good to see you. Come in. I'll make some coffee."

He lowered his eyes, touched the rim of his cap. "I'd like to talk, but not here. Would you mind taking a ride?"

"Oh." I put my hand to my mouth.

We rode silently past the two-story shops on Main Street in Northeast Harbor, everything covered in fog. He parked at the town pier. I smelled the salt in the misty air, couldn't see more than twenty feet ahead.

We shuffled over the planks of the wharf. A gull on top of a wooden piling squawked and flew off. All at once David faced me, and like a magician, pulled out a rose from inside his coat.

My mouth dropped open. I stared at the flower: a single rose, fiery red against the gray harbor. He held it close to my lips, and I smelled its sweet aroma.

I laughed, pushed at him, but tugged him back immediately. "You... you...What an actor. The long face. The silent ride. I thought I would die."

He flashed his wide grin. "I wanted us to remember this moment."

"I can't believe it." I threw my arms around him.

He held my chin, looked at me with great affection. "You know what really gets to me about you? And this may sound silly. It's the way your hair clings to your cheeks. I start to shake inside every time I think about that." He kissed me tenderly, then held me close.

I wasn't able to see the boats in the harbor, but I heard the riggings clanging against the aluminum masts, sounding like bells. I kissed his eyes. "Guess today's my lucky day."

He stepped back and smiled. "We should celebrate, have a drink."

I almost suggested my place, thinking we might finally make love, but I wanted to hear what he had in mind. "What would you like to do?"

He didn't hesitate. "How about the Quarterdeck?"

"Perfect," I said, putting on a wide smile.

David let out a cheer, pulled me by the hand. "Onward to the Quarterdeck."

As we walked across the wharf hand-in-hand, I wondered for an instant if he had really told me everything that was important. Was it possible he had some kind of sexual problem?

Seven

I swept the broom back and forth, trying to loosen the eagle droppings from the floor; then, I brushed them over the edge of the platform. The sea breeze swooped up the fine white dust, blew it onto the green needles of a nearby spruce tree. I stopped working for a moment and glanced out at Seal Cove with its choppy waves. The tower swayed a little in the wind. I felt, as I often did when I was up high off the ground, that I was an eagle, and in a moment I would leap off the tower, and soar along the shoreline. *So free.* Then, I returned inside the eagle cage, and I gathered up a half-dozen, brown wing feathers that Maria and Ismael had left behind, inserted one into each of my braids, put the rest in my backpack.

I came out to the edge of the platform, this time with binoculars, and I followed the craggy coast, looking for Maria and Ismael. In the distance three harbor seals with dog-like faces slept on a small rocky outcrop surrounded by the sea, their skin shining silver in the sunlight. A raft of two dozen ducks, common eiders, brown females and white males, paddled southward. I scanned the western ridge where the maples shone yellow in their fall color, but the eagles weren't there either.

Soon I climbed down the ladder and went to Sal. He had turned the white, wooden dory over, and was scrapping barnacles off the bottom of the boat. I helped him. I liked working with Sal. He usually didn't talk much, but it was fun to watch him. He was very efficient, and every move seemed calculated. When we finished the boat, we started to dismantle the nylon tent, removing the strings from the stakes. Sal saw a bee inside the tent and caught it with a glass jar. He came out, released it, calling after the insect, "Hey, tell your buddies it was Sal DeCarlo that saved your butt." Then he looked at me, waited until I laughed. I did.

A little later I heard a faint, familiar high whistle coming from the north. Sal and I grabbed our binoculars and hurried to the rocky shore. Soon, we saw three large birds soaring towards us. They glided closer, and I recognized Maria, Ismael, and a tag-along friend, a brown, turkey vulture with purple-red skin on its head.

I whistled to Maria, and she returned the call. When she was overhead, she folded her wings, plummeted down, and landed on the branch of a nearby pine tree. She roosted there quietly, tilting her head left and right, searching the sea for food.

Meanwhile, Ismael and the turkey vulture floated upwards on a spiral thermal into the vast, blue sky, their wings outstretched. When they reached the top of the current, Ismael plunged down at the vulture, but braked with his wings just before he touched the bird. The vulture flipped over and sparred at Ismael with his claws. They somersaulted and fell towards jade water, but soon hitched a ride up the warm currents again to play once more.

I turned my attention back to Maria, who was still perched on the branch. Five minutes passed; then all at once, she dove down at the exact moment a white eider bobbed up from its underwater search. The two birds collided in the sea, the eider pulling Maria underneath the surface, but a second later they popped up in a furious splash. Maria paddled madly with her wings, lifted into the air with the duck's head pierced in her talons and its body dangling, and then she headed north along the shore. When Ismael and the turkey vulture saw what she had caught, they followed. Sal and I watched until they disappeared around the tip of a peninsula.

"So long," I shouted after them, knowing that it was time for them to head south any day. I tugged on the sleeve of Sal's sweatshirt. "You think they'll make it back next spring?"

He pulled on his pony tail, seeming to be in deep thought. "As a great American philosopher once said...I think it was Henry Thoreau...Does a moose shit in the woods?"

I laughed, gently punched his arm.

He pranced around in a circle like a stallion, his chest puffed out and his behind riding high. "I'm bad. Don't mess with me." He did some quick dance steps, then more prancing.

I watched in amazement. "Hey, Rocky. When's the fight?"He strutted over, put his arm around my shoulder. "Just trying to keep up your spirits, Sis. A promise is a promise."

"Huh?"

He paused. "Mom asked me to look out for you."

"Come again?"

"You have to know everything, don't you? She was worried about you. That's all. Felt I might be able to help." He stepped back, smiled. "So, how am I doing?"

"Excellent." I patted him on the back. "Mom told me something, too."

"Let me guess." He rubbed his chin. "To make sure I stay out of trouble."

"That goes without saying." I touched his shoulder. "Hey, I could use a cup of that coffee you've been brewing." I locked arms with him, and we moved towards the coffee pot on the campfire. "Yeah, so, Mom told me something about myself. It's not about you. Sorry. She said I'd get another chance at marriage. And when I did, she said I should just be myself. And I should let my husband be who he is. To treat him special. To remember to compromise. To be sure to spend time with my children. Funny thing is Sal, I'm not sure I want kids."

I checked his face to make sure he was listening. It was hard to tell with Sal. I let out a deep breath. "I see David with Rachel. He's under a lot of stress and responsibility, and he's got to give her all his attention. I don't know if I could do that. I have trouble just taking care of myself." I laughed. "I mean, sure, kids are sweet, and I'd like to be a mother, but..."

"Ayyyyy," Sal shouted. He flew to the coffee pot, which was beginning to boil over, and he yanked the pot off the fire. The flames sizzled from the spilled liquid. Sal let out a laugh like a bark, poured two cups, tasted his. "Just how I like it. Burnt." He handed me a cup. "You know, Julia, what you said, it sounds just like Mom. Always wanting the best for us. A good marriage. Kids. Boy, she loved kids. It's kind of sad. We're both single. No kids."

I almost choked on my coffee. "Wait a minute. You're supposed to keep my spirits up."

"Oh." He knocked on his head with his knuckles. "Well, it'll work out. We're still young. Just got to find the right one."

"So, I'm curious. Do you think David is right for me?"

"You guys serious?"

"Who knows?"

"Why not date around a little?"

"You don't like him?"

"Well, he seems a little stuck up."

"You mean he's not macho enough for you."

"Did I say that?"

"He's a businessman, Sal."

"So?"

"You've got to act mature and confident when you're selling stuff to people."

Sal dumped what was left of his coffee into the fire. "I like guys who are down-to-earth."

I felt my body grow tense. "You didn't like him from the start."

"Julia, cool it, okay. You asked me what I thought, and I told you."

I paced for a moment. "You're right. I shouldn't get so defensive." I glanced at my wrist watch. "Say, I've got be back to the office in an hour. How about letting me take a few pictures of you before I go?" He agreed. I shot him mending the fishing weir. I clicked a few pictures as he climbed the tower. Then I positioned him in front of the fire, had him dropping logs into the flames. As I was taking pictures, I was thinking about how to arrange the shots of Sal and others from the eagle project into a display on the bulletin board at the park's reception center. When I finished photographing Sal, I put the camera into my backpack, and then I noticed the manila envelop I had brought along for Sal. I considered waiting to give it to him because I wasn't sure I wanted to deal with his reaction, but I thought there was nothing to gain by putting it off. I handed it to him.

He opened it, took out the photograph. Disbelief swept his face."T-t-t-t-that's Dad?"

I nodded.

"Oh, Christ," he said.

"I found him in Portland."

"Portland? I thought he was in New York."

"He moved."

Sal's hands tightened into fists. "Lucky us. We just can't seem to get far enough away from the bastard, can we?" Sal let out a bitter laugh. "Shit, Julia. Why'd you have to find him? I can't believe it." He gave the photo back to me.

"It's for you, Sal."

"I don't want it."

I stuffed it in his shirt pocket.

"Thanks." He smirked at me; then, dropped it in the fire. Within seconds, it was aflame.

"Cute, Sal."

"I told you I didn't want it."

I picked up my coffee, sipped it, and looked at him over the top of the mug. "You know, Sal, Dad's sober. Has a job. Apologized. Said he was sorry Mom was dead. He was asking about you."

Sal poked at the fire with a long stick. "You're breaking my heart."

I paced a little. "You don't get it, do you? Look at me, Sal. For years I tried to bury him. See what happened. I married an asshole. Now I'm trying to face my past."

"Sounds like your therapist talking."

"It was my decision to see him, not hers."

Sal moved to a nearby chopping block. He lifted a long-handled axe in one hand and with the other set a maple log vertically on the block. With both hands, he brought the axe down, and with one stroke split the log in half. He did this several times; then, he glanced at me. "Let me ask you, Julia. Have you told David about Dad?"

"A little."

"Did you tell David about Rattlesnake Ledge?"

I lowered my eyes. "I had to. He saw the scars."

Sal put another log on the block, chopped it in two. He took a joint from his shirt pocket, lit it, drew in a puff, handed it to me.

I waved it off. "Do you have smoke that stuff right now?"

He smiled. "Helps me think better." He gestured with the joint as he talked. "So, are you going to see Dad again?"

"I don't know."

He sucked hard on the joint, held his breath for five seconds, then exhaled. "Keep me out of this, okay? And another thing. Notice I'm saying 'please'. Don't ever bring him to Bar Harbor."

"Why not?"

He toked, and spoke as he held his breath. "It's like this. When you talk about him, you know what I see? Mom running into our room at night, hysterical, locking the door."

Sal exhaled in a big breath. "Then, Dad breaks down the door, grabs Mom. She's hanging onto the bedpost, screaming: 'Please don't hit me.'

He wallops her, drags her out of the room. Remember that? I thought he was going to kill her. What could we do? We were just kids."

He puffed on the joint in quick tokes, then tossed the stub into the campfire. "Even now, sometimes, I get the feeling like I'm nobody. No better than an ant." Sal tightened his lips, locked onto my eyes. "He did that to me, Julia...So please, don't bring him here. I ain't afraid of him. That's not it. It's my temper. I might do something crazy. You know what I mean?"

Sal stood up, teetered a little, but he quickly regained his balance. "Whoa. That Columbian's strong stuff." He took a deep breath, let out a cough. Then he set another log on the block and brought the axe down with all his force. This time, though, his aim was off, and the axe glanced off the log and lodged in the ground an inch away from his right foot.

Eight

"Ummm. The curry smells good," David said, lingering over the vegetables that I was stir-frying in my wok. He picked out a carrot, put it in his mouth. "What else are we having?"

I opened the oven door, inserted a folk into the center of the quiche, pulled it out. "It's not done, yet."

He lifted a lid off a pot on top of the stove; steam rose from the rice pilaf. "Looks delicious, but not as tasty as you." He nibbled my neck, gave me a hug. Our lips met in a soft and long kiss. He stepped back at arm's length. "You look stunning." He touched my feather earrings, lightly ran his hands over my violet, silk blouse. "Smooth, like your skin."

The evening was unfolding just as I hoped it would. To be alone in David's company, to hear that he appreciated me, to take care of him. And I had high expectations that I would finally find out later what this gorgeous man was like in bed.

I put him to work stirring the vegetables while I set the table. Soon, he said, "So, I've noticed you don't eat meat." He flashed his wide grin. "What's the story? Can't afford it?"

I went to him, pulled on his ear. "Does my lion need his meat?"

He laughed. "So seriously, how come? Health reasons?"

"Partly. But mostly has to do with the animals. I think it's inhumane to kill them. Sorry if that sounds too moralistic, but it's the way I feel."

David scratched the back of his neck. "I admire you, but I don't think I could live without hamburgers and chicken."

"Oh, I'm not perfect. You've probably noticed. I eat fish sometimes. And I can't resist a hot dog at the ball park."

He smiled. "Well, I'll say one thing, Julia. You don't have an ounce of fat on you."

I kissed him quickly on the lips. "Keep flattering me. I love it."

When we sat at the pine table in the kitchen, I lit two red candles in brass holders. We clinked wine glasses. "*L'chaim*. To life," David said. He took a bite of quiche. "Ummm. This cheddar is good. Better than the Swiss that people usually put in."

Our conversation drifted easily and aimlessly from Rachel to our grandparents to the best pizza in town. After I served David seconds, which I took as an unspoken compliment, I began clearing the table. I was standing at the counter, putting leftovers in plastic containers, when David tapped me on the shoulder. I turned around, and there he was, holding a small box wrapped in tissue paper.

"For me?" I asked.

"Only you."

Inside was a gold necklace with a Star of David. I knew that the star was a religious symbol for Jews. I held it up. "Thanks. It's beautiful."

I went to the hallway mirror, and he came to me: "Let me help." I watched in the looking glass as he placed it around my neck and fastened the clasp in the back. The star hung low in the V of my blouse. I kissed him on the lips.

He took my hand. "I have to explain something, though. And I know it's going to sound weird. The star wasn't my idea. It was my mother's. I didn't want to give it to you, especially now so early in our relationship. She made me promise."

"Oh."

"I couldn't say 'no' to her."

"Why?"

"She said it was important that you know we're a Jewish family."

"But I knew that already, David."

"What can I say? My mother is strange at times."

I was in a daze about the gift, and I wandered into the kitchen to finish cleaning up. I had never met his mother, so I didn't want to judge her intentions, but I wondered about David, about his relationship with his mother, that he would do something he didn't think was right.

He followed me into the kitchen, went to the sink and began to wash the dishes. I nudged him aside. "That's very nice of you, but why don't you help by starting a fire? There's wood out on the porch."

It was snowing outside, and each time David entered through the kitchen door with split logs, cold winter wind and some snowflakes blew in. Later, when he was in the living room at the fireplace, I went up to my bedroom and looked in the mirror at the star. I liked it, but I wasn't sure what it meant to David or his mother. I needed to find out. I took it off. From the jewelry box on my dresser, I lifted out the silver necklace and cross that my mother had given me for my first communion. I put it on.

Soon, I came into the living room with tea and pieces of chocolate. David was sitting on the carpet in front of the fire. He pointed to the fieldstone fireplace. "Any minute I expect a chipmunk to poke his head out."

I laughed. "Say, you got that fire going quick." I offered him a piece of chocolate, put it in his mouth; then, I went to the CD player, turned it on. "What would you like to hear?"

"Up to you."

I picked Clannad, a collection of Irish songs with lyrics and the sounds of the harp, guitar, flute, tin whistle and mandolin. The first song was one I had listened to hundreds of times. It was a lively instrumental piece. Suddenly, I felt spontaneous and free, and I broke into a jig, my hair flying, my feet and body bouncing. The cross was jangling, but apparently he didn't see it. *Did he need glasses?*

I took him by the hand, pulled him up, showed him the steps. He was laughing and couldn't get the movements right. "Now Julia, if this was a klezmer band, I'd know what to do."

I whirled him around a few times, then let go of his hand and danced alone with abandon. When the song ended, I took a bow. "Improve on that."

He applauded. "You're good. Where did you learn to dance like that?"

"Learn? Why, it comes naturally." I was breathless, gave out a laugh. "Truth is, I used to dance in the Irish pubs when I was at BU."

I sat down next to him on the floor. He took my face in his hands. "You're so talented." He kissed my lips, then moved down to kiss my neck. He had found the cross. He held it up, looked at me with dismay.

"It was a gift from my mother for my first communion."

He let out a nervous laugh. "You're testing me, aren't you?" He stroked his chin. "Sure Julia, I understand how sentimental it must be, you know, coming from your mother and all, but did you forget how uncomfortable the cross makes me feel?"

"You told me that?"

"I thought I did."

I took his hand. "What I remember is you told me you liked me as I am." I touched the cross. "This is part of who I am, too, and this whole thing with the star—Are you trying to change me? You know, David, I became the woman that Terence wanted me to be, just like you became the man that Alice wanted you to be. And it sucked." I kissed his hand. "I'm falling for you, David. But this gift from your mother...it's really confusing to me."

He pressed his fingers against his temples. "You said you weren't a practicing Catholic, so what's the big deal?"

"Why does the cross bother you, David?"

He rearranged the logs in the fire with the poker. "It's not me, it's my mother."

"You're mother?"

"She's very sensitive."

I bit my lower lip. "She doesn't want you to date a gentile. Am I right?"

He said nothing.

"This is her way of telling me to convert or to stay away from you. Isn't that true?"

He backed up a little. "I'm not as smart as you Julia when it comes to figuring out people. I'm not sure why my mother made me give you the star, but there are a lot of things you don't know, so be careful what you say."

"Now I'm really confused, David. What are you talking about?"

He hesitated. "Things aren't so easy for my mother. She's had a few breakdowns."

I let out a deep sigh. "I'm sorry. I didn't know."

"She doesn't want me to tell anyone. Last year it was two months. She couldn't get out of bed. Then it lifted, and she was fine."

He crossed his arms, stared into the fire. His body tightened. "One never knows with these things. When and if she'll recover? Each time it's like a death in our family. Fortunately, my father takes good care of her. Keeps her at home. Hires private nurses."

"That's good. She's okay now?"

He nodded. "I wish there was some way to cure her. She sees a psychiatrist, but her problem seems beyond him. You know, there are some things in the world that can't be fixed. For her, it's the Holocaust." David lowered his head. "She lost twenty of her family. In Poland. It haunts her. She can't forget."

He moved closer to the fire, held up his hands in front of the flames, palms open. "It's as if she's there. As if she sees it all. The naked children. The German soldiers. The gauntlet of clubs and rifle butts. The pit. Floating bodies. Water and blood. The fatal shots to the head. Children, my God, Julia, just children. They killed everyone in the village. Seventeen hundred people. What did they ever do to deserve that?"

I moved behind David, circled him with my arms. He was rigid, like a rock. "I'm so sorry." There were tears in my eyes.

A long silence.

David stood up, paced back and forth. "History doesn't die, Julia. I see it inside my mother. And the Christian churches...they did nothing to stop it. When Christians talk about the blood of Christ, we Jews think of all the Jewish blood that's been spilled in his name for the past two thousand years. And the great irony, that Christ himself was a Jew." He stopped pacing, studied my face. "Do you understand?"

"I think so."

He eased onto the floor, took my hands. "It's difficult stuff, isn't it? Especially for you and me because of our different backgrounds. I hope it doesn't get in the way."

"Me too."

He kissed my hands. "So, you see, when my mother asked me to give you the star, I couldn't say 'no."

"Ah, I understand better." I unlocked the necklace with the cross, and put it in my pocket.

He let out a deep breath. "Thank you. You know, I was feeling like I was on trial in the Inquisition or something." He laughed, a deep laugh. All the tension was gone.

He lay on the carpet, rested his head in my lap. I clasped his cheeks with my hands. "David, I want you to know that I respect you as a Jew. I mean that from the bottom of my heart."

Silence.

I tapped his chin. "Don't you have something to say?"

He glanced up at the ceiling, thinking. "And I respect you and your beliefs."

I laid next to him, kissed his lips, his eyes, his neck. I pulled away a little, took pleasure in looking at his face, his high cheek bones, his brown eyes. They seemed so familiar to me, so pleasing.

We lay quietly for a while, then he held me close, and I snuggled my head into his neck. I knew there was no way we would make love that night. I was thinking of the Jewish children, and I knew he was, too. It was savage. It was incomprehensible.

We sat up in front of the fire, nestled together in a blanket. Outside the snow tinged against the windows. Inside the flames of the fire hissed and snapped. I moved between his legs and rested my head against his chest.

He stroked my face. "You know, Julia, sometimes when I'm at the store, I think of you pushing the hair off your cheeks, and that thought makes me so happy."

I held his hand against my lips. "I want to be careful not to use the word 'love' until I'm sure."

"Of course. I feel the same way." He kissed me tenderly.

I closed my eyes and lost myself in his embrace. I smelled the smoke of the fire. I heard his beating heart. After a little while, I felt him tracing the scar on my wrist with his finger.

He seemed deep in thought.

I glanced up at him. "What?"

"Nothing."

"You sure?"

He turned my head towards the wall. "Look, Julia. See the firelight flickering. It's us. We're dancing."

I kissed the palm of his hand, my lips lingering. I whispered, "I hope tonight never ends."

Nine

It wasn't like me, not calling ahead, but I wanted to surprise him. Would he be there? I wasn't sure.

I parked my car at the municipal lot in Bar Harbor, and walked down Main Street towards the Royal Florist shop. Snow from the storm last night still hung on the lampposts; several shopkeepers were busily shoveling the sidewalks in front of their busineses. Inside the florist store, I looked at the cut flowers. What flower would a guy like? I wasn't sure, so I bought several white roses because they reminded me of the snow, and they smelled heavenly.

As I left the florist, I had a moment of doubt. Was I pushing things too much, being too forward? No, it was time to resolve this. I had to know once and for all if there was some hope that David and I might have a normal and healthy relationship.

Two blocks later, I walked into Zuckerman's Outfitters at the corner of Main and Atlantic, and the brass bell on the front door rang. In a moment, Trisha, David's young, bouncy clerk, appeared from behind a stack of jeans. She had her hair up, today, and was wearing a tight-fitting turtleneck.

"Hi, Julia. Can I help you?"

"Is David in?"

"I'm not sure. Let me check." She went to the check-out counter, picked up the phone, then set it back down. "Oh, his extension light is on. Must be talking to someone."

I knocked on his door.

His voice sounded muffled. "Come in."

He was sitting at his desk, talking on the phone, dressed in his usual business attire: a white pressed shirt, blue tie and tan slacks. I sat down and waited. David had decorated his desk with a photo of Rachel and himself. In it he was beaming widely, buried in sand, and she was laughing, shoveling more of the beach on top of him. Along the walls, file cabinets dominated the office. On a long table rested piles of invoices, a large calculator and a typewriter.

When David hung up, he said, "Sorry. Had to check on a back order. Supposedly the truck is coming today." He raised his eyebrows. "We'll see. Anyway. Nice to see you. What a surprise."

I handed him the white roses, and he raised them up to his nose. "Ah, sweet. Like you. So, what's the occasion? Have I forgotten something, again?"

"Oh, work was getting to me, so I decided to take a long lunch, do a little shopping, stop in. I missed you." I went and sat in his lap, pressed a kiss on the lips. "This is what the secretaries do in the movies, right? So, pretend you're the boss. What comes next?"

He thought for a moment. "Honey, you better lock the door, just in case my wife decides to pop in."

I went to the door and locked it. He gave me a wide grin. I asked, "And now."

"Better lower the blinds, sweetie-pie."

I wasn't sure where he was headed, but I hoped it was where I wanted to go. I lowered the blinds.

He stood up, pretended for a moment to unbuckle his pants.

I nodded knowingly. "Ah, so this is the way it's done. Nice and quick, huh? No time for foreplay. The boss is a busy man and has to get back to work."

He held his hands out as if to say he was uninformed about these things. I went to him, completely undid his buckle, gave him a deep, wet kiss. His laughter had a nervous edge. "You're not serious, are you?"

"What do you think?"

He smiled, redid his buckle. "Of course you're not." He went to the door, unlocked it and opened it a little. "It's kind of stuffy in here." He talked fast. "So, have you had lunch? Want to go out for a sandwich?"

I raised the blinds back up. "Oh, I grabbed a bite on the way over, but I could use your help with something."

"You name it."

"What a winter, hey? So cold. I've been freezing. Would you help me pick out a new jacket? Something warm."

We went onto the floor and looked through several racks of coats. David was attentive, explaining the different insulation values for each jacket. I had to clench my jaws to keep from laughing. He still had no idea why I had arrived unexpectedly. Sometimes, guys have a malfunctioning radar screen.

After five minutes of checking out jackets, I said, "I like them, David, but I don't see a color that works for me. Do you have any more?"

"Let me look."

He went into the back storeroom, and I followed. There were no windows, and it was completely dark. He fumbled for the switch, turned on the lights. He moved forward, but I held back and quietly locked the door. I had him where I wanted. Narrow aisles ran through the storeroom, and stacks of cardboard boxes and racks of clothes filled almost every square foot. The place smelled of newness. We passed a shelf with more than fifty sleeping bags, and then we came to the coat rack. David picked out a magenta one and handed it to me. I took it, examined it closely, smiled at him. Next, I slowly unbuttoned my blouse, set it on a box; then, I put on the coat, zippered it up, and spun around once like a model. "What do you think?"

He let out a short laugh. "People usually leave their shirts on."

I unzippered the coat, held it open. "What's your expert opinion?"

He moved close, nibbled my lips. "If only I had more customers like you." He flashed his wide grin, ran his hands along my back. I felt myself shiver. Now, we were getting someplace. But then, he stepped away, held me at arm's length, gave me a sideways look. "Did you plan this?"

"Innocent me?"

He crossed his arms over his chest, bounced lightly on his feet. "And I fell for it."

"Well, what happens now?"

"We can't do it here, Julia." He looked around. "There's not enough room. Besides, someone might hear us."

"Who cares?"

"It should be special. In a special place."

I met his gaze straight on. "We've waited long enough, David. I've got to know right now that we can do this thing, and that it can be an intimate part of our lives."

He took my hand. "Let's go to my house."

I shook my head firmly. "We'll have an accident on the way over, or suddenly Rachel's teacher will call and say she's sick and has to come home."

"This room isn't romantic."

I wasn't going to let him win this argument. "The first time doesn't have to be perfect. It's usually not. Don't you know that?"

He glanced around, a look of panic on his face. "Okay, but let me fix things up a little." He cleared some space on the floor. Pulled a large air mattress from atop some boxes. Two blankets. Two camping pillows. Then he found a Coleman lantern, switched it on, and turned off the lights. We could've been inside a cave, the spot so womb-like and small in the middle of boxes and clothes racks, and the yellow light glowing like the coals of a campfire. "How's that?" he asked.

"Good." I gave him a suspicious look. "You've done this before?"

"With Alice. Camping. In a tent."

The memory of her wasn't part of my plan, but I wasn't turning back now. I'd just have to make this new memory better. I cuddled up to David, and he enclosed me with his arms. We stood silently for a while. I could hear an occasional sound from the store or street, but it was muffled and soft, quickly absorbed by the piles of clothes. I pressed my head against his chest, and I heard his heart beating. I liked this side of him, tender, even a bit shy. I had some men who had "taken me" before I was married, but I felt beat up afterwards, not loved. I liked sex, but I liked gentle, caring sex. *Was David gentle?* Finally, I would find out.

He leaned away from me a little, ran his fingers through my hair, gently massaging my head. He continued touching me this way, and my mind stopped thinking, stopped whirling, and I felt my whole body relaxing. He pushed the coat back, slid his hands down to my neck and shoulders, soothing my muscles. I swayed with his motions, breathing deep, letting out soft moans. He moved up to my face, sculpting it lightly with his fingers on my chin, mouth, nose and eyes. *Was it true? Did he understand my body?* He placed his cheek against mine, whispering, "I like how you moan."

I slipped through his lips, danced inside his mouth. He started to breath faster, to release sounds of pleasure. His delight was my delight. I loosened his tie, took it off; then I unbuttoned his shirt, one button at a time, watching his torso emerge, so lean and muscular. So gorgeous, every inch the feel and smell of a man. I moved to his navel, my mouth creating circles of wetness. He groaned. I nibbled his skin, climbed up to his breast, and took it into my mouth. His body shuddered, and he let out an uncontrollable moan. It excited me that he was not ashamed to feel this sensitivity, to let me play him like a piano.

All at once, he seemed out of control, and he yanked off my coat; but then, just as suddenly, he stopped, stared at me in my silk, red bra. "Oh, how pretty." He unhooked my bra, cupped both hands gently on my breasts. He circled my nipples with his fingers, and I began purring.

I closed my eyes, felt the heat stirring inside my body. He put his lips on my breast, twirling my mind around like a merry-go-round. That's when it happened. Somehow, positioned like that, a little off balance, we fell backwards against the coat rack. It teetered, tipped into another rack, and like dominoes, both crashed onto the floor with a bang. David looked shocked; I laughed. Within a few seconds, we heard a knock on the locked door. "David, is that you in there?" Trisha asked.

He squeaked out a simple, "Yes."

"Are you okay?"

Shirtless, he went to the door, as if talking closer to it would be more convincing. "I'm fine. You know how clumsy I am. I knocked over a goddamn clothes rack. Don't worry."

"Do you need help?"

"No, thanks. I can handle it."

He came back to me, shaking his head. "I knew this was a bad idea." He took the lantern, scurried to the back of the room, fumbled for a switch, and turned on a fan in the ceiling, which made a loud whirling sound. He returned, "That should help. God forbid some customers should hear us."

I sat up on the floor, curled my arms around my knees. "Should we pick up the racks?"

"Later." He squatted down in front of me. Held my face with his hands. "You're crazy, you know that, but I like you. My life was boring before I met you."

In an instant, we flew in each other's arms. So much for slow. My mouth tasted his arm; his teeth nibbled my foot. We twirled around each other, wild and free. Soon, we were rolling on the floor, clad only in our underwear. "Whoa," David said, pulling away from me, lying on his back, catching his breath. He started laughing. "If only the chamber members could see me now." He sat up. "I should warn you. I don't have any condoms."

"I'm on the pill. Are you safe?"

"If Alice was, I am."

"Same for me."

"We're almost virgins," he said, letting out an amused chuckle. He stood up from the floor, scooped me up with both arms, held me like a baby. I felt safe like that, but also a little silly that I wanted to be carried away by my knight. *Was it an innate feeling, or had I seen too many movies?* Oh well, I surrendered to the feeling. In a moment, he set me down easily on the mattress, lay beside me and covered us with a blanket. I turned him onto his back, spread myself on top of him, my head in the curl of his neck. He held me tight. "I'm yours," I said. "Only yours."

We lay like that, content, blissful for a minute. Then, he slid down, put his mouth around my breast. I sighed, gripped his body with my legs, arched in and out. *Was there anything I would not give him?* He hungrily pawed my back and shoulders, moved downward along my body, dragged his wet mouth along my navel. His hands and lips found my most secret places. *Was I groaning too loudly?*

I twisted around his body, stripped him, and we looked like Adam and Eve before the Fall, shameless without clothes, pressing flesh on flesh. Desire pushed me to the very edge. I pulled back and saw in the faint light of the lantern that he was hard and strong. Circumcised, of course. I expected that, wanted that. I felt his body tremor and jerk as I surrounded him. He let out a loud groan. I felt the power I had over him. Whatever I might have said to him, 'Give me all your money. Jump off a cliff,' I think he would have done it. Not that I was going to ask him. I wanted his love, his caring. The room spun in colors of silver and ruby. I rolled onto my back. "Oh God, I want you inside me."

I closed my eyes, and he came in gently. My flesh melted with his. We were one body, not two. We dissolved into warmth and light. I threw my head back, heard my ragged breath pulling in and out. I felt the blood rushing to every vessel in my body. He began rocking tenderly at first, but soon he began pounding too hard and too fast. "Please, David, slowly." Then, without warning, he let out a cry and pulled quickly out of me. He fell onto his back. He was breathing wildly. Did I hear a sob?

I was stunned, turned to him, held his face. "What's the matter?"

His eyes were shut. "I can't do it."

I reached down for him. This was my worst fear. Was he limp? I touched him. He was still hard. "I don't understand."

His voice was fast, nervous. "I'm going to come any second. I get so excited. I'll come, and you'll be mad at me, just like Alice was. I hated sex with her. She humiliated me. Dug her claws into my back. "Damn you," she would say." He held his head in his hands. "I'm sorry, Julia. I want to please you, but I can't."

I put my finger to his lips. "Shhhhh. It's okay, David. Relax. Breathe in and out. I told you the first time wasn't perfect." I rubbed the temples of his head. "That's it. Relax." His breathing slowed down. After a few minutes, I said. "Let me show you how to do it."

He said nothing.

"I can teach you."

I rose up on all fours, swooped over his face, sweetly kissing him, rousing him into hardness; then, I took him inside. "Just tell me when you think you're coming, and I can help you."

He closed his eyes. Was he ashamed? I hoped not. We rocked softly at first, and then the rhythm changed. We rode one another, climbing. "Now," he said.

I pulled back a little and reached around, found the place between his pouch and buttocks, pressed hard with my fingers. "Breath deep, David," I said.

After a few moments, he murmured, "Okay."

We picked up the pace, but soon I needed to press again. After doing it a few times, he seemed more confident, and we were able to forget the technique. We fell into the rhythm of the dance. He was smiling, his face astonished. Time seemed endless. We groaned together. He rolled me over, pressed against me, rocking, seeking to match my pace. We drifted into fluidity, into a rising ecstasy. I felt otherworldly, reaching a state I had always hoped existed where love and sex merged. My mind reeled. Quivering skin. Deep sighs. I opened to him. Wider. Wide as the earth.

"Take me." I was silk. I was sapphire. I floated like a cloud, then shone like the sun. "Oh God. Now, David, now."

He let out a final groan, deep and resonant, and cried out, "I love you, Julia."

No silence can equal the silence after sex. Why not stay like this forever with him inside me? Forget the world and its hard edges and cruel people. I belonged here, among softness and caring.

Finally, he gently pulled out, then traced my lips with his fingers. "I've never made love like that before. It was incredible. You're such a good teacher, and so patient. Where did you learn that?"

I wanted to sound humble. "It's the Tao of loving. An ancient Chinese philosophy. Teaches one to relax, to be natural, to enjoy the earthly pleasures."

"Wow. All these years, and I never knew what to do."

"Apparently, it happens to a lot of young guys."

He pulled the blanket up, and we cuddled together, our bodies calm and serene. We didn't talk for a while. I looked at the light on the ceiling. The glass frame of the lantern threw off triangular patterns, and so the room had an abstract quality—a feeling, rather futuristic, and I felt as if I existed in another time and place, in a world that was guiltless, safe and nurturing.

Later, we stirred. I turned David onto his stomach and began rubbing his back, learning his contours and muscles. "I feel so good, David, with you. Sexually, you know."

His voice was sleepy. "Do you mean that?"

I tasted the back of his neck. "You're delicious."

He sat up, buried his face in my hair, nuzzled me like a goat with his forehead and nose, then munched on my hair like it was grass. It seemed strange, but felt affectionate. In a little while, I sat up and drew him between my legs, and ran my brush through his hair. "So David, you have a wonderful daughter, but I'm wondering. Is one child enough?" I didn't know why I was asking this. It slipped out. Maybe the sex was just too good, and I had lost my mind.

He considered my words. "For now it is. I never thought raising a kid could be so hard." He swung the blanket around our nude bodies and wrapped us tight. "I think you're a very caring woman, Julia. I'm surprised you and Terence didn't have a child."

"He didn't want kids with me." My voice was shaking a little. "He said I was too crazy, like my father."

David took my hands. "What a terrible thing to say. Do you believe it?"

"I don't know." I bit my fingernails.

"Come on, Julia. I've seen you with Rachel. You're very caring."

"Except she doesn't want to be with me."

"Not at the moment, but she's a smart girl. She'll figure out you're important to me, and then she'll change."

I lowered my head on his shoulders. "I guess you know her better than anyone. I hope you're right." I glanced at my wrist watch. "Say, this lunch hour has just flown by." I laughed. "I should get back while I still have a job."

We began dressing. David was so sweet, finding my panties, fastening my bra for me. He picked up the brush, combed out my hair, kissed me in a loving way that reassured me I wasn't a one-night stand. I straightened his tie, pressed out the wrinkles in his shirt with my hands. He picked up our bedding; then, we looked at one another, took a deep breath and walked out the door of the storeroom. Trisha saw us almost immediately, and came to David with several phone messages, saying, "I told them you were out to lunch." David blushed. So much for keeping a secret, but it didn't matter. I knew Trisha understood because she winked and smiled at me as she walked away.

One by one, I pulled each tomato plant out of its plastic container, placed it in a small hole, and covered the roots with dirt. Thirty-six plants later, I was done. I looked over at Deb, who lifted a hoe above her head and swung it down, breaking the soil in another part of the garden into smaller pieces. "So Deb, when are you going to open up your own canning factory?"

She leaned on her hoe, pretended to consider it. "Me and Paul Newman, right? Let's see. I'll have my own label. How about, 'Gianelli's Pasta Sauce?" She moved to a wooden cart, retrieved a tray of green pepper plants and handed it to me.

"For your sauce, too?"

"Shhhh, the recipe's a secret." We laughed. She showed me how to plant the peppers, then returned to hoeing. It was just like her to let me do the fun work while she did the hard work. She was nice to everyone. Is that why guys took advantage of her? When I finished planting some of the peppers, I took the hoe from her. "Let's switch for a while. I could use the exercise."

Later, I went into her kitchen and returned with two cold glasses of lemonade. "Break time," I called.

She picked a few spearmint leaves from her garden and twisted them into our drinks. We sat on lawn chairs, stretched out, sunned ourselves. I lifted my bare feet into the air. "Look at me. I'm a little girl again with dirty feet."

Deb wiped the perspiration off her face with her T-shirt, pulled her hair into a pony tail. "I feel like mother earth. I wish I could grow food for everyone."

We sat together, quiet, relaxed in each other's company. I looked around Deb's place, admiring it. She lived inland from the coast in a town called Eastbrook, where land and houses were cheaper. She had about ten acres. We sat near her old barn. In front of us, her large vegetable garden smelled of newly-turned earth. To the right the sugar maples flickered green in the breeze. To the left sunlight danced off the surface of a beaver pond. Peggy, Deb's golden retriever, bounced over, placed her wet nose against Deb's bare leg, and let out a muffled bark. Deb took a biscuit out of her pocket and gave it to the dog. Peggy gobbled it in one bite. Deb turned to me. "So, how are things with David?"

"We were talking about kids." I laughed.

She grinned at me. "Guess the engagement ring's next."

"Are you kidding? We just made love for the first time."

"Weren't you hot for him?"

"He wanted to take it slow. I was getting worried, but he finally rose to the occasion." I paused for effect. "All twelve inches of him."

"My God," she said, throwing her head back, laughing, and then we laughed together. Our clowning around must have startled Peggy, who came to me, licked my knee; and I scratched her back. "Say Deb, do you think you want kids someday?"

"Sure." She put an ice cube in her mouth, sucked on it. "I got it all figured out. I can walk the dog and push the stroller at the same time. Breast feed at night; pump at work during the day...That's my dream, anyway. All I need is a responsible guy. What are the odds? A million to one?" She laughed a little too long.

I put my hand on her knee. "You're a terrific woman, Deb. Any day now the right guy will come along and see that."

She closed her eyes, her mouth tightened. "Thanks. I've been feeling sorry for myself. Kind of lonely, you know." She put the cold glass against her forehead. "How about you, Julia, you want kids?"

"Yes and no. I guess if the right guy comes along."

"David?"

"Who knows?"

All the sudden we saw Peggy, digging in the tomato patch. Deb jumped up, waved her hand. "Get out of there, Peggy." Deb ran towards her, and the dog sprang up and ran off just before Deb reached her. Deb filled in the hole and came back. "She thinks it's a game. See, I already have one kid."

I brushed the hair out of my eyes, rubbed my temples for a moment. "What I don't get about kids is how needy they can be. Like with Rachel. She wants all of David's attention, so I'm thinking, go away girl. I'm jealous, you know. I want David to dote on me. Not my proudest moment, if you know what I mean?"

Deb touched my hand. "What's Odette say about it?"

I let out a deep sigh. How could I answer that question without sounding like a broken record. “She says I was injured as a child. Got to look at the pain. Move beyond it. Learn to love and comfort myself. Then I’ll be able to nurture someone else.”

Deb patted me on the back. “Let’s see. Maybe by the time you’re sixty-five—“

I raised my eyebrows, let out a quick cackle.

“So Julia, is Odette any good?”

“Yeah, she’s helped me a lot. Knows me like a book, too. She’s strange sometimes, though. Sways a little in her seat. Even hums a little when I’m talking.”

Deb stirred the ice cubes in her drink with her finger and took a sip. “Sounds like a black thing, no? Maine is such a white state. It must be hard for her to live here.”

“She won’t say. I’ve asked her, but she said no personal questions. That’s one of her rules.” I gazed off, feeling a bit lost and confused, as I often did when I talked about therapy. “It’s weird to confide in her and not know who she is. A few things I know about. She has a son, and she likes to sail, I think. There’s a photo on her desk. She and her son are on a sailboat.”

Deb reached out, stroked my arm. “Well, you know, I respect you for doing therapy. And you’re lucky. A good therapist is hard to find.”

Our conversation drifted to other things; then, after a little while we returned to the garden and dug more rows with hoes. Next we started to plant corn seeds every few inches. I concentrated on my work, but Deb caught my attention by throwing some seeds at me. I looked up. She smiled. “Saw your brother downtown the other day. Some woman was hanging all over him.”

“Really? What did she look like?”

“Blond. Cute. Young.”

“Sounds like his type.” I flashed a smirk. “Let’s see, if she’s anything like his other squeezes, they might last together about three weeks.”

Ten

A gusty ocean wind swept the top of the tall pine tree I was perched in, and I grabbed onto a branch to keep from falling. The tree rocked for a little while; then, the wind subsided. Was I afraid? I tried not to think about it because I was studying the eagles as part of my job from a canvas blind fifty feet above the ground. Besides, the platform I stood on seemed secure enough.

All at once, I heard a branch snap to my right. Up went my binoculars. I saw a large eagle with a brown body and a white head and tail fly out of an aspen tree with a two-foot stick in his talon. He flapped his long wings and landed on a half-completed nest in another, nearby pine tree; then, he pushed the branch into a nest of sticks with his feet. At the same time a female eagle gathered limbs from the ground. Again and again the two eagles came to the nest that they were building forty feet above the ground.

I felt privileged to be witnessing the resettlement of the eagles on the Maine coast. These two were the first nesting pair in Acadia since the 1950s when DDT decimated them along the Maine coast. Who knows why they were here? They certainly didn't take their first flight here. It was odd. Maybe they moved downeast from Quoddy Head? Maybe they didn't like their relatives there?

Within a few hours they had built a nest three feet thick; then, they took turns jumping on top of it to create a shallow depression in the middle. Next, they wove grass and moss into the bowl. I adjusted my camera, zoomed in and took a few pictures. Later, I shot more when the eagles constructed a corral of sticks around the perimeter of the nest. I had read that the corral would prevent the chicks from tottering off or being blown off by the wind.

About noon the female suddenly appeared with a weathered-looking sneaker in her talon and placed it in the bowl. Then soon, she brought two clothespins. The male stared at her without expression from a nearby spruce tree. *What was he thinking?* I tried not to analyze the eagles with human concepts and feelings. They were a different species. I wanted to see things through their eyes, but the sneaker and clothespins remained a mystery to me.

When the nest was complete, the two eagles perched on the uppermost branch of a dead aspen tree and rested in the hot afternoon sun, rarely moving except to occasionally preen their feathers.

I sat down on the platform, leaned against the trunk of the tree and drank water from my canteen. My blind and the eagle's nest were on a ridge above the rocky shore of Bartlett Island west of Acadia National Park. Nothing happened for the next several hours, so I wrote for a while in my notebook, preparing a report on the eagles that I would present and publish at the end of the summer.

Later in the afternoon, cooler ocean winds began blowing onshore, and the eagles stretched their wings, rearranged their feathers, and flew off together. I watched them with my telescope. They found a warm air thermal, and they soared up a thousand feet into the blue sky. Suddenly, they turned to each other, locked their talons together, and fell downwards, spinning around in cartwheels. About fifty feet from the green water, they separated in a flash, spread out their wings, and glided.

They found another thermal and climbed upwards, again, where once more they locked talons and careened again to the sea in a descent of fierce abandon. How could I describe their wild, graceful display? I wrote in my notebook: *The Wedding Dance.* The word wedding stirred a painful memory for me. *Would I have another chance at marriage, like my mother had predicted? Would I have another wedding dance?* I hoped so.

When the eagles returned to the nest, I knew what they would do next, and I prepared my camera.

The female stroked and pecked her mate's yellow bill. Nudged his chest. Bowed her head low. Opened her brown wings. Called to him in a soft, high-pitched note.

Back and forth they sang to one another. He flapped his wings. Moved his white tail up and down. Jumped on her back, talons curled up, wings outspread.

She sang to him. Moved her white tail sideways. He pressed his cloaca to hers. It was the kiss that would bind them as partners for life. *Such tenderness*, I wrote in my notebook.

Afterwards, they preened one another. Rearranged their nest. Ruffled up the moss and grass. An hour later, they made love again.

When it was dark, I climbed down the wooden slats on the tree. I hiked along the ridge in the woods and came to the white sandy beach where my motor boat was docked, and drove it back to the mainland. That evening at home I browsed through books on my bookshelf, trying to find names for the eagles. I picked Emily and Robert, the first names of two great New England poets. I hoped the names would bring the eagles good luck.

Several weeks later Emily laid two, large eggs. A month after that, the chicks hatched. "It was like Genesis," I said to David as we lifted boxes from the loading dock of his store to a flatbed cart. "Emily stepped off her eggs, and, you're not going to believe this, a small egg tooth started to poke through the shell. So think—"

"What's an egg tooth?"

"Oh, it's temporary. The chick uses it to break the shell. So think about it, David. Seven billion people in the world. And here I was, this nobody in Maine—"

He put his arm around me. "Hey, don't call yourself a nobody."

"Thanks." I placed another box on the cart. "Okay, so I was watching a tiny tooth break the egg. It took hours. Then suddenly, the newborn crawled out. Covered in beige down. Wet. Helpless. Dragging her pink legs—."

"And where was I when this miracle was happening?" He slumped over the boxes. "Stuck in my office, punching keys on a calculator." He fell on his knees, his voice theatrical. "Please, you've got to take me with you."

I laughed. "You know why I can't take you."

He stood up, paced on the dock. "The chicks are older now, Julia. Their parents aren't going to abandon them just because some guy is in the blind with you, some guy who's promised to be quiet as a mouse. I'm begging you Julia. Take me. What do you want? Gold? Diamonds?"

I fumbled with a button on his shirt and looked in his long face. Was this guy for real? So playful and innocent. Suddenly, I melted. "Okay."

He flashed his wide grin, planted a kiss on my lips. "When?"

"Tomorrow."

He put his arms around my waist. "Hey, you know what I read in the town library? Only four out of ten eagles live long enough to breed. Is that true?"

"Keep studying." I pinched his cheek. "We'll have a test in the morning."

He began loading boxes again. "You think I'm a *noodge*, don't you? But do you know what I have to do everyday? Flatter people. So what if they're a size forty-six. 'You look great,' I lie to them." He wiped the sweat from his face with a handkerchief. "I don't mean to complain. I make good money. But your stuff, working with eagles, that's incredible."

Early the next morning when we arrived on the island by boat, it was still dark. At the blind David quietly set up his telescope, and I put my camera on a tripod, Soon, there was enough light, and we looked at the eagles' nest. Emily was lying on top of her chicks. A little later she moved to the edge to preen, and we saw the chicks huddled together in the grassy bowl. They were two beige puffs of down, squatting, too young to stand, tilting their huge heads left and right. David whispered: "You're right. It's like Genesis."

Emily rested back on top them, pulling moss and grass around her to keep them warm. Later, Robert landed on the nest with a fish in his talons. Emily stood, fluffed out her feathers, and let out a loud cry. He released the fish, then flew away. She ripped off a tiny piece, bowed low, and offered it to one of the chicks.

When she finished feeding her young, she lay on top of them again and began to doze off. Everything seemed quiet and safe, but suddenly, Emily jerked up her head. After a few moments, I saw a black-backed gull flying directly towards the nest.

Emily hunkered down. The gull uttered several sharp cries as it passed a few feet above her head. In a flash, Robert appeared out of nowhere, dropping from the sky, his wings tight against his body. I aimed my camera and started taking pictures. The second before he struck the gull, he banked back, ruffling the gull's feathers with his talons; then, he chased the bird and dove at him four or five times.

Soon, he returned and perched on the spruce tree next to the nest. He tossed his head skyward, grunted loudly, and called out, "whee-he-he-he-he."

David tapped me on the shoulder. "I thought he was going to kill that gull."

"The next time it'll be lunch."

Activity at the nest quieted down, and David and I sat on the platform to rest. He put his arm around me, pulled me close and gave me a long, lingering kiss.

"Hmmm. I like that," I whispered.

"Thanks for letting me come today, Julia," he said in a quiet voice.

We busied ourselves for a while, reading and whispering. About noon, David fell asleep in my lap. An hour later, I shook him awake: "Quick. You're going to miss it."

He stood up, half asleep, teetering, a little unsure of his balance on the swaying platform, and looked through his telescope. After a few moments, he gave me a confused look, then readjusted the lens. "All I see is Robert with another fish."

"Really?"

"Oh." He stretched and yawned. "This is some kind of test, right?"

I nodded. "About the life of a naturalist."

"Let me guess." He scratched his head. "Not much happens most of the time, and so maybe running a clothing store isn't so bad."

I patted him on the head. "You're such a smart man."

Later that afternoon, we saw that Emily had moved off her chicks. They stirred and lifted up their huge heads. The smaller chick began swaying his head; then, all at once, he lunged at the larger one, biting her, knocking her down in the nest. He twisted and shook her head with his bill. Emily watched them, but did nothing.

The fighting continued. Several minutes passed. David asked, "How long can it go on?"

My stomach tightened. "What can we do?"

Jab, bite, twist. The larger chick cried out in a high-pitched chittering sound. Finally, Emily grabbed the smaller bird in her bill and shook him back and forth, but he wouldn't release his sibling, who was screaming even louder.

Emily dropped the birds and looked around. Was she looking for Robert? What could she do? Suddenly, she plopped on top of them, and rolled her body back and forth like a rocker; then, she lay perfectly still.

David turned to me, his face distraught. "Why would they fight like that?"

I paused, pushing the hair to the side of my face. "His sister probably pooped on him."

David let out a quiet laugh.

Somewhat later, Emily stepped to the edge of the nest. There in the grassy cup, the larger chick squatted upright. She appeared unharmed, and her mother fed her. "Thank goodness," I said.

When it was dark, David and I climbed down the tree and drove the boat back to Acadia.

That night at home I awoke with a start to the sound of thunder. Every few minutes the rumbles came closer, until it seemed they were overhead. Then, in instant, one shook the house. I went to the window and saw the lightning slice the sky. The air smelled like electricity. I felt my heart quicken, and my hands were shaking.

All at once the rain fell fast and hard like bullets. The wind howled. It tore off branches, leaves and roof shingles.

Suddenly, I heard an explosion like a bomb; then, I saw lightning strike the tree next door, and a huge branch crashed onto my neighbor's porch.

I closed my eyes: *The eaglets...My God, the eaglets.*

I barely slept the rest of the night. Just before dawn I hurried towards the island in my boat. The rain had stopped, and the bay was eerily still and cluttered with uprooted seaweed. Several times I swung the boat around a floating plank. I was whispering: *Please, please...*

On the island I ran along the trail through the woods. When I reached the nest, I covered my mouth with my hands. The upper crown of the pine tree had broken off, and the nest lay smashed on the ground.

I pulled at the sticks of the broken nest and tried to find the grassy bowl where the eaglets would be. Finally, I found it and gently picked away grass and moss.

Inside was a dead chick, her head crushed. I lifted her up, held her in my hand. My legs were trembling. I set her down and searched the shrubs for her sibling, but I didn't find him. What did it matter? He was too young to survive without his nest and parents.

I climbed up to the blind, sat motionlessly. Later I heard a muffled sound, and Robert and Emily landed in a nearby aspen. Soon, they dropped to the ground next to the dead chick. Emily touched her with her beak. She stepped back. She uttered no sounds. She paused, then lifted up into the air and perched in the aspen once more. Robert followed. Occasionally, they stared downward. A while later, they flew away, and I never saw them again that summer.

When I descended from the blind, I picked up the chick and pressed her fluffy down against my cheek. I was crying. Who could understand such things? I dug a sandy hole near the base of the pine tree and buried her. I said a prayer. What else could I do?

Eleven

The *Bay Lady* blasted her foghorn three times and pulled away from the Portland Ferry Terminal. My father, David and I climbed up the metal stairs to the open, second floor deck, sat on one of two dozen wooden benches, and watched the red brick buildings near the wharf fade as the ferry cruised into Casco Bay. The boat was half-full, mostly weekenders with their dogs on leashes heading out to their summer homes on the islands.

"So, Mr. DeCarlo, Julia tells—"

"Frank. Call me Frank."

"Oh, so Frank, Julia tells me you're working at Sears."

My father took a sip of coffee from a paper cup, seemed to be sizing David up. "Yeah. They put me on the cash register last week. They said they wanted to train me first, but I said, 'Don't bother. I have tons of experience from New York'."

I rubbed my chin. "I didn't know that."

"Sure, Julia. At Robert Halls. Couple of my buddies trained me. They were experts when it came to the cash register."

Mischief swept his face. "They were full of good ideas. Step one. You leave the drawer open after a sale. Step two. You wait on the next customer. Step three. You take their cash, but you don't ring nothing up. Step four. You give them change out of the open drawer."

I tapped David's hand. "He's putting you on."

My father looked at me over the top of his black eyeglasses. "Julia, it's not polite to interrupt your father." He faced David. "Step five. Close the drawer. Step six. And now you've got to be careful. You open the drawer and pocket the money when no one's looking. Let's see, right now, I'm making about two hundred extra dollars a day, plus my salary." My father let out a great laugh.

I put my hand on David's shoulder. "Be careful. He's a big joker."

My father reached around, lightly punched David on the arm. "The truth is I'm a maintenance guy at Sears. If it's broken, I fix it."

David smiled. "That's quite a story, Mr...I mean, Frank. You taught me something I didn't know. Guess I'll have to be more careful about my own cash register. Maybe Julia told you. I have a clothing and camping store."

"No, she didn't tell me. Just said she wanted to bring her new boyfriend along. You got a store? Ain't that something." My father took out a cigar and put it in his mouth.

I pointed to it. "Dad, you can't smoke on the boat."

"I ain't stupid." He kept it unlit in his mouth for a while, sucking on the end like it was a lollipop.

A few minutes of silence passed. We stared out at the sea, the wind blowing our hair, the sun on our faces, but the silence was uncomfortable. I had no idea how this would work out with my father and David. Would my father behave himself? Could David accept him? Was I testing David too soon? At first David made up a dozen excuses about why he couldn't come, but finally he relented. I think he wanted to please me, but maybe he was just curious.

Suddenly, my father interrupted my thoughts. "If Sal waits long enough to see me, I might be dead and buried."

He turned to David. "What do you think of that, huh? My own son won't see me. You treat your father like that, David?"

"No, sir."

My father talked with the cigar between his fingers, waving it to emphasize his words. "You know what I think, Julia? Sal just wants to remember the bad things, not the good ones. In those days, fathers didn't have time to be with their kids. I was up at six every morning. On the road for ten, twelve hours. You seen one broken toilet, you seen a thousand. Some nights I couldn't get the smell out of my hands."

My father stood up, walked to the other end of the deck, threw his coffee cup into a trash can; then, he leaned on the iron railing and looked out at the approaching islands.

I took David's hand. "You're being very nice. Thanks."

"He seems okay. A little rough around the edges, but...He never went to college, right?"

"Finished high school, though."

Soon, my father sat next to me again. I said, "Oh, before I forget..." I pulled a photo out of my backpack and gave it to him. My mother was in a white Easter dress wearing a red velvet hat with a veil over half her face, standing on the front porch of our old Milford home.

"You remembered." My father smiled, stared at it for a while; then, showed it to David. "Pretty woman, wasn't she?" He put the photo in his shirt pocket. "Say, Julia, I meant to ask you the last time. Did Maria ever remarry?"

I shook my head. "She was busy working and taking care of us. And once we grew up and left home, she seemed happy to be alone."

My father took off his glasses, rubbed his eyes. "Maybe she still loved me, huh? Maybe that's why she never remarried?"

I studied his face to see if he was serious. Had he forgotten the bruises, cut lips and swollen eyes he had inflicted on my mother? Had he forgotten he nearly killed her? It took all of my self-control not to yell at him, to challenge him, but I wasn't going to create a scene in front of David. It would have to wait for another time. And I would challenge him because

I didn't want to spend my time with a father who deluded himself about his violent past. I glanced at David to see his reaction to my father's comment, but he had moved from the bench to the starboard side and was looking through his binoculars. "Hey, there's an osprey," he called over to us.

I went to the railing with my binoculars and saw the white and brown bird about the size of a hawk, hovering twenty-five feet above the water. I motioned to my father to come and look, handed him the binoculars. The osprey hung in mid-air with beating wings; then, plunged into the water and disappeared below the surface. After a few seconds she rose up with a fish gripped in both claws. She lifted into the air, turned the fish so its head faced forward; and then, flew off.

"Why did she do that?" my father asked.

"To reduce the air resistance. You've got good eyes. Not many people would've noticed."

When we landed at Peaks Island, my father lit up his cigar. It seemed to calm him down, the puffing and blowing. We strolled through the village and came to a country road that crossed the island to the other side. We walked in silence, passing through a forest of spruce and fir trees. Ferns and moss covered the forest floor. I heard a bird calling, "*Cuk, cuk, cuk, cuk, cuk.*" I recognized the sound of the pileated woodpecker and searched for the red-crested bird in the forest canopy with my binoculars. Again the bird called out. This time the sound came from the ground. My father saw it and pointed to it. The woodpecker, large as a crow, was poking a hole in a dead, horizontal tree trunk, digging for ants. "It's a male," I whispered, handing my father the binoculars. "Can you see the scarlet mustache on its bill?"

When we arrived on the other side of the island, the surf pounded the rocky shore and sent up clouds of silver mist. We trekked down Seashore Avenue, a sparsely developed road with a few houses. All at once I noticed a patch of blue-purple flowers along a small brook. I hurried closer. I had seen the flowers before in photographs, but never in the wild. Four petals with fringed edges adorned them. I called David and my father over. "They're fringed gentians. Very rare. Go ahead. Smell them."

They knelt on the ground, took in their odor. "Hmmm," my father said. "Never smelled anything like that before." He pulled himself up from the ground and patted me on the back. "*Mamma mia*, Julia. You know everything about nature."

David stood next to my father. "Has she told you about the eagles?"

"Eagles?"

"Your daughter, single-handedly..." David began, but I didn't stay to listen to him and began walking ahead. Soon, I turned around, and they were following. David was doing all the talking. I was amazed to see that my father was actually listening. I saw him offer David a cigar. I had to keep from rolling on the road in laughter as I watched David blow smoke out of his mouth, pretending to enjoy it.

I stayed ahead of them, hoping they would get to know one another. The next time I turned around I saw David hand my father his business card. My father read it, and I knew in an instant from the look of disdain on his face, that he realized David was Jewish, something I had avoided telling him because I feared he would've skipped the ferry trip. I thought if only he met David, he would like him, and the Jewish issue for him would be mute. Why was everything so complicated? I stared at my father a while longer to see what he would do next, but it seemed he was controlling himself. Still, I was afraid any minute he might say something anti-Semitic, so I rejoined him and David.

Soon, it was David who pulled away at a faster pace, and my father and I were left walking side-by-side.

"Zuckerman?" He moved close to my ear, whispered. "Ain't that a Jewish name?"

"So what?"

He held out his hands, palms up. "Don't get me wrong, Julia. I ain't trying to tell you who to date. But if it gets serious, and you have kids, it'll screw up their lives."

I gave him a twisted smile. "I know what you mean. The horns on the kids will look kind of weird. But now, you know, they have a special operation to remove them."

He tried to look innocent. "Did I say anything about horns?"

"Come on, Dad. I remember all the terrible things you said about Jews."

He stood up straight, his voice almost scholarly. "It's a religious thing, Julia. We're Catholics. We believe in Christ. Jews don't. Do you want to raise your kids without God?"

"The Jews have a God, too."

"But it ain't the right one."

I shook my head. "Do you know how stupid that sounds?"

He glared at me, then threw up his hands up in surrender. "Amen. I don't want to argue. What do they say? Don't talk religion. Don't talk politics." He stopped walking and relit his cigar. I kept on moving and caught up to David. "Why did you give my father your business card?"

"He asked for it." David winked at me. "Maybe he wants to fix my cash register."

I didn't laugh.

About a half hour later, we reached Island Road and came to the outskirts of the village. A red wooden school stood at the edge of a spruce forest. Suddenly, my father bent down on the ground like a sprinter, saying, "Ready. Set. Go," and he ran to the playground of the school. "Watch me," he said, and he clambered up the metal slide, slid down head first, and caught himself with his hands when he hit bottom.

Then he went to the swings and began pumping. In no time he was flying. David and I joined him, each taking a swing.

I began climbing high, laughing, feeling like an osprey above the sea. Then, as it often does, things began to move in slow motion. The chain in my right hand loosened. My eyes flashed upwards, and I saw that it had snapped where it was attached to the upper bar. I was about six feet off the ground. I fell in an instant. Let out a scream. Felt myself scrape on the dirt underneath the swing. I lay still for a moment.

My father and David were immediately at my side. "Are you okay?" my father asked.

I looked at my arms and legs. My elbow was scratched, but not bleeding. I laughed with relief.

They pulled me up. "My silly Lilly," my father said, and he put his arms around me.

It was the first time he had hugged me in eighteen years. I was a little girl again, and I rested my head on his shoulder.

Suddenly, I felt his chest heave, and he pulled away. He went to a nearby maple tree, put his hands on the trunk, leaned his head against it. He stood like that for a few moments. When he turned to me, he had tears in his eyes. "Boy, I screwed up my life, and yours. I'm so sorry, Julia."

As I moved towards him, he held up his hands, kept me at a distance. He wiped his face with his sleeve, then sat on the ground at the base of the tree. "Just give me a few minutes alone, all right?"

I went away and sat at a picnic table with David. "Is he okay?" David asked.

"I've never seen him like this before."

David and I sat silently, and I took out my brush and straightened up my hair. I watched my father out of the corner of my eye as he lit up a cigar and puffed away. Surely, it was a good sign that he was able to express his feelings. Was it possible that he could be the good father I had always dreamed about?

About five minutes later, he came to us. "*Ho fame.* I'm starving. Let's eat."

We found a window seat at Jackie's, a seafood restaurant on the knoll above the ferry landing. Off in the distance I saw the islands of Casco Bay and the Portland skyline.

From the menu I quickly picked out fish and chips, but my father fretted over the selections. When I peeked over the top of his menu, I saw he was studying the back, the beer and wine selection. He pointed to a picture of a beer mug. "That looks good. I'd sure like one."

I put my hands on my chest. "I hope not."

He picked up his napkin, wiped his mouth. "Not a day goes by that I don't want a drink. The doctor said it takes a couple of years for some people. Man, I hope I can make it."

I locked onto his eyes. "You can do it, Dad."

After the waitress brought us our food, my father tapped David's plate with his fork. "So David. You make a lot of money at your store?"

"Business has been good."

My father let out a strange laugh. "Of course. You people are good at business."

David sat upright, his body tightened. "If you mean I work long and hard for my money, then you're right."

I don't know why I didn't intervene. Maybe I didn't see it coming?

My father waved his fork in the air. "Sure, I mean that, but I mean you people are clever, too."

David gave him an icy look. "How's that?"

"Well, everybody knows you charge more than the stuff is worth."

David paused, bit his lip. "That's bull shit, Mr. DeCarlo."

I smacked the table with my hand. "Dad, stop it."

He smiled innocently. "I meant it as a compliment. I'm sorry if you took it the wrong way."

I was at a loss for words. Maybe my father would never change. Maybe Sal was right. I rubbed my leg against David's underneath the table. He looked at me. I raised my eyebrows in dismay, whispered, "Sorry."

The rest of lunch passed in silence, except for the customary comments about the food. I felt defeated.

After we finished eating, we went into the gift shop. My father tried on a black fisherman's cap with a small logo on the front that said "Peaks Island."

I tried to sound upbeat. "It looks good on you."

He convinced me and David to take one. We put them on and went to the front of the store to the cashier. She was in a print dress with her gray hair rolled in a bun on the top of her head.

My father tipped his hat to her, dropped some bills on the counter to pay for all three.

"My goodness," she said, tapping my father's arm. "So this must be your daughter. I'd have to be blind in two eyes not to see it."

As we walked away from the shop to the ferry, I felt both pride and fear. Pride in my father for staying sober, but fear also that David would think my father and I were too much to handle. So, what did my father have to do with David? I knew enough about life to know that when you married someone, you in some ways also married their parents. And I knew, too, you carried your parents' good traits and their shit inside yourself, and like it or not, it affected the people around you for good or ill. Not that David and I were talking about marriage, but it was a fact-of-life I tried to keep in perspective.

A few days later, back on Mount Desert Island, I climbed into Sal's pickup truck, put on my seatbelt and tried to relax. Sal was a fast driver, and today was no exception. He sped off. For a while I kept my eyes on the road, just in case, but he seemed to have things under control. I turned to him, "So who's the cute blond you're dating?"

"You saw us together?"

"Downtown." I lied because I didn't want Sal to think Deb was spying on him. I wanted to protect Deb. I knew she had a crush on him.

Sal spoke with enthusiasm. "Her name's Erin. Irish-American. Has that Boston accent, too, like the Kennedy's. Met her at Sheehan's Cafe. She's a good dancer. And easy to be with. That's important. I hate uptight and pushy."

"What's she doing in Acadia?"

"Waitressing. I can't believe I met her." He whistled. "I'm in seventh heaven."

I patted him on the shoulder. "Good luck."

A little later he pulled into an abandoned sand pit and drove to the far end. We were parked in the bottom of the pit; the sandy sides reached upwards thirty feet to a plateau of pine trees. Just outside my window was a rusted-out dump truck with no wheels. We stepped out of Sal's pickup, and he opened a large tool case in the back, took out a high-powered rifle. "Ever shoot one of these?"

I let out a nervous laugh. "What do you think?"

"I brought a water pistol for you."

I smacked him on the head. "Is that a deer rifle? I didn't think you hunted."

"I don't. It's a M16, like the one I had in Nam." He grabbed a bag full of empty beer cans and went to a dead pine tree that lay horizontally on the ground. Along the trunk he placed about twenty-five cans. When he came back, he lit a joint and took a toke.

He offered it to me; I waved it off. "Better not if I'm going to use that thing. You shouldn't be smoking either. How the hell are you going to shoot straight?"

He took another toke, let out a laugh. "Jesus Christ, Julia. We were stoned half the time on patrol."

He stubbed out the joint on a rock, put the butt behind his ear and picked up the rifle. Within seconds he loaded a magazine, aimed and fired. A can jumped off the log. Another bullet; another can. Five times he did it. I don't think ten seconds had passed.

He smiled. "Not bad, huh?" He handed me the rifle, stood behind me, held the gun with me and helped me sight the target. "Take a deep breath. Pull the trigger slowly." I did. Suddenly, the butt slammed into my shoulder. I think I would've fallen backwards if Sal hadn't been holding me from behind.

I guess he saw the shock on my face. "Now you know. Be ready for it."

"Did we get a can?"

"Of course. Try it on your own."

I sighted carefully and fired. I missed. Sal watched while I tried two more times.

He put his hand on my shoulder. "When you're pulling the trigger, you're jerking the gun, just a little. Pull it smoothly."

I steadied myself. “Whammm.” The can jumped up. Six more times I shot. I only missed once.

Sal patted me on the back. “Who would’ve guessed? Julia, the sharpshooter. Cool gun. Isn’t it?”

“Kind of violent.” I handed him the rifle. “You do this for fun?”

“Clears my head right up.”

“I thought you hated war.”

He raised his fist in the air. “If Nixon and his Mafia try to draft me again, I’ll be ready for them.”

“You and Rambo, right?

He laughed. “Hey, I’m just mouthing off.” He fired the rifle in rapid succession. Each time a can blasted off. When there were about a half dozen cans left on the trunk, he stopped and put the gun on the seat of the pickup. “How about a beer?”

I nodded. He took two from the cooler in the back, and we sat on the tailgate of the truck. I took a sip. “So Sal, aren’t you going to ask about the ferry ride.”

“No, but I bet you’re going to tell me.”

“Dad cried. Real tears. Said he was sorry.”

“You believed him?”

“Maybe he’ll make it this time.”

Sal laughed. “You been watching too many movies.”

I put my hand on his knee. “He wants to see you. It would mean a lot. You know, maybe if we help him, he’ll be able to stay sober.”

Sal took a gulp of beer; then he pulled the joint from behind his ear, relit it, and smoked it to the end. He asked, “Remember that time there was a fire in the Terranova’s woods?”

I nodded.

“Well, somebody told Dad I did it. But I didn’t. He wouldn’t believe me.” Sal rubbed the back of his neck, looked away from me. “He took me in the garage. Called me a liar. Whipped me with his belt. Whipped me bad.”

“Oh my God.”

Sal slid off the tailgate, paced. "It gets worse. He tied me to a post in the garage. Said when I told the truth, he'd let me go. Then, he left me alone. Tied up like an animal. I was eight years old, Julia. I was crying. I thought Mom would come out and help. She didn't. I don't know how many hours passed. I still have nightmares about it." Sal stood in front of me, locked his eyes onto mine. "And you want me to see him?"

I put my hands to my face. "I didn't know, Sal."

"You've been pretty rough on me, Julia. All the guilt. But I don't want to be mad at you. You're a good sister, and I care about you."

"I'm sorry, Sal." I lowered my eyes. I knew he was right. *Who was I to tell him what to do?*

After a moment, Sal moved away from me and finished his beer in one long gulp; then he took the rifle from the seat of the truck, aimed it and fired rapidly, blowing away the last six cans in six shots.

Twelve

David picked me up at my house, and I slipped into the front seat of his van; then, I turned around to Rachel. She was strapped in a car seat and was wearing a pink T-shirt with a picture of Elmo. "Hi, Rachel. I like your T-shirt. Elmo is one of my favorites, too."

She lowered her eyes, turned her head away.

David reached back and tugged on her leg. "Can you say hello to Julia?"

She whispered, "Hello."

"I have something for you, Rachel." I reached into my backpack and handed her a children's book about Acadia's wildlife. There was a color illustration of a mother seal and her pup on the front cover. She glanced at the cover, but set the book down and picked up her black and white panda bear, pressing him to her chest.

David looked at Rachel in the rear view mirror. "What do you say to Julia?"

"Thanks," she said faintly.

As he began driving off, he reached over, touched my thigh and raised his eyebrows as if to say: *Let's hope for the best.*

Soon, Rachel began reading the book, then stretched forward and held up a page for her father to see. "Daddy, what's this bird?"

He shot a quick look. "A loon."

"How's it sound?"

"*Quack-quack-quack.*"

She laughed. "Can't fool me."

He let out a haunting, yodeling call.

"That's weird," she said.

I had hoped she would notice the loon in the book, and I had brought two loon feathers, silky black ones with white spots. I pulled a feather from my braid and gave it to her. "You can keep it. See I have one, too," I said, pointing to the feather in my other braid. She put it on the seat without saying anything. She turned the page. Maybe my strategy of giving her things wasn't working. I wanted today to be the day when I won her trust and friendship. *What would it take? Why couldn't she see that I cared about her?*

Soon, we drove over the bridge at Somes Sound. Gulls swooped in the air and cried out. In the distance, the trees on Bernard Mountain glowed yellow and orange in their fall colors. David called back to Rachel. "How's my daughter?"

"I finished the book." She reached forward and tugged on his arm. "Are we almost there?"

"Ten minutes."

The moment that we parked at the waterfront park in Southwest Harbor, Rachel unbuckled her seat belt and ran around the car, swinging her bear by its arm, calling to her father, "Come on, Daddy." He chased her around a lamppost, caught her and lifted her above his head. She giggled loudly.

After he set her down, I ran to her and tagged her arm. "You're it," I said, then scurried away, but she ignored me and returned to her father, hopping on his back for a pony ride. Later, she pedaled her plastic three-wheeler along the sidewalks with her panda bear on her lap. I took out my camera. She saw me try to take a picture, but rode on. David stopped her; then, they posed together for the photo, and she smiled widely with her arm around his neck.

I'm not jealous, I told myself. Stay focused. *Somehow I'll break through to her.* I went to her, put my hand on her shoulder, kissed the top of her head. She rode off again. I called after her. "Say, do you like lollipops?" She stopped. I had three. She picked the orange one. Well, at least I wasn't batting zero, but I wondered if I was trying too hard. I probably was. I didn't know what else to do.

A little later, she tugged on her father's hand and pointed to a shallow pool of rainwater in the center of the parking lot. A dozen white gulls stood there, some sleeping with their heads buried under their wings. She gave David a mischievous look; then, all at once, she pumped hard on her bike and sped ahead. When she reached the puddle, the gulls fled in unison, squawking. She turned to her father and laughed. In a moment, she pedaled fast towards the pier at the other end of the lot. It had wooden planks, no railings and several lobster boats bobbed along its side. David yelled after her. "Stop. Wait for me."

Did she hear him? We caught up with her just as she had begun to ride onto the pier. David grabbed the handlebar of the bike, stooped down and touched her cheek. "The pier is very dangerous, and you can't go on it by yourself."

She spoke excitedly. "I wanted to see the boats."

"Not on your bike, and not alone." He stroked her hair.

She lowered her eyes. "Okay, Daddy."

He set the bike on the sidewalk, and we went together onto the pier. It smelled like fish. There were ropes, lobster pots and buoys cluttering the planks. He took Rachel's hand. "Please, stay with me."

She lifted up her panda bear. "Take Prince's hand, too." He did.

As we walked to the end of the wharf, I glanced down at the green water. The tide was out and so the sea was a good ten feet below the pier, but the water was still deep here, and I couldn't see the bottom. A strong offshore wind churned up foot-high waves.

All at once, a sea duck popped up from its underwater search. "What's that?" David asked, pulling me to the right side of the pier for a closer look. We took out our binoculars. It was a red-breasted merganser. When the sea duck dove again, I noticed Rachel wasn't with us. I looked around and saw her near the other edge of the wharf, dancing in circles, swinging her panda bear by its arm.

Everything seemed to happen in a nightmarish, slow motion. I saw the look of shock on Rachel's face as she tripped on a rope, lost her balance and began falling off the dock. She screamed. We both leapt towards her, but when we got there, she was gone.

In an instant, we jumped off the dock to the right of where she had fallen. I hit the water and sank below it. Almost at once, I clawed upwards and broke the surface, but Rachel wasn't there. David was frantically pawing at the water, looking for her. I swam five feet in one direction, then another. For a second, I saw her black hair and pink T-shirt underneath the water to my left. I dove, grabbed her, and we bobbed up. She coughed, then shrieked. "Daddy! Daddy!"

David swam to us in a flash. We held her tight, but she swung her arms wildly and gasped for air. It wasn't easy to stay afloat. David shouted, "Swim there." He jerked his hand out of the water and pointed to a fisherman's ladder attached to the pier about twenty feet away.

We held Rachel and paddled. Foot-high waves lifted us up and down. The water was freezing. I felt my wet clothes weighing me down, and for a second I sank underneath, but I kicked my feet forcefully and resurfaced. How long had it taken to reach the ladder? It seemed like forever. David heaved Rachel on his shoulder and began climbing up. I pushed them from behind.

Finally, we reached the top and crawled onto the pier, huddled together on the deck. David put Rachel in his lap and rocked her. She was coughing out water, letting out sobs. He held her tight. "You're safe, now."

She looked around and cried out, "Prince?" I handed her the wet bear. She pressed him close to her face, and her sobbing changed to a whimper. I moved close to her, rubbed her back. She was shaking. We were all shaking. "Let's get to the van," I said.

Once inside, David started up the engine and turned up the heat. I took off Rachel's wet clothes and dried her with a spare sweatshirt; then, we wrapped her in a blanket that David had stored in the back of the van. I held her in my lap. Her teeth were chattering. David kissed my forehead. "You were very brave, Julia. You didn't hesitate for a second." He held Rachel's hands and blew on them. "You were brave too, pumpkin. That was very scary."

I pulled David and Rachel close. "I've never been in water that cold."

David put his arms around us. "God was merciful." He flashed his brilliant smile. "Hey, look at us. We're like survivors from a shipwreck."

Soon, he began driving back to Bar Harbor and cranked the heat up as high as it would go. Rachel was still sitting in my lap, wrapped in the blanket. She had stopped shaking. David turned to her, his face full of amusement, and he began singing: "Row, row, row your boat gently down the stream. Merrily, merrily, merrily, merrily, life is but a dream."

She let out a small laugh.

I gave her a gentle squeeze, rubbed her cold cheeks and ears. She leaned her head back, looked up at me with eyes like a fawn; then, she touched the loon feather in my braid. A moment later she reached into the back seat and picked up her loon feather. "Tie it here, Julia" she said, holding out a strand of her hair. "I want one like you."

I felt my tears come quickly. "Of course, darling."

That evening, when Rachel had fallen asleep, David and I went into his bedroom and made love. Afterwards, he said, "I'm a lucky man, tonight. I'm with the woman I love." He traced my lips with his fingers. "And my daughter has found a new friend." He brushed my lips with his. "Thanks for being patient with her." A little later, he asked me to stay the night, and I did. It was the most peaceful sleep I had in years.

Thirteen

"Take your suitcase," David said to Rachel. She pulled it out of the van, ran across the snowy sidewalk and rang the doorbell of her grandparents' house. David's father, Marc Zuckerman, opened the door, and Rachel jumped into his arms; he kissed her and carried her inside.

David touched my hand. "Nervous?"

"Me?" I let out a nervous laugh.

"Just be yourself."

Suitcases in hand, we moved towards the house, a nineteenth century federal-style building with a widow's walk between two, red brick chimneys. Marc came down the granite steps, his arms open. "It's been too long." He encircled his arms around his son, gave him a bear hug.

David said, "Happy Hanukkah, Dad."

Marc turned to me. "Finally, I get to meet the woman who's been keeping my son away." He laughed, kissed me on the cheek, then ushered us into the kitchen.

David's mother, Harriet, stood at a butcher block counter grating potatoes. She wiped her hands on her apron, fluffed her frosted black hair and kissed David on the lips. "Happy Hanukkah. I was getting worried. You're late."

"Sorry, we had to stop a few times to let Rachel run around." He motioned for me to come closer. "Mom, this is Julia. Julia, my mother, Harriet."

She shook my hand. "Nice to meet you."

"Pleased to meet you, too," I said.

Rachel, and her cousins Alex and Sam, were already playing on the floor with small metal cars. David leaned down, kissed both his nephews on top of their heads. Marc went to Rachel, touched a silver feather hairpin in Rachel's hair. "Say, that's pretty."

"Julia gave it to me. See, she has one, too."

Sharon, David's sister, entered the kitchen and came to me. "David's told me so much about you." She shook my hand. "I'm very happy to meet you."

David kissed and embraced his sister. *What was it with all the kissing and hugging?* It was new to me. My parents weren't affectionate. *So what did I know about these things?* Lately Odette had been asking me to think about the difference between affection and sex. I was thinking that the Zuckerman's affection seemed like a web that linked them together as a family.

Soon, Harriet gathered everyone to make latkes. The adults grated potatoes, onions and carrots, and the children stirred the eggs, matzo meal, lemon juice and salt. Next, Harriet and Sharon dropped spoonfuls of the mix into the sizzling oil of two large skillets. The aroma of fried potatoes and onions filled the air. When the pancakes were cooked brown, she placed them onto paper towels, and David ate one. He flashed his wide grin, "The best in New England."

His mother nodded. "Everyone can have one. Only one. The rest are for dinner."

I had one; it was delicious. David took my hand. "Let's get settled in before dinner." He and I carried the suitcases upstairs, and we entered a small guest room. "You'll sleep here," he said; then, he led me into his bedroom where there were two single beds. "Rachel and I'll sleep here." He motioned with his arms to the white furniture painted with green lines and geometric shapes. "My Mom has barely changed things since I left."

I looked around. Several posters hung on the walls. Wolves in a snowy forest. A ghost crab on a beach. Bob Dylan with his harmonica and guitar. And more than one hundred sea shells decorated the window sills and bookshelves. I picked one up and laughed. "Think you have enough?"

He wrestled me onto the bed, fell on top of me, and gave me a deep kiss.

I lifted his head, looked up at him. "So far, so good, yes? Your mother seems fine."

"She's on her best behavior."

I touched his cheek. "I really like your father."

"Isn't he something?"

David took my hand and guided me to a cushioned window seat. He sat behind me, ran his fingers up and down the back of my velvet shirt. "Some of the best times of my childhood were spent right here. Daydreaming, studying. I read *The Diary of Anne Frank* here. And Kurt Vonnegut's novels too."

"I envy you. I wish I could go back and rewrite my childhood. Turn it into a happy story." I looked out the window at the snow on the ground. There were bare lilac bushes around the slate patio. Across the street, the Piscataqua River glistened in the sunlight.

David fumbled with my glass earrings, then kissed me in the tender spot just below the ear. "I love you, Julia. Does that help?"

I returned his kiss, drew him close. I pressed my face against his. We sat together for a bit, quiet, peaceful with each other. I traced his lips with my finger. "You've been very kind to me, telling me that you love me. You've probably noticed that I haven't been able to say the same."

"I should be patient, right?"

"I've thought carefully about it, and I want to tell you now. I do love you, David." I let out a deep sigh. "There, I've said it. It's a scary word for me. I don't want to get hurt, again."

"Me either."

We kissed tenderly, lingering on each others' moist lips. Suddenly, David's mother yelled up the stairs. "David and Julia. I could use your help setting the table."

In the dining room David reached into a china closet and handed me a silver menorah, a nine-branched candleholder with intricate designs etched into it.

"It's beautiful." I set it on the table.

"From Poland. Seventeenth century." He began putting candles in it. "Passed down through my Mom's family. She and her mother came to the states just before the Holocaust. Otherwise...well, you know the story."

I pointed to one of the candles. "Why is that one higher?"

"It's the *shamesh.* You use it to light the others." He put the candle box back in a drawer.

"You forgot some."

He let out a short laugh. "It's the fifth day of Hanukkah, so we only put in five. You don't know much about Hanukkah, do you? I could tell you, but my Dad will at supper. He does it every year."

David handed me silverware, dishes and glasses, and we finished arranging the table. Soon the rest of family came into the dining room, each carrying something: latkes, baked haddock, salad, fresh rolls and wine. Harriet took off her apron, was dressed in a dusty, rose two-piece dress. "You look very nice, Mom," David said.

After the family settled at the table, Marc struck a match and lit the *shamesh.* In unison, everyone began to pray. *"Borukh atoh Adonoy, Eloheinu, Melekh ha-olaum, asher kidshanu be-mitzvotov ve-tzivonu le-haudleek nair shell Khanukka."* Marc gestured to me. "Now I'll say the prayer in English for our special guest, Julia. Blessed are you Lord, our God, King of the universe, who sanctified us with your commandments, and commanded us to kindle the lights of Hanukkah."

Using the *shamesh,* Alex lit the first candle, then Sam, Rachel, David, and I lit the others. Next, Marc lifted his wine glass, and we joined him, even the children with their glasses of cranberry juice. "To my son, David, and his friend, Julia. All the best." Everyone drank. One by one, Harriet began passing around the platters.

Rachel said, "Please pass the apple sauce, Daddy."

Alex grabbed the sour cream. "Yuk, apple sauce. You'll ruin the latkes."

Sharon tapped the shoulders of each of her sons. "Eat slowly." They nodded, then swallowed a latke in an instant.

"Listen to your mother," Marc said. "Horses gulp their food, not my grandsons." They slowed down. "That's better." He turned to me. "So, I understand you're a naturalist, Julia. Please, tell me something about your work?"

Everyone stopped talking, stared at me.

I straightened up, felt a little nervous. "Well...I've been doing an inventory of Acadia's wildflowers. Some of the prettiest ones are the cardinal and the wild lupine. I..." In a flash, I realized the flower story would bore the children. I paused, cleared my throat. "Alex. Sam. Have you ever been on a cruise ship?"

They shook their heads.

"Guess what? I work on a tour boat in the summer. We sail on the ocean, and I show people the fish, birds and marine life. A lot of children take the tour. How would you like to join me this summer? Rachel's coming, aren't you?"

Rachel's face beamed. "I get to ride with the captain."

I touched her hand. "What else are you going to do?"

"Blow the foghorn." She put her hand over her mouth and giggled.

I turned to Alex and Sam. "But if you come, you got to promise not to get mad at me when I can't show you any sharks. Last year there was a boy who was upset when I couldn't."

Alex blew his lips. "Was he stupid or what? Everybody knows there aren't any sharks in Maine."

Sam laughed.

Alex faced him. "So if there aren't any sharks, what are there?"

Sam thought for a moment, started to laugh. "Dinosaurs." Everyone laughed with him.

"Harbor porpoises," Alex yelled out; then, he tugged on his mother's sleeve. "Can we go on the boat, Mom?"

Sharon glanced at Alex over the top of her thick eyeglasses and smiled. "As long as you don't fall overboard."

Rachel said, "You can stay at my house."

"Yippee," Sam shouted.

A little later, Harriet passed the food around again, and everyone took seconds.

I turned to Marc and smiled. "So, David said you're very busy at your store."

He shrugged. "That's nothing new." He gently tapped my hand. "Do you know how David came to open the Bar Harbor store?"

I said, "He told me he wanted to be near both the ocean, and some mountains."

David moved his head close to mine, gave me a tender kiss on the cheek, pretended to whisper, "Shhh, Darling. That's a secret."

Marc laughed, but suddenly I noticed that Harriet was glaring at me. *Why?*

"You know, Julia," Marc said, "at first I thought David was putting pleasure before business, and I almost said, `No'." He touched Harriet's shoulder. "Isn't that right, darling?"

Her face tightened. "I worry Marc that you don't know how to say `no.' Sometimes David wants too much. At the time he was married to a nice Jewish woman. A lawyer. He had it all." She was talking fast, her eyes darting around. "Now look at you, David. A divorced father with a little girl, and you're not even dating a Jewish woman."

David raised his hands. 'Please, Mom, enough."

It took me a moment to realize what was happening. I was speechless.

Marc stood up, raised his hands in the air. "Please, Harriet, David. Is this how we act with a guest?" He sat down, closed his eyes, let out a great breath. Then he looked up. "So where were we? Oh, yes. The Bar Harbor store. David was right, Julia. The store's very profitable. He tells me, it's because of all the merchandise you buy."

I laughed, but half-heartedly. Unlike Marc, I didn't know how to switch gears so easily.

Marc looked at his wife. "There's only one problem, isn't there, Harriet? David's too far from home."

David flashed his wide grin. "Sometimes not far enough."

No one laughed. There was an uneasy moment; then, the family began eating again and broke into different conversations.

A little later Marc rose, clinked his spoon on a water glass. "I'd like to remind everyone that we're here today to celebrate the Festival of Lights."

David nudged me. "Here comes the story."

"On this day we remember our long struggle for religious freedom. And we hope for a world where all people have the right to worship as they wish."

He stepped behind Alex, placed his hands on his shoulders. "Tell me what happened 2200 years ago."

Alex puckered his lips. "I think it was the Syrians. They put idols in the Jewish temples, and they told the Jews to pray to them."

"Exactly," Marc said. Next, he went to Sam. "And what did Judah Maccabee do?"

Sam folded his hands on the table. "His small Jewish army beat the bigger one. Then Judah went to the temple and lit the lamp again."

Marc patted him on the head, and he went to Rachel. "A question for you. What was the miracle?"

She looked up at the ceiling, then down. Up and down again. "Um... they only had enough...was it gas?"

He gave out a gentle laugh. "Oil."

"Oh, they only had enough oil for one day to burn in the lamp...but it burned for eight days. Is that right?"

"It must be the latkes that make you so smart." He leaned down, kissed her on the back of the neck. She giggled. "And now for the presents."

"Yeah, Hanukkah *gelt*," Alex shouted.

Marc left the dining room, and soon returned and handed out envelopes with silver coins for the young children, and large bills for David, Sharon and me. He touched my shoulder. "Buy something nice for yourself, okay?" He laughed. "From David's store, of course."

Afterwards, Marc came up to me in the kitchen. "I'd like to talk with you." He poured two cups of coffee; then, led me into his first-floor study in the back of the house. We sat together on the canvas couch. I looked around the study. There were hundreds of books on the shelves behind the desk; a framed map of Israel on one wall; and on another, Audubon prints of a crow and great blue heron.

Marc took a sip of coffee; then, said, "I want to apologize for my wife's comments at dinner. I will tell you, at times it is...but I'm a family man, a religious man, so I endure."

Did I hear a faint, momentary sob in his voice?

He leaned back and glanced up at the ceiling; then, he looked at me. "David wants us to like you, and I do. You're a surprising woman, like the way you talked to the children."

I nodded. "They're nice kids."

He put his cup on the end table. "I hope you understand this is Harriet's issue, not mine. I have many friends who are gentiles. And I see, that even though Alice was Jewish, being Jewish doesn't always make for a good match. My hope now is that David is happy, and that you'll be good to him."

"He's an amazing man." I considered my words. "He believes in me. That's a new experience."

Marc nodded, his face sympathetic. "He told me your mother died last year, and that you had a difficult childhood, yes?"

I lowered my eyes. "I wish things had been different." I took a great breath, let my body loosen. "The good news is my father is doing okay right now. Holding a job. Staying sober."

He crossed his legs, sat back in the couch. "So Julia, your father's Italian?"

"My Mom was too."

He stroked his gray goatee. "What does it mean for you to be an Italian-American?"

I tapped my feet on the floor, considering his question. "Well, I can speak a little Italian. I know my family came from Naples. I like to cook Italian foods. Learned that from my mother and my grandmother."

I ran my fingers through my hair. "But to be honest, to be an Italian-American is to be Catholic, too. I was very religious when I was young. Went to Catholic elementary school. Now I've grown away from the Church. It's too conservative. Still, I guess, I'm Catholic in some ways, like my guilt, my compassion, my sense of right and wrong."

"You're a thoughtful woman, Julia." He picked up his coffee, took a sip. "David tells me your father was a soldier. Was he in the Korean War or World War II?"

"World War II. In Italy and Germany. The infantry. Saw a lot of killing."

"That must have been tough. It was a horrible war, like no other in human history. Sixty million dead. David told you what happened to Harriet's family?"

"I'm very sorry." I put my hands to my cheeks. "As you get to know me, you'll see I mean that, from the bottom of my heart."

He paused, pondering. "The way I see it, Julia, everyone today, no matter what religion, lives in the shadow of that war. Look how it's affected my family, and yours." He bent forward, his elbows on his knees. "I was in the Korean War. By the time I got there it was nearly over. I'll never forget the bombed-out cities, the mass graves."

He rose from the couch, sat on the edge of his desk. "Please, bear with me for a few minutes. I want to explain something to you."

He loosened his tie a little. "As you know, Hitler and the Nazis killed six million Jews. But when you kill someone, you also kill their children, and their children's children. Today there would probably be fifty million Jews. But we're only fifteen million." He stood and paced. "We Jews have survived millenniums of persecutions." He looked at me. "Why do you think we've survived?"

I puckered my lips, thinking. "Maybe...Because you're part of God's plan."

"A good answer." He sat on the couch again, folded his hands on his lap. "I do believe God has a special purpose for us. To be a Jew in the twentieth century is to understand the potential for the end of humanity. If there is another world war, and inevitably it'll be a nuclear war, we'll all die."

He closed his eyes, swayed slightly as he spoke. "If humans are to survive, then we Jews must survive. If the world can't accept us, and others who are different, then the end is near."

Silence.

He smiled, touched my hand. "That's why it's important for me to be a pious Jew, and for my son, and for his daughter too. I've taught them to never be ashamed of their Jewishness, and to respect others' beliefs. As for my wife, I guess I didn't do such a good job." He laughed, a quick laugh. "David says I talk too much sometimes, meddling in affairs that aren't my business. Too bad for you I'm a meddler. Have I offended you?"

I held out my hands, palms up. "No. I understand."

He smiled. "David said you would. Thank you."

We sat together silently, sipping the last of our coffee, at ease with one another.

When Marc and I returned to the kitchen, Harriet was standing at the sink washing pots and putting dishes into the dishwasher. I offered to help. Marc left the room, and we were alone.

Harriet smiled as she handed me a dish towel. "That was nice of you to invite the children on the cruise."

"Have you and Marc taken the boat?"

She shook her head.

"You could join us. Acadia is so beautiful from the sea."

"Maybe."

After talking with Marc, I thought I understood Harriet better. I thought I might be able to connect with her. So, as I began drying the pots, I said, "Everything at dinner was delicious. David said you were a great cook."

She adjusted her apron. "I don't know how families eat frozen food. If it isn't fresh, why bother?" She rinsed the wine glasses and put them in the dishwasher. "So Julia, how was your conversation with Marc?"

"Interesting. We talked about your family. My family. About Judaism."

She looked straight at me. "Did Marc ask you about Jesus?"

I set the pot on the table. "Not that I recall."

She put her fingers to her lips. "I'm curious. Do you believe that Jesus is God?"

I studied her face. "My mother did. For me, he's a role model. He was kind and loving. That's how I want to live."

She raised her eyebrows. "That won't go over big with the rabbi."

"Rabbi?"

Her mouth tightened. "David said you were going to convert."

I sat down, steadied myself with my hands on the table. I wasn't prepared for this. I asked, "Where's David?"

Her voice was icy. "Outside with Rachel."

I went out, and in a minute returned with him. Harriet was sitting at the table, and we joined her. "David, you're mother and I have been talking. I'm a little confused. She said you told her I was converting."

His face was tense. "Mom, I said she was thinking of converting."

Harriet looked away. "That's not what I heard."

I tapped David's hand. "I never said that."

He ran his fingers through his hair. "But Julia, we talked about it."

I shook my head firmly. "It was a very general discussion."

"I wasn't...what I mean is..." He slumped in his chair, put his head in his hands. There was a long silence. When he raised his head, he said,

"All right. I haven't been completely honest. But Mom, Julia, you're to blame too. I can't stand this. I wanted to smooth things out." He rose and paced. "So, how do I do that?"

Harriet stood up. "Lying to your mother isn't the way." She went to the sink, began rinsing more dishes.

I turned to David. "I can see you're trying to help us, but I'm afraid you're making things worse. Do me a favor, okay? Your mother and I need to talk. Please leave us alone for a while."

He started to speak; then, slipped out of the room. I moved close to Harriet. "I have a Hanukkah present for you. It's upstairs. I'll be back in a minute."

When I handed her the gift, she hesitated to take it, but then, she sat at the table and slowly unwrapped the pink tissue paper. Inside was a gold frame with a photo of Rachel on her three-wheeler, her arm around her father, her face beaming. Harriet stared at it for a few moments. She asked, "Did you take it?"

"Just before Rachel fell into the ocean."

"It's a nice picture."

"You love them, Harriet, don't you?"

She said, "Sometimes too much."

"I know they love you."

I saw a tear in her eye, and I touched her hand. "But they care about me, too. So, you see, we have something in common."

She lowered her head.

I leaned towards her. "Look, I know you don't like me because I'm a gentile. But even if I was to convert, and I'm not saying I will, I'd still come from a gentile past."

She locked her eyes onto me. "You know, Julia, you're assuming a lot. Who says David's going to marry you?"

I gave out a nervous laugh. "Marriage? Is that what this is about? You think I'm trying to hook your son? We haven't even talked about marriage. We're both coming off bitter divorces."

She looked confused. "So why are you dating him?"

What could I say to get her to understand? I put my hands over my face; then, I looked at her. "I'm not a bad person. I want to like you. David tells me you're a good woman and a good mother. I believe him."

I heard my voice breaking. "But you've got to see the good in me, too." I pointed to the photo. "I care about them. I'd die for them if I had to. That's a helluva lot more than Alice has done." I held out my hand, and let out a sob: "Please, Harriet. Let me in, just a little."

She looked blankly at me; then, she left the room without saying another word.

Fourteen

One evening my father phoned collect. "Listen, Julia...I got trouble. The cops tried to kill me last night."

I pressed the receiver closer to my ear. "What?"

His voice sounded drugged. "They wanted to give me a ride. I told them to get the hell away. I...I ran down the street."

A long silence.

"Hello, Dad, are you there?"

"The cops. They said they'd give me a lift to the bridge. They...they would've tossed me in the bay." He coughed, and I heard him spit. "Those fucking assholes would've killed me."

The words. The tone. It was all coming back to me. "Dad, you've been drinking."

"They would've killed me."

"I don't want to talk when you're drunk." I hung up the phone.

A minute later he called collect again, but I refused the charges. I sat down in the living room at the desk in the corner. I didn't move from there for a long time, and I stared out the French windows, but all I saw was a vague picture of the evening light fading into darkness. I felt my mind jumping back and forth between my childhood and the present, and I didn't know where I was. I tried to think. What now? Maybe it was just a temporary slip. My father would remember family was more important than alcohol. But I had to be firm. No matter what he did, my mother always forgave him the next day. I took a piece of paper out of my desk and wrote to my father, telling him not to call me if he was going to drink. The following week he phoned collect again, and I immediately asked, "Did you get my letter?"

"I'm the father, you're the daughter, and I don't want you telling me what to do."

I felt my hands shaking. "So, you're drinking?"

"I live the way I want."

"Then we have nothing to talk about."

He raised his voice. "Yes we do and you better—"

I hung up.

A week later, he sent me a letter on yellow, lined paper. His handwriting was scribbled, words crossed out. "The boss had me coming and going. Do this. Do that. The damn coloreds sat on their asses all day. I complained. The next day he fired me. *Bastardo.* Freedom of speech. I don't have any money left. My landlord said he would kick me out if I don't pay the rent next week. *Per favore*, Julia. Help me." He asked for nearly half my monthly salary.

I mailed him a check and wrote: "This is the last time I'm giving you money. Please Dad, you've got to stop drinking. I can't bear to see you suffering like this, and you're making me suffer right along with you."

When he phoned collect a week later in the middle of the night, I absent-mindedly accepted the charges. I wasn't sure if I was awake or dreaming.

"Julia? Is that you?"

I sat up in bed, fumbled for the switch on the light. "It's me."

He sounded fearful. "The cops are fucking crazy. They handcuffed me. Beat me with clubs."

"Are you drunk?"

"No."

He didn't sound drunk.

"They pushed me into the cruiser. I screamed at them, 'Let me out of here.' They said, 'We have a nice cell for you.' They would've strung me up. I got down on my knees and begged them to let me go. They laughed at me. They let me go, but said they'd get me the next time." My father coughed a few times. "They're wacko. They're on drugs. I'm never going back there."

"Where are you now?" I pulled the blanket up to my neck.

"Boston." He spoke loudly. "Those Portland cops are killers. I saw them shoot a man at the Gulf station."

My father's voice sounded far away. "What happened to that man? He's gone. They kicked him and killed him. They know I saw it. Now they're out to get me." He spoke as if he were crying. "I'm hungry. *Sono stanco.* I have no place to stay. Come to Boston. Help me out."

"What happened to the money I sent you?"

"It's gone."

"Eh?" I pulled my hair into a knot at the nape of my neck. I had no idea if I should believe him or not. A dozen emotions swept through me at once. "Go to a shelter."

"Young punks are running the place."

"You can't live in the street."

"Help me. *Per favore.* Come to Boston."

I said nothing.

"Come Saturday. At noon. I'll be at the duck pond in the Public Garden."

A long silence.

"I'll be waiting for you." He repeated the time and place, then he hung up.

After work the next day I stopped at David's store and found him still working in his office, sitting behind a pile of invoices, writing out checks. He came to me, gave me a tender hug, brought his lips to mine.

I sank in the chair next to his desk.

"More problems?"

"My father wants me to come to Boston."

"Boston?"

"He said the Portland cops were trying to kill him."

David sat down, tapped a pen on his desk. "You believe him?"

"He's having a breakdown."

"Oh, God."

I put my head in my hands. "He wants me to meet him Saturday. He needs money."

David leaned forward. "Do you want my advice?"

I nodded.

He paused. "Stay out of it. You tried to help him, and I admire you for that, but I see him sucking you into his shit. You know, from what I've read about alcoholics, you can't help them if they don't want to help themselves."

"But he's schizophrenic, too."

David put his pen to his mouth. "What does Odette say?"

"That he needs professional help." I stood up, paced from the chair to the window and back. "But how do I get him to do that? I'm sleeping terribly. The thought of him living in the street is maddening."

David straightened up in his chair. "You know he seemed unstable, even when we went to Peaks Island."

I sat back down. "At least he wasn't drinking."

David raised his hands in the air in a gesture of surrender. "Sal might be right about him."

I clenched my hands, put them to my face. "I've got to have some hope, David. After all, he's my father."

David came around, still standing, gently pressed my head against his chest, ran his fingers through my hair. "I'm sorry you've got to deal with this."

After a moment, I stood up, pacing a little. "If I went to Boston, would you come with me?"

He moved away, thinking, his hand on his chin. "I promised Rachel I'd spend the day with her."

I sank back into the chair, heard the pleading in my voice. "I could really use some company."

"You're going?"

I shrugged.

He said nothing.

I locked onto his eyes. "What if it was your father?"

"He's not." David looked away, his voice cold. "I'm sorry, Julia, but I can't take on his problems. I have too much to handle in my own life. Besides, he's not exactly my favorite person."

"Meaning?"

"You think it's easy for me to like someone who's anti-Semitic?"

I hesitated. "You know, David, if it was your Dad in trouble, I'd help you."

He looped his thumbs around his belt, lowered his eyes, and walked to the other side of the office; then he looked at me. "Please, Julia, don't make me feel guilty. You have a choice. You can always decide not to go."

When I walked onto the pedestrian bridge above the frozen pond in Boston's Public Garden, I had a good view of the entire park. There was snow on the ground, but the sidewalks were clear. All at once, I saw my father in the distance, sitting on a park bench, smoking a cigar and wearing his black fisherman's cap. I went to him. He smiled. "Julia, I didn't think you'd come."

I sat next to him on the bench, and he shook my hand. I noticed the stains on his long, winter coat, the scab on his unshaven chin and the smell of urine. "Dad, I hate seeing you like this."

His voice was gravelly. "Where am I supposed to clean up?"

"You had an apartment."

"I told you why I left Portland."

I spoke hesitantly. "I know the cops can be rough, but I don't believe that story about the man at the Gulf station."

He curled his fingers around the handle of a wooden cane, and he tapped it loudly on the sidewalk to emphasize his words. "They killed him."

"Dad, the story sounds...paranoid."

He looked at me, his eyes narrowed. "I saw them kill that man. You don't believe me? Believe me."

"What man?"

"The cashier. *Un uomo simpatico.* A good man. He let me take my time fixing my coffee. Let me warm up in his place. I'd tell him to keep the change. He always thanked me."

"And the cops killed him?"

"Isn't that what I just said?" My father drew hard on his cigar, but it had gone out. He lit it again; then, spit tobacco juice onto the ground. "I went in there one night. There were two cops. `Get out," the fat one yelled. I left fast. When I looked back, I saw him knock the cashier to the floor. He kicked him. Shot him in the head. I ran away. The next day the cashier was gone. Nobody knew what happened."

"Maybe he just quit."

My father stared off. "I don't know what they did with the body."

"But there would have been blood. People would've asked questions."

"The cops know I saw them. They're after me."

"Maybe it was a hallucination?"

He banged his cane against the bench. "I know what I know."

Suddenly, I was afraid of him. The banging. The coarseness. The anger.

He smoked his cigar, exhaled in hard noisy puffs. An elderly woman strolled by with a poodle, and her dog stopped to sniff his shoes. He kicked at the dog. "Get that damn thing away from me." The woman pulled on the leash and hurried along the sidewalk.

I moved further down the bench, away from him. "What can I do to help?"

"I need some money. I need a room."

I shook my head. "I can't keep giving you money." I handed him a piece of paper with an address, a phone number and a name. "I called the Veterans' Administration. They're only a couple blocks from here. A social worker said she'd help you."

He squinted his eyes, studied me closely. "You mean a shrink?" His voice became hoarser, louder. "Did your mother ever tell you what they did to me in the hospital?"

I pulled my coat tightly around me. "I don't want to hear about it."

He poked my arm with his finger. "They strapped me to a table, greased my hands, feet and head, taped wires on me, turned on the juice. They fried me. I pissed and shit my pants. They killed me inside. I ain't never going to no headshrinker again."

I stood before him, gestured with my hands. ""Please Dad. I care about you, but I don't know how to help you. You need professional help. *Per favore.* Go to the VA. For me and Sal."

"Sal doesn't give a shit about me."

"And that surprises you? He told me you beat the hell out of him."

"He's lying."

"Go for me, then."

He spit and turned away.

I paced. "Dad, try to—" All at once I noticed a wine bottle in a shopping bag next to him. I pointed to it. "That won't help you one damn bit."

He laughed. "It's my birthday. I'm celebrating."

"That's not funny."

He tapped me on the arm with his cane. "Come on, what happened to my silly Lilly?" He shrugged. "Okay, you want to know the truth. Every now and then I have a nip. My arthritis is killing me."

"What about the tranquilizers?"

"I'm not taking them anymore."

It was happening all over again, just like in my childhood. My voice was shaking. "Since when?"

"A couple weeks ago. They made me feel like a zombie."

I shook my finger at him, my voice a half cry, a half whisper. "You're scaring the shit out of me. I won't go through this again."

He glared at me. His face turned red, his body tightened; then, he jerked up, took his bag and hurried away. I called after him. "This is great." I caught up with him. "I come all the way down here, and you just walk away."

"*Mi lasci in pace.*" He kept moving.

I followed him. "Do you need money for food?"

"What do you care?" He kept walking. "All you want to do is lock me up again."

"No, I want to help you get better." I held his arm. "Please, Dad—" Without warning, he pushed me away and knocked himself off balance. He recovered; then, he hobbled around a bend. I ran after him, pulled him to a stop and gave him several hundred dollars.

"*Molte grazie.*" He looked in my eyes. For a moment, I thought he remembered who I was, that I was family, that I meant no harm. "I don't want to be any trouble, Julia. Thanks for the green." Then he tramped off, using his cane for support.

"*Ciao*," I called after him.

Soon, I began heading back to my car on Beacon Street. Just before I walked out of the park, I stopped and looked at the bronze statues of the mother duck and her ducklings, statues commemorating the children's book, *Make Way for Ducklings.* I knew the story well, knew that the mother duck had managed to bring her ducklings to safety, but I had failed to do the same for my father, failed like my grandmother and mother had years ago. As a child, I had wondered why they weren't able to find some way to fix my father's problems. Yet, here I was, an adult, and I was feeling powerless and hopeless, just as they must have.

No sooner did I return from Boston then I heard bad news about Sal. It seemed to me that sometimes one piece of bad luck attracted another, and then another. *Was it the stars? The moon?* I sure as hell didn't understand it. *What could I do?* Deal with it and hope the streak of bad luck ended soon. Still, I was feeling weary of it all.

When I went to console Sal in the park service's old sheep barn the next morning, I saw him, lifting a large rock out of a hole and dumping it into a wheelbarrow. He was in a winter coat. It was cold in the barn, and his warm breath turned misty as he puffed with exertion. I went to him, put my hand on his shoulder. "I'm sorry about Erin."

He shuffled his feet in the dirt floor. "I told Jim to keep quiet. I was going to tell you. Just wasn't ready."

"Want to talk?"

"What can I say?" He lifted a pick above his head and swung it into the hole with a force that shook the ground. After a few swings, he stopped, pulled on his Red Sox cap, brushed the dirt off his denim jacket. "You want to know if I'm hurting? I cared a lot for her. I was even thinking about an engagement ring."

He chewed on his lower lip. "What fucking bullshit." Without warning, he raised the pick above his head; then, flung it across the room. In an instant, it hit the wooden wall with a bang.

I stepped away from him.

"It's okay," he said. "I got it out of my system."

"Are you sure? Because you're scaring me."

"I'm sure."

He took a shovel, lifted dirt out of the hole and dropped it into the wheelbarrow. "I was just part of her Maine adventure."

"She told you that?"

"I should've seen it coming." He shook his head. "Yesterday morning she showed up at my apartment. I was barely awake. She said she was going back to Massachusetts. Leaving in an hour."

"Just like that?"

"She blamed me, naturally." He shoveled more dirt. "Said I was too jealous. Never gave her any space." He paced away a few feet, came back. "Truth is, I think she was going back to her old boyfriend."

"I'm so sorry, Sal."

"Yeah, it sucks."

"Can I help?"

"Let's not talk about it anymore, okay?" He coughed nervously. "The more I do, the more it hurts."

"If that's what you want."

He rolled the concrete mixer next to the hole and dumped the cement into it; then, he smoothed it out with a trowel. He covered it with a plastic tarp. He saw by my face that I didn't understand what he was doing, and said, "To keep it from freezing."

Bad luck all around. It was getting to me. As Sal worked, I wandered off and walked around the barn, looking at the dirt floor, broken windows, and slits in the walls. It was hard to imagine, but I knew once Sal and the others finished the work, the park service would have an excellent building for an exhibit on lake ecology. For a moment I tried to picture the long sweeping room with recessed lights, exposed posts and beams, and a pine floor. There would be glass cases, maps, photographs, dioramas and graphic displays about lakes and their plants and animals. It was my job to work with the interior designer. I came back to Sal and tapped my foot near the hole with the wet cement. "What's the cement for?"

"It's the footing for a new post." He pointed to the old beams of the barn. "They're in good shape, but we've got to knock out these rotten posts. Put in new ones. Should straighten up the roof."

"That's terrific. It's great to see things finally beginning." I pulled on his coat sleeve. "By the way, Sal, what day is it?"

He looked at me like I was stupid. "Sunday."

"Since when does the staff work on the weekends?"

"I don't want to think." He shoveled more gravel and sand into the cement mixer.

I tugged on his arm. "Come on. I've got lunch in the car. And our skis, too."

"Can't."

"Might be the last snow of the season."

He ignored me.

"Please."

He leaned on the shovel. "Did you say lunch?"

"Subs and macaroni salad from Noonie's deli."

"You twisted my arm."

When we drove off, I handed him a tuna sub. He took a bite. "It's weird. I felt like a little kid this morning. Wanted to stay in bed all day. Like when I had chicken pox. Wanted Mom to take care of me. Give me ice cream. Let me watch TV forever."

I nodded. "Remember *Stuart Little*?"

Sal laughed. "Why the hell did she read that to us all the time?"

"Maybe she wanted us to feel sorry for him instead of ourselves."

Soon, I drove through the entrance to the park's carriage roads, a fine place to ski, walk, bike or ride a horse because of the wide trails and moderate slopes. We put on our skis and headed north along a snowy road that hugged the west bank of Jordan Pond.

When we came to a fork in the road, Sal said, "Follow me. Got something to show you." He sped ahead, his legs pumping like a steam engine, his pony tail bobbing. "I'm smoking," he called back, and disappeared around a bend. I laughed quietly, remembering what a powerful halfback he had been at Worcester High, busting through defensive lines.

Ten minutes later, I saw him standing in one of the four buttresses of a cobblestone bridge that crossed Jordan Stream. He gestured with wide arms. "Here it is. Found it last month. Isn't it something?" He pointed out the texture and color of the cobblestones; then he led me down underneath the bridge. We looked up at the arch. "Awesome," he shouted into it, and the word echoed.

"Awesome," I yelled; then, he called, and I called, and we shouted together until the space under the bridge was filled with a dozen echoes. It was magical.

Back on top of the bridge, I took a thermos out of my backpack and poured coffee for us. We brushed snow off the stone wall and sat down. Sal patted me on the back. "Say Julia, thanks for getting me out."

We sat in silence, sipping our coffee. The wind shook clumps of snow off the spruce branches, and they fell on the ground with a thump.

After a few minutes, I turned to Sal. "I'm sorry to trouble you with my problems. I know you're hurting right now, but I don't have anyone else to talk to." I paused. "Dad's having a breakdown." I told him about the phone calls and the episode in the Public Garden. "Just like you said, he didn't stay sober for long."

Sal looked at me blankly, said nothing.

I bit my fingernail. "Aren't you going to rub it in?"

He took off his ski cap, smoothed back his hair, tugged on his pony tail. "I'm worried for you, Julia. If you take on too much, you're going to crack, too."

I stood and paced. "I can't just give up."

Sal went to his backpack, took out a joint and lit it. He took a long puff, held it out to me. "Toke?"

I took a puff, handed it back to him. "No more, thanks."

He walked to the other end of the bridge and finished the joint. When he returned, he said, "Don't you see what he's doing, Julia? Mr. Crisis. Everybody jump. Forget you have a life of your own. Daddy-O is the center of the universe. And his universe is hell. Am I right?"

"He's draining me."

"Have you told David?"

"He's staying out of it. Can't handle it."

"I didn't think he was that smart."

"Haha, Sal. Personally, I think David's being selfish. I could use some support."

Sal closed his eyes, pondering. "Okay, Julia. I think I know what we can do." He paused, his face lit up. "There's a guy in Worcester that I know. He might be able to help. He's a male nurse. A good one."

Sal paced and talked fast. "Here's what he does. First he gives the patient a shot to put him to sleep. That way there's no pain. Now, the second shot, that's the cure. It's an overdose. No guns, no blood. Then, that night, he takes the body to his buddy's crematorium. Afterwards, he sails his boat out of Marblehead. Even says a little prayer before he scatters the ashes in the water." He smiled at me. "All for only $10,000, Julia. What do you think?"

I smiled back. "Spent all my money on subs at Noonie's."

"Maybe we could take out a loan?"

I rapped him on the head. "Thanks, Sal. You've been a big help."

I put on my skis and headed north on a carriage road to Eagle Lake. I stretched my legs in long strides, gliding, almost weightless. The grouse feathers on my ski poles flapped in the breeze. Soon, Sal caught up with me, and we skied side-by-side. I looked at him. "Why do you keep joking about killing Dad?"

He kept his eyes straight ahead. "Who says I'm joking?"

"What are you talking about?"

He didn't answer; he pushed ahead on his skis and began climbing up a steep slope of the trail. I tried to keep up with him. I was breathing hard. When I came to the crest of the hill, he was already gone. I looked down the slope to the valley and mountains to the east. All at once, I realized for the first time that I wasn't helping Sal by bringing my father back in our lives. It was eating away at him, and that was dangerous.

I skied down the slope and found Sal at the bottom, sitting on the rail of a small wooden bridge that crossed over a frozen wetland. He stood up. "There's something wrong over there." He put his hands to his ears. "Do you hear that?"

I listened. It was a faint screeching sound coming from the far end of the wetland. "Let's check it out," I said, skiing down the bank onto the icy pond. We had skied halfway across the wetland when the sound stopped. We waited. A minute passed; then, it started up again. We skied on and saw in the distance an animal lying in the snow near the edge of the forest. As we came closer, a red fox caught in a leg-hold trap let out two barely-audible yaps, her ears upright, her eyes open. She tried to stand, but couldn't even raise her head.

"She's starving," Sal said. "Damn trapper never checked his gear." There was blood in the snow. I pointed to the half-severed black leg, let out a gasp. Suddenly, Sal took out his hunting knife, and before I could say anything, he grabbed the fox's muzzle and slit its throat. The body trembled; then, it went limp.

I knelt on the ground and ran my hand along its yellow red fur. I saw she had eight nipples and her belly was large. I glanced at Sal. His face was expressionless. "She was pregnant."

He wiped his knife in the snow and put it back in the sheath; then, he pulled the trap apart and released her leg. "There was no other way, Julia. She was too far gone."

I said nothing.

He picked up the trap and threw it into the woods. "Fucking things should be banned."

We left the fox's body in the snow for other animals to feed on. It was nature's way. Then, we skied back across the pond and picked up the carriage road again, skiing through a green forest of spruce trees with wide trunks and tall canopies. There was no sunlight, and it seemed like dusk in the woods.

I glanced at Sal in his wool cap and denim jacket. He was looking straight ahead, and seemed deep in thought. I cared deeply about him. We had been through so much together. He was my family. He was my blood. It was the Italian way.

We left the spruce forest and skied along a road on the west side of Eagle Lake. A heavy snow began to fall, and it clung to our faces. I could taste the ocean's salt in the snow. Everything was white: the sky, the lake, the trail. I couldn't see more than twenty feet in front of me. It seemed like I was skiing in a dream. Some of it was a good dream, but some of it was a nightmare.

Fifteen

After David parked his van next to the town hall in Somesville, we opened the back door, and he handed me my ten-speed bike. "Say, Julia, I've been meaning to tell you, but it keeps slipping my mind. Next weekend, Rachel and I are driving to Boston. She's really been bugging me to see her Mom."

Once the date registered in my mind, my mouth dropped open. "You're kidding, right? That's the weekend of Sal's party."

He rubbed his face with his hands. "Damn, I forgot."

"Please, go the following weekend."

"Let me think...Can't. Alice said something about a business conference."

"But David, I told you weeks ago."

He ran his fingers through his hair. "I'll make it up to you. How about you and Sal coming over for dinner when I get back?"

"It's not the same."

"You're being difficult, Julia."

"Is that so?" I turned away from him.

He rested his hand on my shoulder. "Why are you making such a fuss?"

I tightened my hands, put them to my mouth. "I have a bad feeling about this, David."

A long pause.

"And I don't like it. Especially—"

"Julia—"

"Especially when it could have been avoided."

He threw his hands in the air. "What do you want me to do? Rachel will be very disappointed if we don't go. But I swear I won't screw up again. I'll start writing down the dates."

I puffed my cheeks, blew out a big breath. "Don't you see, David? You're only thinking of yourself. How about me? My father's having a breakdown, and if you haven't noticed, I'm having a tough time."

A long silence; then, he came to me, put his arm around my waist. "I'm sorry, Julia. I don't know what else to say. Please, let's not argue all morning. Remember? We're supposed to be having some fun."

"Fine." I flicked him away with my hand. *What do you do when a guy won't compromise?* I hopped on my bike and began pedaling southwest on Route 102. He followed. As I glided down a winding hill, I crouched low on my bike and picked up speed. I flew around a bend, and, just ahead on the road, I saw a crow eating a dead raccoon. I whistled like a hawk, and the crow cawed, lifted upwards, and vanished into the forest.

A little later, after I had calmed down, I looked back. David wasn't there, so I slowed down. When he caught up, I asked, "Too fast?"

He flashed his wide grin. "No, it's just that, when you're mad at me, I feel safer behind you."

I rolled my eyes and pedaled ahead. We rode along the coast past Pretty Marsh and Seal Cove. Everything was muted in fog. Clanging buoys and fog horns called out warnings to lobster boats and schooners.

By the time we stopped at the headland above Goose Cove, the fog had lifted. Offshore I saw a raft of a hundred eiders floating in the sea, and I watched them with my binoculars. The white and black males and brown females rose up and down on the crest of each wave. Several opened their wings, leapt upward, and lunged into the water head first, diving downward for muscles, crabs and urchins. Gulls swam among the eiders, waiting for scraps. All at once, I spotted a king eider in the group. "Oh, my God." I handed the binoculars to David. "Look there, in the middle of the ducks."

Soon he found him. "She's beautiful."

"It's a he."

"In orange?"

"Why not orange?"

"Blue...maybe."

"You're thinking like a human."

He lifted up the binoculars; then, he nodded knowingly. "Of course, orange is perfect."

I stared through the binoculars again. "Such dignity." Suddenly, I felt myself shrinking amidst the duck's grandeur. "Wish I felt that way today."

David put his arms around me. "It's my fault too, Julia. I'm really sorry I forgot, but I want you to know you're very important to me. I mean it."

He was in a sleeveless T-shirt, and as he hugged me, his firm biceps pressed on my sides. Inside his embrace, I felt safe, and I placed my head in the curve of his neck. "You know, Odette said I overreact when things don't work out. Has something to do with being disappointed a lot as a kid."

He pulled me close, squeezed me tightly. Was it the squeeze that did it? In an instant, I let out a loud fart. "I can't believe it." I hid my face with my hands.

He laughed.

"Don't, I'm so embarrassed." I moved away.

After a few moments, he came to me, put his arm around my shoulder. I pressed my face against his. "I wish I wasn't so neurotic about things. I hate it when things don't go my way."

"Will you stop already? We worked it out."

I whispered, "I wish I believed that."

The day of Sal's party I stopped at the post office to check my mailbox. There was a post card from my father. On the front was a photograph of the Boston skyline, and on the back he had scribbled a note: "Went to the VA. They're giving me disability checks. Found a room. Don't worry. Call your brother. Keep Smiling?!? Your father, Frank."

Did I think he had fixed things? Not for a moment. As long as he was drinking, and as long as he refused to take his medication, he was a propane tank waiting to explode.

That evening, when Deb and I walked from the car to Sal's apartment, I was unusually quiet. She pulled me to a stop. "You okay?"

I hesitated. "I feel a little weird. It's like, I don't know what I'm supposed to do at this party. I know I'm not looking for a guy. Do I dance? Do I drink?"

She touched my hand. "Just be yourself."

I took in a deep breath. "By the way, thanks for coming. You know, it's a drag to be alone at a party."

"Sure."

In Sal's kitchen a dozen people in T-shirts and jeans milled around, drinking beer and wine. Deb and I greeted two of Sal's friends from work; then, we made our way into the living room. Sal was bopping with a troop of others to the sounds of the Rolling Stones: "I can't get no...no, no, no, no satisfaction..." I gave Sal a hug, and Deb shook his hand; then we three returned to the kitchen. He took a sip of his beer, put his hand on my shoulder. "I know you're bummed about David, but try to enjoy yourself tonight, okay?"

"Everyone looks so young."

"Want me to introduce you to some of my friends?"

"Maybe later."

He pointed to the food on the table. "There's plenty to eat. So, what can I get you to drink?"

We asked for wine. After he brought each of us a glass, I said, "Go on. Circulate. It's your party."

He turned to Deb. "Want to dance?"

She smiled, and off they went.

I couldn't believe it. I needed Deb's company tonight. As usual, Sal was about as perceptive as a rock.

I drank the wine in one long sweep, then poured another. The second one, I sipped slowly. A little later I crossed the room to a man in his early twenties who had been staring at me. He had long brown hair and a beard, and gold, wire-rimmed glasses.

I held out my hand. "Hi, I'm Julia DeCarlo. Sal's sister. You must be John Lennon."

He laughed, then shook my hand. "Derrick...Derrick Smith. Who's Sal?"

"My brother. He's throwing the party."

"Don't know him. Creighton invited me. I think he knows your brother." He reached behind my shoulder and touched the feather in my braid. "That's cool."

"It's an eagle feather."

"Oh, I thought they were illegal."

I pulled the braid up front and held up the feather. "This one isn't. I raise eagles at the Park Service." I talked a little about my job, about how I picked up the preened feathers of the eaglets from their cage. He told me about the business courses he was taking at the community college in Ellsworth. Soon, he tapped his empty beer bottle with his fingers. "Say, I could use another. How about you?"

With fresh drinks, we went into the living room. The lights were dim, and the room was hot with gyrating bodies. Jimmy Cliff was singing: "I'm going to get my share right now of what's mine. And then the harder they come, the harder they fall, one and all..." Derrick and

I moved onto the dance floor, and I spun him around, backed away, danced and clapped, then came back and took his hands.

"You're good," he said.

The music was loud. I moved close to Derrick's ear and shouted. "Ever see Jimmy Cliff live?"

"Not yet."

"I saw him at U Mass. Wow, he was stoned out of his mind."

We danced for a while, and when I finished my wine, he brought me another. A slow song by Jimmy Cliff came on. I pressed close to Derrick, and we danced check-to-check. Derrick could've been anyone; it didn't matter to me because I was feeling no pain. I felt as if Jimmy Cliff's words were meant for me: "And this loneliness won't leave me alone. It's such a drag to be on your own. My woman left and she didn't say why. Well, I'll guess I'll have to cry. Many rivers to cross..."

After another glass of wine, I was wrapping my arms around Derrick's shoulders as we danced, snuggling my face in his hair. Someone passed a joint around on the dance floor, and I took a few tokes. Was that Deb glaring at me? Why shouldn't I be having a good time?

Several fast songs later Derrick and I, sweaty and breathless, stopped dancing and sat on the sofa. I kissed his cheek. "Derrick, untie my braid, okay?" When he was finished, I brushed out my hair; then, I went to Sal's sound system and put on an album by Janis Joplin. On the dance floor I rhythmically bumped my hips into Derrick, then backed off. *Was he panting?* I flung out my arms, jumped up and down. My hair flew wildly. For a moment, I was no longer Julia DeCarlo; I was Janis Joplin.

When the song ended, Deb came over and pulled me aside. "This might be a good time to leave."

I waved her away. "I'm just starting to have fun."

Later, and I'm not sure how much later, Derrick and I, as if in a some drugged dream, left the party and strolled arm-in-arm several blocks to his apartment.

Inside there was a Formica bar in the corner of the living room. He went behind it, took out a leather pouch and rolled a joint. I sat on a barstool, toked as he held the match and took a deep puff. "Mexican?" I asked, passing him the joint.

He inhaled. "No, Columbian."

"Wow, it's strong."

After we finished the joint, he pulled me close and gave me a long kiss. I don't know how long it lasted. I was drifting in and out of reality. When I tried to regain my bearings, I stepped back, touched his face, his beard. Who was this man?

All at once, he dropped to his knees, pressed his face against my belly and looked up at me, his blue eyes looking innocent. "I adore you." He lifted my T-shirt and nibbled my skin, and I started laughing.

He stood up and threaded his fingers through my hair, pulling my head back, bringing his mouth to mine, but he didn't kiss like David, didn't seem tender at all. *But David wasn't here, was he? He was taking care of his needs. Well, I had needs. I don't like being left alone. Was he alone? No, he was with Rachel and Alice. What did he do when Alice opened the door? Hug her, kiss her, forgive her?* I didn't want to know. All I wanted to know was that I was with Derrick or John or whatever his name was, and he was happy to be with me.

Whose hands were those on my breasts? David's? Derrick's? When did he take off my bra and T-shirt? Were we playing some game? I took off his T-shirt. Such broad shoulders, taunt muscles. "What's that? A birthmark?" He didn't answer. I felt him unsnapping my pants. I had no idea if I wanted him to continue or not. Such strong grass.

Suddenly, Derrick pulled me down onto the carpet and climbed on top of me. He fumbled with himself and entered me. I felt like he was poking me with a stick. I looked around the room. There wasn't any furniture, just pillows on the floor. "What the hell?" I tried to push Derrick off, but he wouldn't move. I dug my fingernails into his back. "Get off." I shoved again, and he rolled onto the floor.

I sat up, and my head was pounding. I stood up dizzily. I crossed the room with my arms over my breasts, searching for my clothes. Near the bar I picked up my shirt and jeans. Derrick was still lying on the floor, and I poked him with my foot. "Help me. I can't find my bra and panties."

He looked for them half-heartedly; then, he came to me, still undressed, and opened his arms. "We don't have to make love. We can just fool around." He stroked my hair.

"Don't touch me." I moved back, put on my jeans.

He put on his wire-rimmed glasses. "Hey, it's me. John Lennon." He began singing: "I need somebody, not just anybody."

"You want to know what I need? I need to get the hell out of here." I pulled on my T-shirt.

Suddenly, he grabbed my arm, raised his voice. "Listen, bitch. I didn't rape you, you know."

I threw his hand off. "Go fuck yourself." He backed away, and I hurried out the door.

Should I have driven myself home? No, but I had to get away from him as fast as I could. I was lucky I made it to my house without killing someone.

Once inside, I went into the living room, sat on the sofa and wrapped myself in a cotton, Indian blanket. I didn't turn on the lights. I closed my eyes. I was nauseous from the wine and grass, and my head was spinning, so I opened my eyes, trying to stop the dizziness. A little light from the streetlamp shown into the living room. I could vaguely see the shape of the fieldstones in the fireplace. Suddenly, I was exhausted, and I lay down on the couch, but I felt like I was going to throw up, so I sat up again. That helped a bit. I wanted someone to take care of me. *Who was there to help me? No one. Not when I was a child. Not now.*

Who was that woman with Derrick? She was the old Julia. She was back. I tried to leave her in Massachusetts. I tried to exorcise her in therapy with Odette. I tried to replace her with the new Julia that was loved by David, and that loved David and Rachel. But the old Julia just wouldn't go away.

Exhausted, I lay down, again. I curled up under the blanket, hugging my knees, placing my lips on my arm. *Sleep, Julia. Sleep.*

The nausea was too much. My stomach began to heave. I ran upstairs to the bathroom. Somehow, I made it just in time, and I fell on my knees, held onto the seat, and vomited for what seemed forever. *Did I deserve this? Of course. This and more.*

When I was finished, I moved to the sink, rinsed out my mouth and washed my face and hands. I looked in the mirror. Touched my puffy eyes. Pulled at my stringy hair. I saw wrinkles on my forehead that I had never seen before. Would I ever get it right? I knew that I wanted what most women wanted: a home, a husband, kids. *Was I any more successful with family than my father?* I didn't think so.

I took off all my clothes because I didn't want to smell the vomit or any trace of Derrick, and I put on a nightgown; then, I went into my bed, propped up the pillows and pulled up the blankets. But I was afraid to lie down; I didn't want to be sick again. The window was open and the wind ruffled the lace curtains. I breathed in the cool air, trying to relax. I was so exhausted, I just wanted to sleep.

Fifteen minutes passed. An hour. I couldn't fall asleep. Images of Derrick, David, my father, my mother and Rachel spun around in my mind. All my relationships seemed twisted. How would I ever fix them? I was on a highway with a dozen other cars going at high speeds, squeezing me from all sides, tailgating me, and I couldn't get off the road.

After a long time, I rose from my bed and paced to the window and back. It felt good to move. *Maybe the walking would help me sober up? Maybe I should take a walk outside in the night?* No, I didn't want anyone to see me like this. I kept shaking out my arms, stretching my neck, trying to get comfortable. Everything in the room seemed out of place. I moved my Chinese flower vase from the night table to the dresser. I took cosmetics from the top of the vanity table and put them in drawers. I straightened the paintings on the wall. I made my bed. Still the room looked disorganized and broken.

Finally, the tears came like the sudden downpour in a rainstorm. I wailed loudly, gulped air.

I moved to my vanity table, sat on the stool. I didn't look in the mirror. All at once, I lifted my fists into the air and pounded them into my thighs. Pain, but pain's release. I jabbed my thighs again. And again. My heart was racing. I saw a nail file on top of the table, and I picked it up. In an instant, I brought it down into my thigh, and I punctured my skin. A few drops of blood trickled out from the wound.

Suddenly, I saw myself once again at Rattlesnake Cliff. The pearl handle knife. The blood in the snow. I dropped the nail file on the floor; then, I dragged myself to my bed, collapsed and wept again. *Did I fall asleep?* I didn't know. When I looked out my window much later, I saw that the morning sky was brightening. All at once, I knew what I had to do.

Within a half hour, I reached Deb's house and pulled into the gravel driveway; then, I hurried to the porch and knocked on the kitchen door. Almost immediately, she opened it. I fell into her embrace and burst into great sobs. "I'm in a lot of trouble."

She held me for a few moments; then, she led me into the living room, eased me down on the sofa. "What did that guy do?

I couldn't catch my breath.

She lifted my chin with her hands, looked at me. "Breathe in and out...Slowly...That a girl."

After a minute, I felt a little calmer. "I'm sorry to bother you."

"Bother? You're joking." Deb put her arm around my shoulder. "Did he hurt you?"

I buried my face in her hair. "We went to his apartment. I was so high. He penetrated me. It was my fault, too. When I realized what he was doing, I stopped him. I really messed up this time. I've been up all night. Can't sleep. Oh Deb, all the work I've done, and I'm still—" I let out a loud cry. I collapsed in her lap, crying.

She stroked my hair. "Hush, Julia. Try to relax."

A few minutes passed. I stopped crying. "I'm so tired."

"Well, sleep then. Everything will be okay. We'll talk later. Here, lie on the pillow." She covered me with a red afghan, knelt down beside me, kept stroking my hair. I whimpered for a little while; then, I fell asleep. When I awoke, Deb was sitting on the floor next to me, handing me a cup of tea. I sat up dreamily, took a sip. She patted my hand. "Feeling better?"

I nodded. "How long have I been sleeping?"

"Maybe an hour."

I held the warm cup in my hands, breathed in the steamy vapors. I looked around the living room. It was dimly lit, shaded by the large maple trees outside. Deb had decorated the room with second hand furniture that she had bought from antique shops. There was an old oak dresser, a stained glass lamp, and a matching green velvet chair and sofa. The floor was covered with an oriental rug.

"Head hurt?" Deb asked.

"My whole body."

"You were really chugging them down last night. Why didn't you leave with me? I was pissed at you."

"I'm sorry. I was drunk, stoned, acting crazy. That's no excuse, I know."

"Yeah, you were somebody else."

"Drinking like my father. It's my worst fear."

"How's that?"

I rose, moved to the marble fireplace and stood with my back to her. I ran my fingers through my stringy hair, then turned to Deb. "I must look awful. Do you have a brush?"

She brought one from the bathroom, sat me on the sofa, began brushing my hair. "So, that's your worst fear, the drinking?"

I pulled my legs up under me, sitting cross-legged on the sofa, while she continued brushing my hair. "Sure, drinking is a big worry. But my worst fear? That's my father." I paused. "I'm afraid someday I'll have a breakdown, just like him."

All at once, Deb's dog, Peggy, stirred from a cushion in the corner, came over and nudged my hand, so I scratched her back. "My life was crazy when I was a kid. One time my Mom asked me to visit my Dad in the VA mental hospital. The place was like a prison. A nurse and I went looking for my father. All the metal doors were locked. There were grates on the windows. Guards with keys. Crazy-looking patients. Some catatonic. Some shouting. After a while, the nurse and I found my father in his bedroom. He wouldn't get out of bed. The nurse left me alone with him, said she was busy. My father was in green pin-stripped pajamas. His head was shaven."

"They shaved his head?"

"And he wouldn't talk to me. I sat in a chair next to him for a long time, asking him questions. I wanted to help him." My voice broke, and I wasn't able to go on for a moment. "All my father did was stare out the window. I was so scared."

Deb rested her hand on my shoulder. "I would've been scared, too."

"The next day some psychiatrist called up the nuns at my school. Told them to keep an eye on me because mental illness could be hereditary. That stupid phone call. You know, I've spent my whole life waiting for the big one."

"You mean last night—"

"Exactly. I was so crazy after I left Derrick...that I tried to hurt myself again."

"Oh, Julia, I'm so sorry."

"This time it was a nail file." I pointed to my thigh. "It was just a scratch."

She put her hands to her cheeks. "Jesus, Julia. Why didn't you call me?"

"I was too ashamed." I gave her a hug. "But thanks for helping me now." I pulled back, let out a bitter laugh. "Damn my father. It's like he's inside me."

Deb reached out, touched my arm. "You're not your father, Julia. You know that. Look at all you've accomplished. A master's. The eagles. A great boyfriend. I mean, look at you. You're in good shape, better than most people." She started brushing my hair again. "And you've never been in a mental hospital like your father. Sure, you're in therapy, but that's a good thing."

"Yeah, that's a good thing."

Deb gently knocked the brush on my skull. "You're going to talk to Odette about all this, right?"

"Tomorrow."

"Thank God." Suddenly, her voice caught. "If anything happened to you...I mean...You're my best friend—" She leaned her head against me and began crying softly. I felt her shaking.

I held her for a while. We didn't say anything. We didn't have to.

Soon, Deb stirred. She went into the kitchen and returned with coffee and muffins. It dawned on me how much I loved her, and how self-centered I could be. *Time to forget your own problems, Julia. Think of Deb.*

I asked, "Say, how did you and Sal get along last night?"

She smiled a little. "We danced a lot. It was fun. He's a good dancer. But after you left, he and his buddies went into the kitchen, and they were singing, playing drinking games, so that's when I drove home. But, you know, and this may sound stupid, I like your brother."

"That makes two of us."

"Think he might ask me out?"

"Is that what you want?"

She nodded. "Don't say anything to him, though."

"Of course not."

Peggy let out a moan, put her head in my lap, gave me that keep-scratching-me-forever look, so I continued scratching her; then I looked up at Deb. "I could use some advice. I don't know what to do about David." I paused. "How do I tell him about last night?"

She thought for a moment. "Sometimes, it's better not to say anything."

Sixteen

Several terns, white and black seabirds smaller than gulls, darted in the sky looking like miniature jets, letting out high-pitched squeals. They flew about twenty feet above the water in Northeast Harbor. Suddenly one dove beak-first into the sea, completely disappearing; then in an instant, shot back upwards in the sky with a silvery, minnow-sized herring in its mouth. I sat on a park bench overlooking the harbor and town wharf, sipping coffee in a paper cup that I had picked up at Mom and Pop's grocery store on Main Street. It was early Monday morning, and when I had the energy, I enjoyed taking a walk before work from my house to the wharf. It was an exquisite time of the morning. Few people were up and about yet. The town and wharf were quiet and still, so I could savor the wildlife and misty morning fog that muted everything in surreal gray. Even the ferry to the Cranberry Islands was quiet now, with a lone boatman sweeping the deck before scores of tourists began arriving in the next hour.

After finishing my coffee, I ambled along the harbor, peering down into the floating rockweed, noticing horseshow crabs, one-foot wide, ancient-looking sea creatures with a huge protective conical shell and wagging, scaly tail, slinking about on the bottom of the harbor, searching for food. That's what I liked about the ocean. There was always something interesting to see. Soon, walking back to my house, I stopped at the post office to check my mailbox. There, I found a post card from my father with a photo of the Statue of Liberty. The card was wrinkled and stained. The writing was barely legible. Clearly, my father had been drinking when he wrote it.

"Dear Julia, Got evicted from the Boston apartment. Damn landlords. Am stay at the Y (big gap) in New York. Don't worry. Still getting VA checks. Could use a change of (word crossed out) scenery. How's about I catch a bus to Bar Harbor? (blotched ink) Would be nice to see you. Keep Smiling?!? Your father, Frank.

As soon as I arrived home, I fired off a note to him at the Y: "Dear Dad, No way do I want to see you in Bar Harbor. You've got to get sober first. That's the rule. The way you're living, bouncing from city to city, something bad is going to happen. I want to be a good daughter, but it's a two-way street. You've got to be a good father, too. Mom did everything for you, but you used her up, almost killed her, and I won't let you do that to me. Love, your daughter, Julia."

Wednesday morning, when I heard David's horn honking in the driveway, I hurried out of the house and flopped into the passenger seat. He kissed me on the cheek. "Feeling better?"

"Okay, I guess." I pushed the hair to the side of my face. "Thanks for coming today. I didn't want to go alone."

He squeezed my hand, started up the van, and we headed northwest to Bangor, Maine.

I let out a loud yawn.

"Tired?" he asked.

"Didn't sleep well."

He ran his fingers through my hair. "Stay at my place tonight. I'll make you some tea, put you to bed early."

"Early?" I winked at him. "I don't believe it."

He laughed.

There was a school bus ahead on the opposite side of the road with flashing lights, and a half dozen kids were getting on. David saw it and stopped. He turned to me. "Say, a customer was in the store yesterday, said two nesting eagles have returned to Bartlett Island. Is that true?"

"Sure is."

"And you didn't tell me?"

"Sorry, I've had a lot of things on my mind."

"I'd love to see them."

"You and half of Maine."

"But I'm David, your boyfriend, remember?"

I let out a short laugh. "Let me think about it."

The bus turned off its flashing lights, moved ahead, and we started up again. Soon we crossed the bridge to the mainland. The rising sun shone orange on Frenchman Bay. We drove on, listening to the morning news on Maine Public Radio. After stopping in Ellsworth for take-out coffee and bagels, we headed northwest on 1A.

David tapped my knee. "You never mentioned Sal's party. How'd it go?"

"Fine."

"You left early?"

I glanced out the window to avoid his eyes. "I was with Deb."

"And?"

"We had a good time."

"So you didn't leave early?"

I hesitated. "I was dancing."

"With Deb?"

I faced him, suddenly feeling defiant. "And some guy."

"So I heard."

"You heard?"

"Small town."

"A girl's not allowed to dance with a guy?"

"Did I say that? I just thought you were going to leave early."

I forced my voice to sound irritated. "You're not jealous, are you?"

"Of course I am."

"So come with me the next time."

He paused for a moment, stared at me as if he were studying my face. Then he asked, "Nothing else to tell me?"

"About what?"

"The party."

I let out a kidding laugh. "Oh yeah, I forget to mention, I slept with this guy who looked like Paul McCartney."

His face tensed up, then he laughed, and looked relieved. "Sorry, Julia. I didn't mean to cross-exam you, but I'm feeling a little insecure."

I reached over and kissed him on the cheek. "I missed you David. I really did. I'm glad you're back."

We drove without talking. I turned on the radio to a rock station. Aretha Franklin was singing, "You Make Me Feel Like a Natural Woman." Soon, we came to a red light in East Holden, but David wasn't paying attention, and suddenly, he had to stop short. Several cardboard boxes hurled forward to the front of the van, striking the backs of the seats. One box tipped over, and T-shirts spilled out. I squiggled between the seats, put the T-shirts back, and re-stacked the boxes. Just as I returned to the front, the light turned green, and David took off. "Thanks, Julia. I should've unloaded them at the store. Didn't have time. Rush, rush, you know. So our appointment's at nine?"

I nodded.

He gave me a quick glance. "You're father's not going to be there, right?"

"Right."

"Good, I don't know what I'd say to him." He kept his eyes on the road. "It's great you keep trying to help him, but I thought you were beginning to see it wasn't working."

I stretched like a cat trying to wake up. "It's Odette's idea. She's always challenging me. Says if you've got a problem, stay cool, and think about how to solve it. Try different things. See what works."

"Makes sense." We came to another red light, and he stopped.

I tapped him on the shoulder. "You know, David. We're both alike when it comes to family. We're loyal. It's in our blood." For a moment, I felt a pang of guilt. Loyal? I had just lied to him about Derrick, but I wasn't going to let one slip-up ruin the best relationship I've ever had.

The light turned green, and he took off quickly. "And the Ten Commandments."

I shook my head. "What did you say?"

"We're loyal because of the commandments."

"Right. Honor your parents."

He picked up what was left of his bagel and ate it in one gulp. "Say, Odette's not Jewish, is she?"

I let out a surprised laugh.

"There are black Jews, you know. Ethiopian Jews. African-American Jews. Even Japanese Jews."

"Well, I don't think she's Jewish. I figured she was Haitian because of her French name. I even asked her. But she wouldn't tell me. Said it would interfere with our work. Said we had to keep the focus on me. Strange, isn't it?"

"You'd think she would answer your question."

"I mean, I'd like to be her friend, too. See her for lunch once in a while, talk about everyday things. She won't hear of it. Said she never socializes with clients, even when the therapy ends."

"Well, maybe it's for the best."

A half hour later we pulled into the garage at the Veteran's Administration in Bangor. Although we had a nine o'clock appointment, the social worker, Bernie Landon, didn't come for us in the reception area until ten. I was furious, but said nothing, not wanting to make a scene that might jeopardize my chance for his help. As he escorted us into his office, I noticed that his red tie ended four inches above his belt. Inside his narrow room, an American flag hung on the wall and a photograph of President Reagan stood on his desk. He arranged the chairs, and we sat facing one another. "So Miss DeCarlo, and you're—"

"David Zuckerman." David shook Landon's hand. "I'm Julia's fiancée."

I raised my eyebrows at David. *What was he saying?* He gave me a mischievous grin.

Landon let out a loud sigh. "Tell me, how can I help you?"

I leaned forward, my hands on my knees, and I talked briefly about my father's troubled life. Then I said, "Right now, he's in New York City. He's had a lot of trouble with the police. Thinks they're trying to kill him. He's been drinking heavy. I was hoping you could get him into some kind of program."

"Is he married?"

"Divorced. My mother's dead."

"Children?"

"Me and Sal. And Sal doesn't want anything to do with him."

"How old is Sal?"

"Twenty-seven. He's a vet, too."

"Where does he work?"

"Same as me. At the Park Service in Acadia. We're both federal employees, just like you." Landon's face looked blank. *So much for my hope that I might have some influence because I worked for the government.*

"Father's hometown?"

"Milford, Massachusetts."

"Hmmmm." Landon was silent and played with his pen. "We wouldn't have your father's records here. We'd have to get them from Massachusetts." He spoke with his lips tight and his jaw immobile. "Can you tell me more about your father's mental illness."

I described his history of violence, his schizophrenia, his VA hospitalizations.

When I finished, Landon tapped his finger against his cheekbone, pondering; then he leaned back in his chair and crossed his arms over his chest. "I'm afraid I can't help you, Miss DeCarlo. Your father has to come to us on his own free will. Doesn't sound like he wants to. And we can't force him into a program. You know, he has rights, too. The only time we can force him is when he's threatening someone's life."

I lowered my head and looked at the floor. "But he's no good to anybody right now. He's in constant trouble with the law. He can't take care of himself. He doesn't trust me. Please, can't the VA in New York at least call him into their office."

Landon said nothing.

I heard my voice shaking with frustration. "You've got to help him. He's a vet. You're the Veterans Administration. Surely you have a responsibility to do something."

He said nothing, arched his back in his chair.

I stood up, felt my legs trembling. "So what do we do, Mr. Landon? Just wait until my father's dead in the street."

"I'm not saying that." He turned to his desk and began straightening up papers. "My hands are tied."

I bit my lower lip. "So it's a hopeless situation. Is that what you're telling me?"

"Hopeless? No. Maybe someone else can help him. Maybe some non-profit program. But, I'm afraid I can't help you, as I said, unless he threatens someone. That's the law. Now, if you don't mind, I have a lot of other work I need to get to."

David raised his hand. "Hold on just a—-

"I'm sorry I can't help you more." Landon spread out his arms, moved forward, and ushered us out of his office. David and I stood in the reception area for a minute, speechless, shocked at Landon's actions.

In a daze we took the elevator, and when the door opened at the parking level, David let out a snort. "We should recommend him for a promotion." He shook his head. "Government at its worst."

I took his hand and we began walking to the van. "You know, David, Landon's right about one thing. There's something to be said for free rights. But the truth is, society doesn't give a damn about the mentally ill anymore than they do about the poor."

"I'm sorry, Julia. I thought they would help." He put his arm around my shoulder.

"I did, too. Maybe if we had gotten another social worker? Guess my father's on his own. Too bad for him. And for me." When we came to the van, I perked up, pulled David towards me, kissed him on the lips. "Hey, at least something good came out of it." I held up my hand. "Did you bring the engagement ring?"

He opened his mouth wide, unable to say a word.

"I'm waiting." I clicked my fingers.

He smiled sheepishly. "I...I thought I'd have more clout if Landon thought I was related."

I let out a long laugh, then I pinched his cheek. "Well then, tomorrow, okay? And please make it a topaz set in gold."

I was working in my office at the Park Service when Father McBride called me back from his detox center in New York City. "Of course I remember you, Julia. Not many daughters try to help someone like your father?"

"That's kind of you to say, but it seems I'm not doing a very good job."

"I don't believe it. By the way, sorry my cousin had to let your Dad go."

I held the phone, stretched towards my office door, and closed it. "I understand...I wanted to tell you that things have gotten worse for my father. He's been hopping from city to city. First, Boston. Now, New York City. Drinking heavy, again, of course. Has he tried to contact you?"

"Afraid not."

I sat down at my desk. "He said he really liked you. Said you were the reason he got sober."

"Thanks, Julia, but that's not true. Every recovering alcoholic does it on their own...with the help of Jesus. I've worked with hundreds of alcoholics, and the one thing I've learned, is, if they're going to recover, it's got to come from inside themselves."

"Inside?" I heard him light up a cigarette and inhale.

"They've got to have some desire, some spark, that says I'm better than this drunk. Anything less just doesn't cut it."

"He did have it."

"People slip. Maybe he'll bounce back. Jesus is always looking for his lost sheep."

I twisted the braid of my hair. "Please Father, tell me, what can I do?"

"Well, what have you done so far?"

I told him about the Public Gardens, about the VA in Bangor.

When I finished, there was a long pause. Then he said, "Sounds like you've done all you can. Even tried to confront him, yes? The problem is the alcoholic lives a deluded life. They love the bottle more than anything or anyone, even though it's killing them. Somehow they've got to wake up. And like I said, and it's got to come from inside."

I leaned over, slumped on my desk. "It seems hopeless."

"You can pray, Julia."

"Yes, Father."

He hesitated. "Have you been going to Mass, taking communion?"

I sat up, felt my body stiffen. *Should I lie? How do you lie to a priest?* "Not exactly."

"That might help."

I glanced at the photo of David and Rachel on my desk. I thought of their Jewishness, and my Catholic skepticism. I was confused, so I said nothing.

He coughed, a smoker's cough. "Well, Julia. I should be going. I have a meeting in a few minutes."

"Before you go, Father. One more thing. Would you please keep an eye out for my Dad? He might drop in."

"Sure, I'll let you know if he does. And I'll keep you and your father in my prayers."

"Thanks."

"God bless. Don't lose hope, dear."

Seventeen

Rachel sat in my lap, her hands on the steering wheel, and we piloted the boat together, riding towards Bartlett Island, but we went slowly, because it was still dark out, and the lights on the boat weren't that strong. There was a moderate northeast wind with two-foot waves. We approached the waves head-on with the bow, which caused the boat to bounce, and Rachel to giggle with excitement. To the east, I saw the vague tops of the spruce and fir trees on Mount Desert etched on the blue-white light of the morning horizon.

David sat next to Rachel and me, sipping a take-out coffee. "Hey, there's Cassiopeia," he said, pointing to the night sky. He took Rachel's hand and used her finger to find each star, drawing the outline of Cassiopeia's chair.

After a few moments, Rachel dropped her head and glanced at me, "How big are the eaglets?"

I stretched my arms to show her their long wings. "They've grown a lot, but they only weigh as much as a newborn baby. That's why, with their wide wings, they can glide and soar above the mountains."

"Like a kite."

"But no strings."

We laughed together.

"When are you going to teach the eaglets to fly, Julia?"

"Oh, you think I'm a circus trainer. No, their parents will teach them. And they'll learn by trying."

"Today?"

"Maybe."

After landing on a small sandy beach, we carried our gear to a clearing near the eagle's nest and began quietly setting up a camouflage blind in the emerging light. David took one end of the tarp-like cloth, and I the other, and we fastened the bottom to the ground with small stakes, and tied the top with ropes to two aspen trees. Rachel came to me. "Where's the tower and cage?"

I put my finger to my lips. "Remember, sweetheart, you promised to whisper, okay?"

She nodded.

I spoke softly. "They're on Seal Cove, not here. That's where Sal's taking care of them. This is another eagle family, and they don't live in a cage because they're wild. Last year they built a nest on this island, but a storm blew it down." I took her to a slit in the blind and pointed to the faint outline of a nest atop a pine tree. "That's the new nest with two eaglets. I'm studying them as part of my job. They're very special. Not many eagles have been born in Acadia for a long, long time."

David set up his telescope next to us; then, he tapped Rachel on the head. "Guess what Julia and I named the eaglets?...Bianca and Aaron. Remember who Aaron was?"

She thought for a moment. "Moses' brother." She squinted. "Who's Bianca?"

"She was my grandmother," I said.

"Can I name an eagle, Julia?"

"Sure, we'll need names for the eaglets in the tower."

She puckered her lips. "How about Harriet? For my grandmother."

"Harriet it is." I was happy to do something for Rachel, but it crossed my mind the name might help David's mother warm up to me. *Was I being too calculating? I hoped not. Authentic – that's the kind of woman I wanted to be.*

David began setting up my 35mm camera on a tripod, and I sat on the ground with Rachel, sharing milk and a bagel with cream cheese.

Soon the sun rose, and we looked at the nest with our binoculars through the slits in the blind. From the ground all that we saw was the bottom and sides of the nest, but no eagles. It was an unusual angle for me. I had observed and photographed them for the past two months from the blind sixty feet up in the nearby two-hundred-year-old pine tree. The ground blind was the only safe way for Rachel to see them.

Every few minutes we checked the nest. After a little while, David announced, "They're awake." He helped Rachel look through the telescope. "Ooooo, I want to hug them," she said.

I went to my camera and zoomed in. The two eaglets stood on the rim of the nest. They fanned out their wings and preened their feathers; then, they pranced around like joggers in a gym. I clicked away. The eaglets looked larger than life, more mythic from the ground.

"Where are Robert and Emily?" David asked.

"Looking for food, I imagine."

Soon the eaglets began flapping their wings rapidly, lifting and hovering over the nest. Bianca pumped higher, and she landed on a branch just above the nest. She began whining softly.

"Is something wrong?" Rachel asked.

"She's hungry."

A half hour passed, then all at once the eaglets began screaming and flapping wildly. In a moment Emily arrived and soared over the top of the pine tree with a fish in her talons. I had seen her land many times on the edge of the nest, drop the fish, then fly off before the eaglets swarmed all over her. Now though, she didn't land. Instead, she circled several times above them and dangled the fish from her talons.

The eaglets jumped and pumped their wings. They rose into the air. Emily swooped down, called to them in a high-pitched cry, and then retreated to a branch on a nearby birch. Still, they screamed and flapped at their mother. They clung to the edge of the nest, teetering, almost falling off, crying for food.

David nudged me. “What’s going on?”

“You’ll see.”

Three more times she flew above the nest, dangling the fish, and three more times she perched in the birch with her catch.

The eaglets lost whatever patience they had. They began crying even louder and flapping their wings more frantically.

Again, Emily flew above them.

Suddenly Bianca lifted off the nest, her wings beating fast, and she drifted out into the open air. She hovered for a moment, then glanced downward.

“Go for it, girl,” I whispered.

Emily, who was gliding above her, took off with the fish, and all at once her daughter followed. Bianca flew for about a hundred yards, then seemed to run out of steam, and tried to land on a large limb in an aspen tree. She wasn’t steering very well and crashed into the leafy branches. I took a picture. Down she fell, slapping her wings against the tree until she hit the ground.

“Ouch,” Rachel said. “Is she hurt?”

“Maybe just a scrape. They’re tough birds.”

Emily let out a series of cackling sounds, then swooped down on the ground to her daughter. Bianca stood up, her wings stretched out, her head bowed, and Emily dropped the fish before her. I clicked away. She stood guard over her daughter and in a few minutes Bianca ate everything. Then, Emily flew off. For a moment Bianca looked around bewildered and alone; then, she hobbled into the shrubs and hid.

David pointed up to the nest. “How about Aaron?”

“He’s got to work for his food, today,” I said.

Aaron stood at the rim and seemed to be searching for Bianca on the ground, occasionally calling to her. After a while he disappeared into the middle of the nest, and we couldn't see him. An hour passed. Where were the parents?

Finally, I flung my binoculars and camera over my shoulders and said, "I'm going to climb up to the platform. I want to get a closer photo of Aaron."

"Can I come?" Rachel asked.

"The ladder's sixty feet up, darling. It's too dangerous."

"Please, I can do it, Julia."

"When you're older."

She twisted her feet into a V on the ground. "Oh, all right."

David put his arm around me. "Be careful. It's windy up there."

I circled behind some shrubs and came to the bottom of the white pine. Then, hand over hand, I pulled myself up, grabbing branches and wooden steps screwed into the trunk. Halfway up I stopped to rest on a large limb for a few moments. When I reached the platform I looked down dizzily and saw the blind where David and Rachel were hidden. The wind was strong and whistled through the pine needles. I held onto a branch to steady myself. The tree and the platform were swaying back and forth. It took me a minute to get my sea legs.

Hidden by the blind on the platform, I focused my binoculars on Aaron, who was resting in the nest like a hen sitting on eggs. A little later, he stood up, tossed his head skyward and emitted a squealing cackle. He kept calling.

Soon Robert appeared, and like Emily, he hovered above the nest with a fish hooked in his talons. Had he and Emily talked to each other about this? I could hear Emily saying, "Today's the day, Robert. It's time for the kids to leave home and start flying on their own." Aaron obviously disagreed. He screamed at his father, flapped his wings, floated a few feet above the nest, but refused to leave it.

Then, like Emily, Robert perched in a nearby aspen with his fish. After a little while, he flew to the nest again, trying to coax his son away, but to no avail; so Robert flew back to his perch. Yet, a third time he hovered and dangled the fish. Aaron screamed loudly, but didn't budge. Now Robert perched farther away from his son in a tall pine. Aaron kept screaming. After about five minutes Aaron lowered the volume to a soft whine.

Suddenly, Robert perked up when Bianca cried from below in the shrubs. He looked and listened, then dropped out of the tree with his wings tight against his body, opening them at the last second to brake and land on the ground. He dropped his fish, wobbled toward the shrubs and called for Bianca. She didn't answer. He left the fish on the ground, flew back to a branch on the pine, and watched for her to emerge.

Meanwhile, Aaron cried out in a begging sound. He paced around the nest, whining, unrelentingly. Robert ignored him.

Bianca, still hidden in the shrubs, called out in a plaintive high-pitched cry, and I searched for her with my binoculars. Cautiously, she poked out of the shrubs, then moved towards the fish, but stopped about ten feet from it.

I was focusing my binoculars when all at once I saw Rachel in the clearing. I let out a gasp. She bent down and picked up the fish. I lowered the binoculars, rubbed my eyes. Was I imaging things? I looked again. Rachel was moving towards Bianca, reaching out her hand, offering the fish to the eaglet. I looked at the blind. Where was David?

Suddenly I was startled by a swishing sound. Robert was diving to the ground. I yelled down to Rachel, cupping my hands to my mouth. "Drop the fish, Rachel." Did she hear me? I shouted, "Help, David, help."

In an instant I began clambering down the ladder. My hands and feet frantically grabbed branches and steps. I missed a step, slipped for a moment, but caught a limb with my hand. In no time I was halfway down. I didn't pause to look for Rachel. My only thought was to get to the ground.

I unconsciously lowered my foot down into the crook of a branch, but in a second I realized I had made a big mistake. It was stuck. I tried to pull it out, and suddenly I lost my balance. I was falling. In a moment

I was upside down. My hands leapt out, looking for something to latch onto. I grabbed a step with both hands.

I let out a cry and looked up. My foot was stuck in the branch and my leg was twisted. I pushed up, lifted my body, tried to relieve the pressure on my leg.

I looked around. Everything was upside down. I felt dizzy. I glanced at the ground. I was about twenty feet up. I searched for Rachel. She was standing motionless, and then I saw four figures lined up in a row.

David came first, then Robert, then Rachel, and finally Bianca at the edge of the shrubs. No one was moving. Rachel was still holding the fish in her hand. Robert was facing David, and the eagle tossed his head skyward, grunted loudly, called out, "whee-he-he-he-he." He turned to Rachel, moved a few feet towards her, spreading out his wings, sweeping them along the ground.

Rachel began crying. "Help me, Daddy."

I didn't know what I was doing until I heard my own sound. I let out a call like an eagle. It was almost an innate call. Robert looked up. He must have thought I was some alien from another planet. I whistled to him. Did he recognize me? Was he able to make sense of this crazy situation? Did he know we meant him no harm?

All at once I felt the step I was holding shift a little. I looked closely and saw that the screws of the step were slipping out of the trunk. What could I do? There was nothing else to grab onto. In a second the step popped out, and I dropped downwards. I felt my ankle snap, and I let out a shrieking sound.

All that was holding me was my foot, still stuck in the branch. I wrapped my arms around the tree, tried to push myself up, tried to ignore the excruciating pain.

David looked up at me, then back at Rachel. He yelled at her. "Throw the fish to Bianca and move away. Now."

She was paralyzed, unable to speak. Robert moved his head from side to side, looking at her, then me.

David moved towards me, then stopped. He moved towards Rachel and spoke loudly, firmly: "Rachel, do what I said. Drop the fish. The eagle won't hurt you."

She was frozen.

He folded his hands, his voice begging, "Please, drop the fish."

She did nothing.

Finally, he threw his hands up in the air. "*Oy*, Rachel. I give up. Julia's hurt. I've got to help her." He turned and ran towards me.

In an instant Rachel threw the fish to Bianca, circled wide around Robert and hurried towards us. Robert let out a loud cry, then pranced to Bianca.

David rushed up the tree. When he reached me, he said, "This is going to hurt," and he pushed me upwards with his arm and shoulder. I was sobbing openly. He kept pushing until I was able to sit on a branch; then, he wiggled my foot, trying to loosen it. I thought I would faint from the pain. Finally, it came free. "Be brave," he said.

He maneuvered me onto his shoulders, so that my legs were straddled around his neck like a horse rider. I tried not to cry. He moved down. Would the steps hold? He took a long stride over the broken step. Down another. It seemed like forever. Finally, we reached the ground.

He laid me down. My foot was at rest, and the pain subsided a little. He kissed me and put a backpack under my head as a pillow. "There. Better? How do you feel? Can you speak? What can I do?"

"Water," I whimpered.

He held the canteen, and I sipped. He gently removed my boot and my sock. When he touched my ankle, I shrieked.

"Sorry, Julia. It's broken all right. Could be worse, though. No protruding bone. No blood."

Rachel sat down next to me, wiped the sweat off my forehead. "You're shaking, Julia."

"It hurts terribly." I looked around. I spoke through clenched teeth. "What happened to the eagles?"

She pointed. "They went into the shrubs."

I reached out, stroked her hair. "Are you okay?"

"He didn't bite me."

I let out a little laugh. "That was nice of you to give the fish to Bianca."

David tapped her on the head. "I turned my back for a second. Why in the world?"

She lowered her eyes. "I wanted to help."

David held my hand, then said, "Got to splinter it. Keep it from moving." He hurried off, and returned with several sticks. First he wrapped his T-shirt around my ankle and then tied the branches vertically along my calf and ankle with some rope he had cut from the blind. "Too tight?"

I grimaced. "I wouldn't know the difference."

Soon I was on his back with my arms around his neck, and he moved slowly along the trail to the boat, trying not to rattle my foot. Suddenly, he tripped momentarily on a rock. "Oh, God," I yelled out in pain. When we reached the boat, he put a blanket on the floor and laid me on top. In a flash he started the boat and headed towards the mainland. I heard him call the Coast Guard on the radio. "Got a woman with a broken ankle. We're boating back from Bartlett Island. Think you can guys can get an ambulance to Pretty Marsh? We'll be there in about ten minutes."

Rachel stayed by my side. "Here's some water," she said, holding the canteen to my lips. She pushed my hair to the sides. "You're so hot."

The wind was gentle and the waves were small, or so I thought; then, we hit a big one. The boat bounced up and landed roughly. I screamed. Rachel kissed my cheek. "We're almost there, Julia."

When we arrived at Pretty Marsh, I heard the siren as the ambulance approached. In no time the two EMT's placed me on a stretcher and put me inside the van. As we headed to the hospital, one of the paramedics injected a painkiller into my rump, and he replaced the make-shift splint with an official one. David and Rachel sat on the floor at my side.

"So what's the verdict?" David asked the paramedic. "Think she'll live?"

He touched my foot. "Probably have to amputate." He laughed. "Just kidding. Looks like a simple break. You'll be up and around in no time. What happened?"

Rachel said, "She was up in a tree. I was on the ground. I had a fish in my hand and the eagle wanted it, and I thought he was going to bite me, and Julia hurried down the tree but got stuck, and that's when it broke."

The paramedic gave David a skeptical look. "She's joking?"

"You never heard about Julia DeCarlo, the eagle lady?"

He pointed to me. "That's you?"

"If I live," I said in a weak voice.

Everyone laughed.

The paramedic gently tapped Rachel on the shoulder. "Show me the bite."

She shook her head. "I gave up the fish, so he let me go."

I squeezed David's hand, brought him close, brushed a kiss over his lips, said softly, "You're the best. Thanks. I'd still be dangling in that tree if it wasn't for you." I pulled Rachel close. "And you too honey. You're the greatest. You're taking good care of me."

She stared away. "You're not mad at me?"

"For being nice to Bianca?" I kissed her cheek. "How could I be." *I was taking the higher ground. I knew five-year-olds interpreted the world differently than we 'wiser' adults. Still I wasn't looking forward to months of rehab. But did I love Rachel, regardless? You bet.*

The paramedic moved David and Rachel aside. "Sorry to break this up, folks. Got to take her blood pressure." He wrapped the sleeve around my arm and felt my pulse. "A-okay," he said, giving me a thumbs-up. Then he moved to the front of the van and sat in the passenger seat next to the driver.

David came near, caressed my face with his hands. "Sorry I wasn't watching Rachel. Truth is I was taking a piss in the woods."

I lifted my eyebrows at him, then let out a little laugh. "When I saw the four of you standing in a row, I couldn't believe it. You really had to make a quick decision."

"It was a gut reaction."

"Weren't you afraid for Rachel?"

"I trusted Robert. And I thought you were going to fall on your head."

Rachel sat in David's lap. "Does it still hurt, Julia?"

"Some, honey. But the shot was a big help."

She twisted a little of her hair into a braid. "Gee, I hope Aaron flies today."

I spoke in a whisper, still in shock. "He may not. But tomorrow for sure."

"He'll be starving."

"Oh no, they'll feed him before he goes to bed."

A look of relief came across her face. "Yeah, they're not that mean, are they?"

"They're good parents. Just tough. It's the only way their kids will survive in the wild."

She chewed on her finger. "I'm glad I don't have to survive in the wild."

I could hear the sarcasm in my voice. "Oh, you will."

"What do you mean, Julia?"

I paused. "I'm afraid you're still too young to understand."

"But, you'll explain it to me when I'm older, right?"

"I will, darling." I pulled her close and hugged her.

She nestled her face in my hair. After a moment, she pulled back a little and smiled. Then she laid her head next to mine, and I held her like that all the way to the hospital. I suddenly realized that she and David were like family to me, the family I had always dreamed of.

Eighteen

"This is dumb. What the hell am I doing here?" Sal asked, as he stepped in front of me just before we entered the revolving door of the Veteran's Hospital in Boston.

"We've been over this, Sal. Let it go." I moved him aside, and pushed ahead through the spinning door, trying to carefully maneuver my cane and the cast on my leg.

Inside the lobby, he grabbed my arm and stopped me again.

"I'm worried, Julia."

"He's in a wheelchair, for God's sake."

"Right, how could I hit a disabled man?"

We rode the elevator to the eighth floor and came into a hallway that smelled of urine. As we walked down the corridor, we passed piles of dirty sheets and blankets stacked outside the patients' rooms.

"Hi, I'm Julia DeCarlo," I said to a nurse in a blue-stripped uniform, who was sitting behind a counter, scribbling notes into a report. "I called yesterday. My brother and I are here to see our father, Frank DeCarlo."

She glanced up over the top of her eyeglasses. "Nobody told me nothing. You picked a bad time. Morning shift is just cleaning up."

"We flew all the way from Maine," Sal said.

The nurse tapped her pen in her hand. "Your father's one of our worst patients. Doesn't get along with the other vets. Won't take his medication."

"I'm sorry." I nodded knowingly. "It hasn't been easy for us, either."

Her face softened; then she pointed down a long hallway. "He's probably in the TV room, last door on your left."

We entered the room and stepped into a thick cloud of smoke. I saw my father in a wheelchair, drinking a cup of coffee, staring out a window. A half dozen other men dressed in bathrobes and pajamas sat in the room. They were smoking cigarettes and watching a war movie on a television set hung from the ceiling. I went to my father; Sal trailed behind. "*Buon giorno,* Dad." I kissed him on the cheek, then pulled Sal alongside. "Look who I brought."

He gazed at Sal, but from the puzzled expression on his face, I knew he didn't recognize him.

Sal whispered to me. "Are you sure you have the right guy?"

"Of course."

My father wheeled in front of us. "The nurses are trying to kill me, Julia. You've got to get me out of here."

I raised my eyebrows, put my hand on Sal's shoulder. "Dad, don't you know who this is?"

"A doctor."

"It's Sal."

He looked closely at him. "Sal?" He reached out his mobile hand, his left hand, and Sal shook it. "*Mi scusi.* I didn't know you. It's been so long."

Sal fidgeted and slipped his hand away.

"*Tu sei molto grande*, Sal." He wiped the tears from his eyes. "Who'd have thought I'd have such a big boy?"

Sal glared at him. "I'm not a boy anymore."

"Hey," my father yelled above the sound of the television. "Look who's here. It's my kids." One man glanced at us, then turned back to the movie. My father motioned to a row of green vinyl chairs. "Sit, sit."

I sat and patted his hand. "Sorry they screwed things up."

"*Essi sono asini.*" He slapped his hand on the arm of his wheelchair. "Your phone number was right in my wallet. They never even looked. What if I had died? Who would've known?" He shook his head bitterly. Then, he took a pack of cigarettes from his shirt pocket and offered us one.

"We don't smoke," Sal said.

My father, using his good hand, tipped a cigarette from the pack into his mouth.

I took his lighter and lit it. "I thought you were in New York?"

He took a long drag. "Had to get out. They're crazy there. Got a buddy here in Boston. McNamara. Nice guy. He put me up. Things were going good. Then this damn stroke hit me."

"Any better?" I asked, pointing to his right arm.

"It's dead."

"And the leg?"

"The same. Goddamn doctors, and they ain't doing nothing to help me."

"Well, at least you can talk again." I tried to sound optimistic.

"What good is talking?" He shook his finger. "I'm no cripple. I'm a free man. I want to be able to move around, go places. This wheelchair is killing me. Tell the doctors they've got to do something."

"They said the damage is permanent."

"And you believe them?" He took a puff on his cigarette. "One week they try to help me; the next they give up. Talk to Dr. Jong, will you?"

"Okay." I closed my eyes, rubbed my temples, felt a headache coming on. "But I'm not promising anything."

He took several puffs on his cigarette, then stubbed it out in an ash tray he had taped on the arm of the wheelchair. He pulled at his thin chin and looked at Sal. "Didn't think I'd ever see you."

Sal shifted in his chair. "Julia put a gun to my head. Made me do it."

"You haven't changed, have you? Still a smart ass." He let out a short laugh.

Sal clenched his teeth. "At least I don't beat up women."

He glared at Sal for a few moments, then shrugged his shoulders. "Amen. Let bygones be bygones."

We sat together, quiet, uncomfortable with one another. He lit another cigarette. "So where you living, Sal?"

"Acadia. Like Julia," Sal said, staring at the floor.

"Got a job?"

"Work at the park service." Sal shuffled his feet on the floor. "Been renovating a sheep barn. I do other things. Help with the eagles. Keep the—"

"Ow. Ow." My father lifted his paralyzed leg up. "Oh shit, it's my thigh." He moved his leg around, then set it down in a different position. He took a puff on his cigarette. "I've got to get a good job like yours, Sal. My boss in Portland was a bastard. Always riding me. Let the coloreds sit on their ass..."

For several minutes he moaned about his job. *How often as kids had we heard him rant like this?* I saw Sal's face tense up, his hands tighten. I chimed in: "What do you say, guys? It's kind of stuffy here. Why don't we go downstairs and get something to eat?"

"Downstairs?" My father leaned forward, cupped his ear. "Why not? I could use a fresh *caffe*."

I stood up.

All at once my father noticed my cane and cast, and pointed to my foot. "Say, Julia, what happened?"

"Fell out of a tree."

"You're lucky," he said. "At least you're not in a wheelchair like me."

So much for his sympathy. I was a fool to expect it. I leaned down, pulled off one of the eagle feathers I had taped to my cast and attached it to his wheelchair.

"What's that for?"

"It's magic. Cures most everything."

He laughed. "My silly Lilly. Hey Sal, remember that name?"

Sal nodded.

I began pushing my father through the hallway. He directed me like a traffic cop. "*Sinistra*, Julia, go left. Are you listening to your father? Watch out. Oh, my bad leg. You're going to hit it." We went inside the elevator. "Wrong button, Julia. It's in the basement. Don't you know nothing?" Sal moved behind him and made a choking gesture with his hands.

In the cafeteria we bought coffee and donuts, then moved to a table where my father parked himself and his wheelchair at the head of the table. A few tables away, an elderly woman fed soup from a thermos to a frail-looking vet. I looked around the cafeteria. It was painted in a faded-green color and was empty except for us and the elderly couple.

I took a sip of coffee; then, I pushed my chair away from the table and began slowly lifting my leg with the cast up and down.

"What are you doing?" my father asked.

I winked at Sal. "Getting ready for a dance performance next week."

"How can you dance with that cast?"

"Got you." I laughed. "The doctor wants me to exercise it. You know, keep my muscles strong."

"See, you've got a good doctor. Wish I had one." He lit a cigarette, then pulled out a bundle of tattered photographs from his pants' pocket. He carefully removed the rubber band and showed us a picture of Sal as a young boy sitting on a tree swing in Milford. "That's how I remembered you, Sal. I have a lot of memories. Some good, some bad."

One by one, he handed us a photograph. In a faded picture I was a young girl in shorts and no shirt, smiling, holding up a fish I had caught from the Charles River. There was a photo of my father, my mother, Sal and I sitting on a park bench in the Boston Commons.

In another my father, dressed in Army fatigues, clutched a submachine gun. "Damn Nazis nearly killed me," he said. He pointed to a shrapnel scar above his right eyebrow and opened his shirt to reveal another on his chest. "Was in the hospital for a month before they sent me back to the front. They said, 'If you can walk, you can fight."

Next he handed us his wedding picture. He and my mother were posed in front of a white, marble altar. He wore an army uniform, and she was in a white lace gown with her black hair uncovered. At the time she looked to be in her early twenties; he in his mid-thirties. I studied their faces. What did my mother see in him? My mother had called herself a "war bride," and in this photograph my father looked dignified, even heroic. Who's to understand such things, such times?

He passed Sal and me the immigration photo of his parents in their old-world clothes, their stark expressions. And, there was a picture of our Milford house with its asphalt-shingle siding. I noticed that he handled each photograph with pride and care, and I realized all that he had left was the past, his time of success and love.

Then he showed us the picture of my mother that I had given him on our trip to Peaks Island. In it she stood on the front porch of our Milford home in an Easter dress wearing a red velvet hat with a white veil over half her face. "Marisa was *una donna gentile*," he said. I looked at him admiring the photograph and saw in his face that he still loved her.

I glanced at Sal. He was looking at a photo and smiling. *Good. He's relaxing.*

After several more pictures, my father gathered them all up, wrapped them with the rubber band, and put them back in his pocket. We sat together quietly for a bit.

My father sipped his coffee. Mischief swept his face. He held a donut up against his forehead and cried out, "Help me, Sal. I've got a hole in my head."

Sal didn't laugh, but I did.

My father wheeled behind Sal and pulled on his pony tail. "Lost your sense of humor?"

Sal swung around, lifted his hand. A moment passed; then he lowered it and pointed his finger at his father: "Don't fuck with my hair."

They looked angrily at one another. Finally my father said, "Okay. Peace. I didn't know you were so sensitive." He wheeled back to the table, took a big bite of his donut. "The food ain't bad here, not like the time I was in North Africa. We marched fifteen miles a day. All we had to eat was smoked herring and bread. The bread was like gravel. Damn herring bones got stuck in your throat. You ate it anyway. It was that or starve."

He finished his donut in a gulp. It seemed to invigorate him, and he talked non-stop, making no connection between ideas, jumping around in time, funny one moment, angry the next.

After a few minutes Sal rose from the table and stretched his arms upwards, almost touching the ceiling tiles. "We should get going."

My father looked dejected. "You just got here."

"Our plane leaves soon, and we have to work tomorrow." Sal began walking out of the cafeteria.

My father caught up with him. "Before you go, I want you to show you the king's castle."

We rode the elevator upstairs to his room, a wide space sparsely furnished with a tan metal bed and dresser. A carton of cigarettes and a urine jug rested on top of the night table. On one wall he had taped several photographs, including a color picture of Jackie Kennedy.

My father picked up a package of vanilla-cream cookies from the top of his dresser and offered us some. I took a few, but Sal passed. I poked him in the arm. "Since when do you pass up cookies?"

Begrudgingly, he ate one.

"*Sedete*, take a load off your feet." My father motioned to two tan metal chairs along the window. Then he lit a cigarette, holding it between two fingers stained brown from smoking.

Outside the window I saw a park in the distance with jade green fields and woods. "Hey Dad, you got a nice view here. Nothing like nature to soothe you. That's why I like Acadia. The mountains inspire me."

"What mountains?" He flicked an ash into the tray on his wheelchair.

"The ones in Acadia, where we work. About a dozen of them. They're surrounded by the sea."

"Sounds nice. I'd like to live in a place like that." He took a long drag on his cigarette. "I've lived most of my life in cities. Boston. Portland. New York. They're vicious places. *Il popolo sono pazzo.* I don't know why I'm alive today. Damn cops. They almost killed me a dozen times." His voice became harder, deeper. He sneered his words.

Sal grew restless, stood up to leave, tugged at my sleeve.

My father looked down at the floor, his voice sad. "I know you've got to get going. Don't let me hold you back. Oh, before you go, I got something for you."

He opened a drawer and took out two plastic coffee mugs inscribed with American flags and the words, "Veterans of Foreign Wars." We watched as he scraped off the price tags with an old penknife; then he handed one to each of us. "The receptionist sells them. They're good for the road. The coffee won't spill."

"*Grazie*," I said.

Sal stepped to him and handed him several large bills. "For cigarettes, food, whatever." They shook hands, and Sal headed for the door.

I called after him. "Just a few more minutes, Sal. There's something I want to talk to Dad about."

Sal stood just outside the doorway, and I moved my chair closer to our father. I hesitated for a moment, then reached out my hand. "I want you to know, Dad, and I mean this, that I love you, and I forgive you."

His face was blank. *Had he even heard me?*

"I want you to get better. Not just from the stroke. I want you to stay sober, too, and I'll do anything I can to help."

My father swung his wheelchair around, turned his back to me, lit another cigarette.

"Dad, this is important. You might not be in that wheelchair...God, the drinking...Not taking your medication—"

"I don't want you picking my brain, all right." He swung around, his face seething red. "Why don't you just go home?"

I took several deep breaths. "You've got to face the truth."

"The truth? I had a few beers with friends. So what?"

I let out a sarcastic laugh. "Dr. Jong said you detoxed here for two days."

He spit out his words. "They tied me to a bed and left me alone. That's why I shit myself."

"Dad, it's not—"

"Enough of this bullshit. Get the hell out of my way. I'm leaving."

With surprising speed and agility, he used his one good hand and leg, began moving towards the door of his room. He didn't wait for me to get out of the way and rammed the footrest right into my shin.

A stabbing pain shot up my leg. In an instant Sal was behind our father's wheelchair, pulling him back. Then Sal bent down, grabbed him in a choke-hold. "You miserable piece of shit!"

My father tried to squirm free, but Sal only tightened his grip.

"Help. He's choking me. Help!"

"Stop it." I pulled on Sal's arm.

He pushed me aside and swung my father around by his neck. "How's it feel? Hurts, doesn't it, you bastard." Sal gave him another squeeze.

My father cried out loud enough to bring two nurses running into the room. Sal saw them and backed off.

My father coughed, unable to catch his breath for a moment. He pointed to Sal. "That sonofabitch tried to kill me."

"That's a crock." Sal smiled at the nurses. "He got mad and hit my sister with his wheelchair. All I was trying to do was restrain him."

The nurse from the front desk looked at me suspiciously. "What really happened?"

"They both lost their tempers."

She threw her hands in the air. "You, Mr. DeCarlo, should be ashamed of yourself, hitting your daughter like that." She went and stood next to Sal. "And you...you better leave right now, before I call security."

"My pleasure."

I caught up with Sal down the hallway. "What the hell was that?"

His face tightened. "I warned you."

Inside the elevator I pressed the lobby button. "You could've hurt him, Sal."

"You...Playing social worker, living in some fantasy world, pretending like everything's fine. He's crazy and all the 'I'm okay/you're okay' bullshit in the world isn't going to solve anything."

I closed my eyes, rubbed the back of my neck. "Odette...she said it might help Dad stay sober if I could get him talking about his drinking."

"Some fucking plan. And what was that I-forgive-you shit? Was that Odette's idea, too?"

"Get off it, would you?" *Why even try to give him a straight answer?*

The elevator stopped at the fourth floor and the door opened. There wasn't anybody there. When the door closed, Sal said, "How could you forgive him? For Christ's sake, he tried to kill Mom."

I felt like he had slapped me. "Nice, Sal. So, it's okay to strangle your invalid father in public? You could be on your way to jail right now."

"At least I didn't kill him."

"What if they hadn't stopped you?"

He smiled arrogantly. "Are you kidding? I knew exactly what I was doing. I could've snapped his fucking neck in a second."

I glared at him. The elevator arrived at the lobby, and I hobbled out the building. My head was spinning. *So much for my plan to bring us closer as a family. I've been praying, too, Father McBride. It's not working.* I crossed the street without looking and hurried into the park.

"Hey!" He yelled after me. "Where are you going?"

"I need some air."

"We'll miss our flight."

I didn't answer.

Sal caught up with me, and for a while we moved across a field without speaking; then, I said, "I loved Mom just as much as you did, Sal. You know that. And I'll never forget what he did to her. But I'm trying to get better." I locked onto his eyes. "Do you want me to blow this thing with David?"

"David? What's he got to do with this?"

"My relationship with him has everything to do with it. The anger you're feeling, it's like a poison in your life, you know that?"

He said nothing and walked ahead of me.

I hurried next to him. "We can't ask Mom for advice, can we? So why not trust Odette?"

He scowled. "Do you always do what your shrink tells you?"

I pulled him to a stop. "When I think she's right, I do."

"Christ, Julia. When are you going to learn to stand up on your own two feet?"

"You say that a lot."

"I believe it."

"I'm talking about the word 'Christ.' I wish you'd stop."

"Do I tell you how to talk?"

"It's disrespectful."

"Says you."

"Said Mom."

"Okay, if Mom said it, I can respect that, but as for Dad, he can go to hell."

I held onto his arm. "Sal, I spent most of my life feeling the exact same way. Where has it gotten me?"

"You're doing fine, Julia. Some people just don't know how good they have it."

"I'm lonely, Sal, and I'm still fucked up over what happened with Mom and Dad. You know, maybe that's why I sabotage every relationship I've ever been in."

"What's this Odette woman done to you?"

We came to a small brook with a footbridge crossing it. I stopped on the bridge, glanced down, briefly looking, like I always have, for something interesting in nature. All I saw were a dozen empty beer cans in the water. I moved on, caught up to Sal. "So, about Odette. You're going to think this is weird, but she's teaching me to heal myself. If forgiving Dad means feeling better about myself and having a shot at making this thing work with David, I'm damn sure going to do it."

Suddenly Sal let out a sound like a sob and his shoulders and arms shuddered. "I'm so fucking angry sometimes, I can't think straight."

I reached out to touch his face, but he pulled away. I said, "Don't you get it? Look at us, Sal. We're almost thirty. Still single. No kids. What do you think's going on?"

"Hey, I'm trying to learn, aren't I? You asked me to come today, right? Said a dying man needed his son. So I came. And look what happened."

"I...I...What can I say, Sal, except...Hate the disease, not the man."

He paused, ran his fingers through his hair. "You're a better person than me, Julia." He opened his arms wide and gave me a bear hug. "I'm sorry I lost my cool like that. I certainly didn't plan it."

We held each another for a few seconds; then he pulled away. "How's that ankle? Want to turn back?"

I was so wired I hadn't even thought about it. I lifted my foot off the ground, testing it. "Good idea. It's a little sore, and we have a flight to catch."

We headed back on a gravel road shaded by a row of maples. He patted my shoulder. "I hope things work out with David."

"Thanks."

"You deserve it. He seems like a good guy." Sal let out a deep breath. "Being alone sucks."

I had been waiting for just such an opening.

"How about asking Deb for a date? She's interested in you."

He picked up a stick and twisted it in his hands. "We're too different. She's got all kinds of degrees."

"She's Italian. You both enjoy the outdoors."

He shook his head. "She's plain-looking."

"Oh, bullshit." I rapped him on the leg with my cane. "She's pretty. Maybe not stunning, but definitely pretty."

"So what. Even if I was attracted to her, you wouldn't want me dating one of your friends."

"Why not?"

"Think about it, Julia. Think about what I just did back there."

A week later David and I went into Woody's Café on Main Street in Bar Harbor. It was about ten in the evening and a band in the back was playing Dixieland jazz. All the musicians were white men with gray hair. I looked around for Sal. He and a friend were throwing darts to the left of the bar. I moved through the smoky air, tapped him on the shoulder. "How come you haven't returned my calls?"

"Hey, Julia, David. How are you? The calls? Right. I told my secretary to get in touch with you. Just can't find good help these days." He looked at his friend Neil, and they laughed.

"I was getting worried, Sal."

He picked up his mug from the bar and took a sip. "You? Worry?" He pointed to David. "Ain't I right, David? Julia never worries."

I stepped closer to him. "Jim said you haven't been to work for two days."

Neil put his arm around Sal's shoulder. "That's cause we've been on vacation."

"Vacation, right." Sal lightly punched him on the arm.

I tightened my lips. "I've got to talk you, Sal. Alone. Without Neil. Let's get a table."

Sal raised his eyebrows to Neil. "Oh no, guess I'm in trouble."

I moved towards a table away from the band, and David followed. I watched Sal at the bar getting a refill; then he strutted to us and sat down. He took a sip from his mug, squinted at me. "What's on your mind, Sis?"

"Been her all day?"

He raised his finger. "Tell you in a moment. Before I forget—" He faced David. "Did you get those backpacking stoves in yet?"

"Yesterday."

"Put one aside for me, okay, amigo?" He turned to me, then back to David. "Oh, by the way, how's Rachel?"

"She's fine."

"Heck of a daughter you got there."

I tapped Sal on the hand. "Jim said you didn't even call in sick."

Sal whistled the first few notes of some rock song. "Jim's got a big mouth."

"He's concerned about you."

"Everybody's worried about Sal, but Sal can take care of himself." He swaggered in his seat.

I locked onto his eyes. "What are you doing?"

He folded his hands to his lips, sat up straight. "I love you Julia. And I forgive you for taking me to Boston." He laughed. "Can't you see I'm dealing with my anger?" He lifted his beer and chugged it down; then, he stood and moved towards the bar. After a few steps he turned around. "Can I get you guys something?"

"No. And you've had enough." I tried to speak with authority.

He looked at me like I was crazy and went to the bar.

I touched David's hand. "He's worse than I thought."

David's voice sounded nervous. "What are you going to do?"

"I don't know."

Sal came back with Neil, and they each had a mug of beer. They sat down, and for the first time I looked closely at Neil. I had never met him before. He was wearing a Jefferson Airplane T-shirt, had long black hair, and had a deep scar on his left cheek. Sal faced me. "Julia, this is my therapist, Neil. The only one who understands me. Cause he was in Vietnam like me. Ain't that right, Neil?"

"Brothers in arms," Neil said, raising his mug, and they clinked together.

Sal patted Neil's back. "Okay, buddy, help me out here. My sister's been asking me over the years if I killed anyone in Nam. Now as my personal therapist, I thought you might like to comment."

Neil looked at me and seemed to sober up for a moment. He stood to leave the table. "This isn't funny, Sal."

Sal grabbed his arm, squeezed it. "Come on Neil. Did I kill anyone?"

Neil tried to free himself. Sal stood, towered over him, and gripped his arm tighter.

For a moment Neil hesitated, then said. "He did."

Sal shook his hand. "Thanks, buddy. Now go play some darts. I'll be there in a few minutes."

Sal was still standing up, and he picked up his beer, took a swig; then, he tried to lift up his leg and put his foot on the table, but suddenly he lost his balance. David caught him just in time, helped him sit down.

Sal smiled, put his elbows on the table and leaned towards me. "But never kids or women, Julia. That's why I can still sleep at night."

"My God, Sal."

He crossed himself. "Bless me Julia, for I have sinned."

"Please stop."

"Two were teenagers. Probably fifteen."

I was shaking. "I've heard enough."

His voice sounded deep and foreboding, like my father's. "It was a tight situation. Had to slit one's throat."

"That's enough." David said, standing, placing himself between Sal and me.

I put my head in my hands and began to sob quietly. "You're right, Sal. I never should've asked."

He picked up his mug and moved towards the bar, then turned back. "By the way, Julia, I've been meaning to tell you. Deb and I went out the other night. She's nice. Real nice. So, maybe there's hope for me. But whatever you do, please don't tell her I killed anyone."

A few days later I was eating supper at home when my father called collect. I was foolishly thinking he might have something good to tell me.

He coughed into the receiver. "*Come stai*? Haven't heard from you in a while."

"Just saw you."

"A lot can happen in a week. Big things that a daughter should know."

I took a bite of salad. "Like what?"

"They fixed me up with an electric wheelchair. Works good. I'm getting around on my own. Riding in the street."

"*Congratulazioni.*"

"And there's more news. Got my own place."

My hands began to sweat. "Huh? You're out of the hospital?"

"You got wax in your ears. Yeah, I'm out. My buddy McNamara found me a room in South Boston. It's on the ground floor. Easy to get in and out. I'm calling from there now. McNamara's a big help. Runs errands for me. You'd like him."

"How's that?"

"He worked in a dog pound. Likes animals, like you."

"Does he drink?"

"What are you, his wife?"

I knew what that meant.

In a moment, my father whispered into the phone, "Had to get out of that hospital. One night a colored man came into my room. He'd of killed me."

"What man?"

"Never seen him before. He was *uno uomo grande*. Standing next to my bed. Looking down at me. I woke up. I shouted for help. He ran out of the room. He'd of killed me. *Essi sono pazzi*. They're wacko."

"What'd the nurses say?"

"I didn't tell them."

"Why not?"

His voice sounded fearful. "They were in on it. The place was bugged. There were two guys in the cafeteria. The same two guys I saw in New York. They travel everywhere. Government guys. They were in the cafeteria at a table next to me. They were whispering, saying the place was bugged."

"You're talking paranoid again, Dad."

"No, true story." I heard him light up a cigarette.

I pushed my plate away from me, too nervous to eat anymore. "You know, Dad, the only way you're going to make it on the outside, is if you take your medication."

He smacked something. "I don't want to be a zombie. *Capisce*?"

"What about the booze?"

He raised his voice. "That's my business."

"*Bene*, then don't call and ask me for help."

"I'll take care of myself. Always have. I need my freedom. Amen." I heard him let out a long puff of smoke. "Anyway, I just wanted to let you know about my new place and the wheelchair." He gave me his address and the phone number of the rooming house. "Don't give it to Sal, though. I don't want to see him, again. He's crazy."

I said nothing. A wave of hopelessness swept over me.

His voice was subdued. "I don't have anymore news. So I guess that's it." Suddenly he sounded upbeat. "Keep smiling. *Arrivederci*."

"*Arrivederci*, Dad."

Nineteen

Rachel held up her hand to stop me. "What's the pass word?"

"Hermit crab."

"Okay, come in." She moved aside.

I stepped over the wall of the large sand castle and dumped a bucket of water in a pond. "Enough?"

Rachel picked up a scallop shell from the water and gestured with it like a puppet, saying, "More, please. I need to swim in an ocean, not a puddle."

I took two clam shells and placed them over my eyes, bobbing my head from side to side. "Yes, Ms. Scallop. I'll see if I can move the ocean up here."

She laughed.

I hauled several buckets of water from the sea to the castle. Soon David appeared with things he had collected from the beach. He handed Rachel a half dozen gull feathers, and she stuck them in the top of the turrets like flags; then, he unraveled a clump of rockweed and set it in the pond.

"Good idea, Daddy. My friends need some shade." She took lobster claws, sand dollars, sea urchins and dog whelks from the castle walls and put them under the rockweed.

I positioned David and Rachel in the center of the castle and shot several pictures.

"Your turn," David said, taking the camera, ushering me inside the walls with Rachel.

When I sat down with her in my lap, she looked up at me and smiled, then jumped up. "Wait, Daddy." She went to the turrets, removed two gull feathers, and stuck one in my hair and one in hers. "Now we're ready."

After David took the picture, I said to Rachel, "Let's move into some shade ourselves." We sat on a blanket underneath a beach umbrella and drank water from canteens.

It was a hot day, and Sand Beach was crowded. Everything shown in a silver-white light from the radiant sun and reflective water. Next to us two teenage girls lay on towels, sipping cans of soda and reading magazines. In the surf dozens of children rode the waves on foam boards. I gazed to the left and saw the granite cliffs of Great Head. Beehive and Gorham Mountain rose to the right, and the broad expanse of Frenchman Bay stretched out before us.

I drew Rachel between my legs, kissed the top of her head, brushed the sand out of her hair.

She fumbled with the straps of the removable boot on my foot. "Does it come off?"

"Sure." She helped me untie the straps, and I removed the boot.

She touched it. "Does that hurt?"

I shook my head.

"It's all swollen and bruised."

"Not for long. The doctor said I'll be running in a month."

"Will you still limp?"

"Probably, to start."

"I'm glad it's getting better."

I kissed the top of her head. "Thanks, sweetheart." I pressed my finger on her neck, and her skin turned white, then red. "Say, you're getting a little burnt." I pulled down the straps of her orange bathing suit and rubbed more sunscreen onto her skin. Such delicate arms, thin like branches. I dabbed sunscreen on her nose, and she giggled. I embraced her, felt my body shudder.

David flopped down on the blanket. "Hey lady, what's for lunch?"

I took a lobster claw from Rachel's bucket and handed it to him.

He put it in his mouth, pretended to chew. "Delicious."

Rachel laughed, pulled it out.

I passed around peanut butter and jelly sandwiches, and we began eating. David set his hand on my knee. "Sexy bathing suit. Can't keep my eyes off you."

It was a pastel lavender bikini, something I thought went well with my black hair and darker skin. I leaned over, nibbled David's arm. "You make me feel very pretty."

He sat up, touched my face. "You know something, Julia? I've been thinking lately, and I know this is going to sound a little strange, but I feel like I've known you all my life...or something like that."

All at once I remembered a secret I had learned about him. Mischief swept me. "I've had the same feeling, David. Even felt I was with you the day you were born. I remember the hospital, your mother, the breech birth—"

"What's that?" Rachel asked, tapping my arm.

"It means when your Daddy was born and came out of his mother, he came out feet first, not head first, like most babies." I closed my eyes, put my hands to my face. "I'm trying to imagine it. Here he comes. Oh yes, the strange second little toe on each foot, a toe curled under the others, twisted." I opened my eyes, looked at David. "And I thought to myself, this is the mark of a prince, and someday he'll be mine."

David's mouth dropped open. "I don't believe it."

"Like you said, we've known each other all our lives." I held out my hands, palms upright.

He let out a laugh. "Who told you?"

"No one." I gave him an offended look.

He crossed his arms over his chest. "I never told you that."

"I was there, David. Maybe as a spirit, but I was there." I tried to put on an innocent face.

All at once he leaped up, pushed me over and pinned me down on the blanket. "Who told you?"

"I'm psychic."

He tickled me and wouldn't stop.

Rachel came to my defense, tried to push him over.

I was laughing, holding out as long as I could, finally I blurted out, "Your sister."

He smacked himself on the forehead. "I should've guessed." He rolled on the blanket, laughing. "And I almost believed you."

I rolled next to him, pulled him close.

Rachel snuggled in between us. She started to speak, then stopped.

I tapped her lips. "What is it, honey?"

"Have you known me all your life too, Julia?"

"Oh yes, darling, I've been dreaming about you for as long as I can remember."

Later, David and I strolled hand-in-hand along the beach. Rachel tagged behind, collecting more shells in a bucket. Ahead of us I saw six sanderlings, darting back and forth at the edge of the surf, picking at the foamy water for food. I laughed. "Look how they run away from the waves, like they don't want to get their feet wet."

I hugged his arm, burrowed my face in his neck. "Oh, by the way. I really missed you last week."

"I missed you, too. But it was great talking to you on the phone."

"I didn't call too much?"

"Are you kidding?"

"You weren't too busy with the exhibition?"

"Only during the day."

He looked for Rachel. She was in the surf up to her knees, searching for treasures. "Don't go in too deep, honey."

"I won't, Daddy."

I brushed some sand off David's back. "I thought you'd be doing business in the evening, you know, talking clothes and outdoor gear."

"People just party then."

"Not you?"

"Used to. Now, I'd rather be quiet. Read in my room. Think of you."

I chewed on my fingernail. "I was a little insecure, you know."

"I'm all yours, Julia." He kissed me, deeply, tenderly.

I stroked his hair. "Do me a favor next time?"

"Name it."

"Call me, too."

He knocked on his head with his knuckles. "What a guy. Guess I'm still back in the old days, wanting a woman to handle the domestic matters."

"Phoning is a domestic matter?"

He rubbed his chin, let out a short laugh. "Sometimes I don't know what I'm saying."

We sat down on the sand and kept an eye on Rachel. I put my arm around David, pulled him close. "I get pretty lonely when you're gone. Odette and I have talked about it. People leaving me is a big thing, you know, because I was abandoned as a child, emotionally, that is."

"Sorry," he said, with a concerned look.

I hesitated. Now was the hard part. "And sometimes I start feeling a little weird. Rebellious. Like I want to drink, screw around. Crazy stuff."

"Screw around?"

I lied. "Just in my imagination." I took his hand, placed it on my cheek. "But Odette's taught me other choices. That's why I called you so much. She told me to let myself miss you. To think about what you're doing. To tell myself how lucky I am to have you."

"And I should call you, right?"

I nodded.

"Thanks for telling me, Julia." He brushed my hair to the sides of my face. "I'd do anything for you."

Would he? I hoped so. Only problem was guys often promised more than they could deliver. I supposed a lot of women did, too.

Rachel caught up with us. "Look Julia."

She held up a large clam shell; the inside of it glistened in colors of pink, purple and blue.

"How beautiful," I said.

"It's for you." She moved down the beach. We stood up and followed. I took David's hand. "Can I tell you something else?"

"Certainly."

"I'm not being too touchy-feely?"

"It's okay."

"I'm worried about Sal."

"Me, too."

I let out a deep breath. "He's been keeping to himself."

"I thought he was back at work."

"Jim says he's not the same." I shook my head. "Dammit, I never should've taken him to Boston."

"Water over the dam, Julia."

"What can I do?"

David rubbed the back of his neck, pondering. "He's made it clear he doesn't want our help."

Later, towards evening the wind changed directions, and it swept cold ocean air onto the beach. I wrapped myself and Rachel in a blanket, and we lay on the sand. It was still warm from the afternoon heat. Everything was bathed in gold light from the setting sun. Rachel pressed against me, snuggled her head against my chest. I heard a distant foghorn. I breathed in the salty mist of the surf. I gazed up at the sky, saw the thin sliver of the crescent moon. Soon, David lay with us. Rachel was in the middle, and we cuddled together, barely moving, hardly speaking.

Despite the peace and love I felt, I was a little uneasy. I had learned from experience that such times rarely lasted. *When would the next storm hit?* I caught myself. *Stop, Julia. Enjoy the moment.* And I did.

Twenty

With a soapy sponge I scrubbed the hood of my station wagon, then turned on the hose and rinsed it. When I finished washing the car, I sat in a lawn chair along the driveway. I closed my eyes, tilted my head backwards, felt the warm sun on my face and bare arms. I kept my eyes closed and breathed in and out like Odette had taught me. My body loosened, my mind stopped thinking. Perhaps five minutes passed when I heard a car pull into my driveway.

A police officer in a Bar Harbor cruiser waved to me. For a moment he stayed inside the car, took another puff on his cigarette, smoothed back the gray hair of his balding head; then, he stepped out, his face somber. "Are you Julia DeCarlo?"

I nodded, and felt suddenly afraid. It was the way he said my name, the fact that he even knew my name.

"I'm Officer Joe Campbell." He reached out as if to catch me. "I have some bad news."

"Not Sal?" I snapped away from him, brought my hands to my mouth.

Campbell blurted out. "I'm sorry to tell you this, but your father's dead."

My legs gave out, and I sank to the ground. I couldn't breathe. I straightened up, threw my head back, and took in a great gulp of air.

Campbell pulled me up by the elbows. "Sit here," he said, resting me in the lawn chair. I was shaking. He took a blanket from his cruiser and wrapped it around me. For the first time his voice sounded nervous. "What can I do to help?"

"Water." My throat burned.

He hurried into the house, then ran back.

I tried to take the glass with trembling hands. He held it with me, and I took a sip.

"I'm really sorry." He sat on the ground next to me. "Are you okay? Do you want a doctor?"

I whispered. "What happened to my father?"

He took out a cigarette and offered it to me.

I shook my head.

Campbell stood, lit a cigarette and inhaled. "We found your father's body in Hamilton Pond."

"Hamilton Pond?"

"Off Route 3. Near Salisbury Cove."

"But...but he was living in Boston."

Campbell took a piece of paper from his shirt pocket and unfolded it. "Was his name Francis DeCarlo and was he just discharged from the VA hospital in Boston?"

I nodded.

"Did he use a wheelchair?"

I nodded again.

"Seems like it was him, then, Miss DeCarlo. We found an ID on his body in the pond. That's where his wheelchair was, too."

"Oh, my God." I shut my eyes, bit my lips hard.

He waited a few moments. "Looks like an accident, or a suicide. He had a campfire. We found some empty liquor bottles."

I spoke softly, as if to myself. "It can't be. I just spoke to him last week. He was in Boston. What was he doing here?"

Campbell paced away a few steps, came back. “Lots of things seem strange about this. I don’t know what’s going on. We didn’t find any money on your father.”

I struggled to breathe again. “What are you saying?”

“Might have been a robbery.”

“Someone killed him?” I let out a brief cry.

He nervously patted my shoulder. “It’s okay, Miss DeCarlo. Calm down. We’ve just started the investigation.”

“Investigation?”

“As I said, things aren’t clear.” He took a long drag on his cigarette. “Well, I shouldn’t be asking you questions right now. You got enough to deal with...Sorry I had to tell you. I didn’t want to. The chief made me do it. Said an old soldier like me would understand what it means when another old soldier dies.” He drew on his cigarette again. “I know this is tough on you. Were you close to him?”

“Off and on. He had mental problems. Drank too much.”

“The war did that to a lot of men.”

I looked up at Campbell. “I loved him.”

“That’s good.”He rubbed his balding head. “Like I said before, I know this is a bad time to ask you anything, but my chief wants you to identify your father’s body. It’s at the hospital. Think you could do that?”

I pulled the blanket around me tightly. “I don’t know.”

“Maybe someone can help?”

I paused. “My brother.”

He gave me an odd look. “Sal? Don’t you know? He’s not in town. I went to his place first. A neighbor said she saw him packing camping gear into his car yesterday.”

I closed my eyes, wiped the tears from my face. “My boyfriend, then.”

“Good. Go to the emergency room. They’ll be expecting you. Think you can get there soon?”

“I guess.”

He took one last drag on his cigarette, dropped it on the driveway and put it out with his shoe. “Anything else I can do for you?”

I tried to think clearly. "Nothing, right now."

Campbell shuffled his feet on the ground. "Guess I should be heading back to town. You going to be all right?"

I stood and teetered for a moment.

He held my hand to steady me.

I walked a few steps forward.

"You're limping."

"Broke my ankle last month."

"Well, it's coming along good." Campbell patted my hand. "Sorry again about your father. I should get going." He went to his car, waved and drove off.

I stood in the driveway, unsure of what to do next. My father dead? It didn't seem possible. Not this way.

Soon after David and I entered the emergency room of Mount Desert Island Hospital, a short, overweight man shook my hand. "I'm Dr. Dan McClane. I did the autopsy on your father. And you're..." He faced David.

David shook his hand. "David Zuckerman. Julia's boyfriend."

"Zuckerman. I know that name."

"Have a store downtown."

"Sure. My daughter shops there. Loves to hike. Not me. Golf's my sport." He tapped his stomach. "Too bad I ride the cart. I should know better. Just too damn busy to walk."

He glanced at his watch. "So, you've come to identify the body. Oh, by the way, Miss DeCarlo, my sympathy to you." He started walking away: "If you'll follow me, please."

He led us into a brightly lit room with white linoleum and white walls. In the middle of the room there was a body inside a thick plastic bag on top of a stainless steel table.

McClane grabbed a can of air freshener from a shelf and sprayed it above the table. "He's bloated a lot. The water does that. You may not recognize him."

McClane started to pull the zipper down, and I swallowed hard, held onto David's hand. When he went past the body's chin, I told him to stop. A sickening odor rose out of the bag, and one glance at my father's face told me he was my father no longer. I hated to look, but I had to find the shrapnel scar over his right eye. It was there. "I've seen enough." I turned away, dizzy.

McClane zipped up the bag and squirted more air freshener. "Some people get sick when they see a body like that, especially when it's their mother or father. Are you okay?"

"I won't be able to sleep tonight."

"I never have that problem." McClane moved to a stainless steel sink along the wall and rinsed his hands. "By the way, did they find the person who killed your father?"

I collapsed into a chair along the wall. "Killed? What do you mean killed?"

"Didn't Officer Campbell tell you?"

"About the robbery?"

"Someone choked your father. There are bruises on his body. He must've fought back. It's all in my report."

"But they found him in the pond."

"Believe me, Ms. DeCarlo. Your father was dead before he hit the water."

The room began to spin. In a moment, David was next to me, holding me up, keeping me from falling out of the chair. I closed my eyes, concentrated on my breathing. After a minute, I opened my eyes, and the room was steady. "I've got to get out of here," I said, moving quickly to the door.

"Oh, before you go—" McClane stepped into a side room and returned momentarily with a black plastic bag. "Maybe you want this stuff? It was your father's."

I set the bag on the counter, looked inside. A smell like urine came out. There were some dirty clothes, his black fisherman's cap, his penknife, some coins, his wallet and a bundle of wet photographs. I handed the bag to David. I tried to put my mind in order, tried to understand what was happening; then, I asked in a low, defeated voice, "Dr. McClane, do you know what time my father died?"

He took a folder off the table and looked inside. "Friday evening. Probably about nine." He ran his finger down the chart. "Hmmm. I hadn't noticed this before. The alcohol blood level. Guess your Dad had quite a bit to drink."

That evening David offered to stay with me, but I felt I needed to be alone. I sat in a wicker chair on the patio. It was late evening, and the sky was clear and bright like crystal. I saw the constellations, the Milky Way, and the crescent moon descending in the west. A warm southern wind rattled the leaves in the trees. It was the perfect evening, and it made my father's death seem even more tragic.

I remembered my father stroking my hair with his hand on the church steps. I remembered fishing on the Charles River with him. I remembered when he bought us peanuts and hot dogs at Fenway Park. And I felt love.

I saw him punching my mother in the face. I saw him in his green, pin-striped pajamas and black slippers lying on a green bed in the mental hospital. I saw him homeless with his shopping bag in the Boston Garden. And I felt sad.

I heard the old Italian songs he hummed as we picked raspberries. I heard the fear in his voice when he called at my Acadia home in the middle of the night. I heard the words he used each time we parted: "Keep smiling. *Arrivederci.*" And I felt deep regret. I curled up in the wicker chair, hugged my knees, and heaved great sobs. They took a long time to subside.

I looked over at my lawyer, Josh Vilinsky, sitting next to me. He was a big man, bigger than Sal. About David's age. I imagined him towering over a jury. No wonder he won so many cases. Now, he nodded to me, giving me the go-ahead to speak. I faced Maine State Trooper Tim

Keough, who was sitting on the other side of the table. He turned on his tape recorder and asked me about my whereabouts on Friday evening.

"I was with my boyfriend, David Zuckerman, and his daughter, Rachel, the entire night."

"Sorry to have to ask you that, Ms. DeCarlo," Keough said. "It was just a routine question. You're not a suspect in the murder."

"I certainly hope not," Josh said.

Keough cleared his throat. "We found a bus ticket in your father's backpack. I checked with the company. The driver remembered your father. Especially the wheelchair. But, Officer Campbell tells me..." Keough nodded to Campbell who sat at the far end of the table. "...you didn't know your father was coming."

"Absolutely not. My father had serious mental and alcohol problems. He had said once he wanted to visit here, but I told him I didn't want to see him in my town until he sobered up. I didn't want him making trouble for me."

"Did your brother know he was coming?"

A voice came over a police scanner in the next room. Keough paused and listened. When it stopped, he asked, "So, did your brother know he was coming?"

"No, sir."

Keough wrote something down on a piece of paper. Everything about him looked perfect: his crew cut, his straight posture, his shirt with the badges and insignia. But one thing was wrong. He was about five years younger than me. Too inexperienced, I thought, to be a detective.

After a moment, he glanced up at me. "The bus driver said he saw your father with someone at the station. Said the guy had a pony tail. Does your brother have a pony tail?"

I looked at Josh, and he shrugged.

"Yes," I said.

Keough tapped his pen in his palm. "Don't you think it's strange your brother skipped town the day your father was murdered?"

I sat upright, tightened my hands on the table. "My brother didn't murder him."

"Did I say he did?"

"My brother likes to camp."

"But he didn't tell you when or where he was going, right?"

"So what?"

"Isn't that unusual?"

"I'm not his keeper." Josh had warned me that the police were considering my brother as a suspect, so I was prepared for Keough's questions.

Keough shuffled some papers, and looked at one of them. "I phoned the VA hospital today. The nurse said your brother tried to choke your father about a month ago."

I felt an ache in my stomach, pressed my hands against it. "My father rammed me with his wheelchair. Sal tried to restrain him. Lost his temper. It wasn't anything more than that."

"That's not what the nurse said."

"I was there. She came into the room after it happened."

"How often did your brother see your father?"

I looked at Josh, and he nodded. I said, "The hospital visit was the first in many years."

"Was he angry with your father?"

Josh cut in. "No comment."

"Did he ever threaten to kill your father?"

Josh leaned forward. "We won't respond to that line of questioning."

Keough shuffled the papers again, and selected one. He began reading from it. It was a summary of my father's mental history.

All at once there was a knock at the door and the receptionist poked her head in. "Call for you, Officer Keough."

Keough stood. "Excuse me." He left the room.

Campbell stirred at the end of the table, reached out his hand towards me. "Sorry he's grilling you. I'm out of the loop now. So's our department. You know, once the case becomes a homicide, the state troopers take over."

I smiled. "I understand." I looked around the room. There was nothing in it but a table and chairs. At the top of the wall was a small window with bars.

Keough reappeared, sat down. "So, where was I? Oh yes." He continued reading from the paper in a matter-of-fact voice. When he finished, he looked up at me. "Sounds like you had a pretty rough childhood. Did your father ever beat Sal?"

Josh answered. "You'll have to ask Sal that."

Keough reached down to the chair next to him and lifted up a small plastic bag. Inside was an aluminum lighter with a shamrock on it. "Do you recognize this?"

"Not a clue."

"Wasn't your father's, or your brother's?"

"My father used matches. My brother didn't smoke."

Keough pulled out another paper. "Says here your brother was arrested for marijuana possession two years ago."

"I told you. He never owned a lighter."

"How often did he smoke grass?"

Josh waved a pen in the air. "Come on, Tim. You're wasting our time with that question."

I tapped my fingers on the table to catch Keough's attention. "Where did you find the lighter?"

"At the murder scene."

"So it might belong to someone else?"

"Maybe." Keough took out another paper. "Says here your brother was in Vietnam."

"And discharged honorably." I spoke firmly.

"No post-traumatic syndrome?"

"No."

Keough was silent, reviewing the papers in front of him. I twisted my hair into a knot at the nap of my neck, pondering. "By the way Officer Keough, there's something you should know."

He sat up.

"My father moved out of the hospital a week before he came up here. Got a room in a guest house in South Boston. Said a buddy of his found it for him. Maybe someone there knows something."

"Do you have the guy's name?"

I tried to think. "McNamara. That was it. My father never mentioned his first name. I've got the address and phone number of the rooming house." I took out my address book and gave him the information.

He wrote it down, then he arched his back, put his hands behind his neck. "That does it for my questions." He folded his hands on the table, then turned off the tape recorder. "There is one last thing. I'm afraid...I'm afraid I have to issue a warrant for your brother's arrest."

"Oh, my God." I let out a gasp.

After a few moments Keough stood. "I'm sorry. I hope you understand. I've got a job to do." Then he picked up his papers and left.

The deputy sheriff at the Hancock County Jail escorted Deb and I into a small room with benches that looked like they came from a set for *Oliver Twist*. He motioned for us to sit. "I'll be back in a few minutes with your brother."

I looked around. The yellow paint on the walls was peeling and the floor boards were warped. There were two barred windows.

"Creepy," Deb said.

Soon the deputy returned with Sal. He was in handcuffs and his feet were linked together with a chain.

I pointed to the chain. "Is that really necessary?"

"Rules are rules, Miss," the deputy said, guiding Sal onto a bench and locking the foot chain to a metal ring in the floor. Then, the deputy left the room.

I went to Sal, gave him a big hug. "You hanging in there?"

"Trying to." He stared at Deb and whistled. She had dolled herself up with lipstick, nail polish and a silk, flower-print dress cut just above the knees. She came to him and gave him a big kiss. He pulled her down on his lap. "I should get busted more often."

She ran her fingers through his hair. "Do they have a double bed in the cell?"

He laughed. "Hey, stop that, Deb. My sister's here."

Deb moved from his lap, sat next to him. This side of Deb was new to me. *Maybe she was just trying to cheer him up? Maybe they were a lot closer than I knew?* I tapped Sal's hand, said, "Josh told me the cops roughed you up."

Sal talked fast, like he had drunk too much coffee. "I didn't know what the hell was going on. I was pissed, you know, being pulled over for no good reason. There were two of them. They threw me on the hood, handcuffed me. Then they told me I was being charged for the murder of my father. I almost shit in my pants. They grilled me the whole way back from the Allagash. Was I ever happy to see Josh. Once they saw him, they lightened right up." He patted me on the shoulder. "Thanks for getting me a good lawyer."

"That's what family is for."

Deb stood up, offered Sal a pack of gum.

He put a piece in his mouth. "Bring any beer?"

She laughed.

"The food really sucks here," he said.

Deb moved behind him, rubbed his shoulders. "You're having pasta tonight with Gianelli's homemade sauce. I gave it to the guards."

He rolled his eyes. "Oh great, then I'll never get any."

"I made plenty for everyone, so don't worry."

"Say, you really know the routine."

"My Dad was a cop."

"I didn't know that. Did you know that, Julia?"

I squinted at Deb. "You never told me."

"Just never came up."

Maybe I didn't know Deb as well as I thought?

Suddenly, Sal's face turned serious. "You should know, ladies, I'm dying in here."

Deb sat down again on the bench next to him, put her hand on top of his. "Josh told us he'll have you out on bail in a few days."

"The sooner, the better. I'm scared. There are some wicked mother fuckers in here." He used his two hands to smooth back his hair. He was in a dirty white T-shirt and jeans, and was unshaven. He must have seen me staring at his clothes. He said, "I know I look like shit." He had an embarrassed look on his face. "Maybe Josh could talk to the guards? I'd sure like to shower."

"I'll ask him," I said.

"So, enough about me, Julia." He patted my hand. "How are you holding up?"

"Just keeping my head above water."

He lowered his eyes, talked softly. "Sorry for all the trouble. Sorry about Dad, too. I hated the guy, but it ain't right someone killed him."

I felt a surge of anger. "Then why did you joke about it all the time?"

"You told the cops that?"

"Of course not. Josh was with me when Keough was questioning me." I pointed my finger at him. "But you see Sal, all that bull shit of yours was out of line."

He made a fist, put it under his chin. "I was pissed at Dad. Bad-mouthing him was a way to release."

"They might use it against you."

He let out a defiant laugh. "Who's going to tell them?"

"Maybe one of your buddies? They'll pressure them. And the nurse already told them you choked Dad."

"Oh, Christ."

"Would you please not say that?"

"Right, I forgot." His forehead started to sweat. "You know I'm innocent, don't you Julia?"

"Of course." I locked onto his eyes. "But it doesn't look good, especially skipping town the day he was murdered."

Sal let out a big breath. "How was I supposed to know? Had to get away. Clear my head. You saw me in the bar. I was a wreck."

"I never should've taken you to Boston."

"I wasn't ready." He took the pack of gum out of his pocket and gave Deb and me a piece; then, he put another piece in his mouth. "So, when's Dad's funeral?"

I looked down at the floor, closed my eyes. "Can't think about that right now. Need all my energy for you."

"Where's his body?"

All the sudden, weariness enveloped me. I couldn't speak anymore.

Deb said, "They moved it to the state morgue in Augusta." We were silent for a minute.

I rubbed the back of my neck; then, I looked at Sal, my voice barely audible. "Help me with this one, Sal. You told me you'd kill Dad if you ever saw him in Bar Harbor."

He puffed out his cheeks and blew. "I never even knew he was here. Not for one minute. They got a lot on me, don't they?"

"The bus driver saw a guy with a pony tail wheeling him around the station."

"Fuck."

I went to the window, stared outside; then, I faced Sal. "Where were you Friday night?"

"On the road. Slept in the truck. Reached the Allagash the next morning."

"Did anybody see you? Any witnesses?"

"I stopped for gas. Bought some food. But who would remember?"

I paced. "Any receipts?"

"Might be some in the truck."

Deb said, "The state police have it."

He jerked up. "What?"

I held up my arms. "Hello, Sal. They're investigating a murder." I wasn't a smoker, but suddenly I had an urge for a cigarette. "I'll ask them to look for receipts." I sat next to him, tapped my feet on the floor. "So Sal, what time did you leave Bar Harbor?"

He hesitated. "I don't know. Six. Maybe seven."

"Come on. Six or seven?"

"What's the difference?"

"Dad was killed about nine."

"Six." He tried to stretch out his legs, but the chain on his legs was too short. "God, Julia, you're acting like Keough."

"I'm trying to save your butt. Do you own a lighter?"

"No."

"A silver one with a shamrock?"

"I said 'no'."

"They found one at the murder scene."

"Why didn't Keough tell me that?" He frowned.

Suddenly, I realized that my father's case was like a game of chess, moving clues around, and no one really knew what the truth was. *We had to be careful.* "Sal," I said. "Remember, don't answer any of Keough's questions without Josh."

"I won't." He swallowed hard.

I swept my hair back, shook my head. "I hope Keough follows up on the lead I gave him."

"What lead?" Sal asked.

"Dad moved to a rooming house the week before his murder. If the cops ask around in Boston, they might come up with something."

I fumbled with my handbag, took out an eagle feather, gave it to him. "For good luck."

He stuck it behind his ear and smiled. I could see his face, his mind working, playing with something. "Here's the news headline they're going to write about me. `Jailbird Uses Eagle Feather to Fly Out of Prison'."

We laughed. The room suddenly didn't feel so bleak and heavy.

"Say, Julia. How are the eaglets doing?"

"They're getting too big for the cage. Have to release them soon. You know, Sal, they've missed you the past two weeks. They're a bit lethargic. They must miss your jokes."

"Ha, ha." His voice was subdued. "I messed up. I'll make it up to them when I get out."

All at once, the deputy appeared. "Time's up, folks."

I stood up and embraced Sal. "Stay strong," I said, then I moved to the door.

Sal picked up Deb's hand, kissed it. "Thanks for coming today. A lot of woman would've run the other way."

She gave him a hug. "I'm not afraid of trouble, Sal. I know you're innocent."

David sat on the swing next to me, swaying a little. "Any news from Boston?"

"Still waiting to hear." I lowered my head and twisted my feet in the dust. "I don't know how much longer I can take this. Everything's so damn slow."

He came behind me, ran his fingers through my hair. "It sucks. Wish I could speed it up."

"Keough's already made up his mind."

"But he called the Boston police."

"He's not serious. If he was, he'd be there himself."

David took the chains of my swing and rocked me gently. "Josh said he's a decent cop."

"Well, I hope he's right."

I glanced around David's yard. Scattered on the grass were balls, a tricycle and wagon, and in the sandbox were shovels and buckets. Rachel was playing with her small plastic horses underneath a nearby maple tree. She saw me looking at her and waved.

I waved back; then, I twisted the swing around to face David. "Josh is doing a super job. You picked a great lawyer. How did you guys meet?"

"Went to UNH together. Never close friends, but we hung out some."

"Maybe I should give him a call? Maybe he can convince Keough that the Boston stuff is crucial to the investigation," I said.

"Go for it." David sat on the other swing, pumped a little. "I've been trying to help out, too, asking around."

"Find anything."

He nodded.

"And..."

He stopped swinging. "It's not good news. Mike told me Sal was at Woody's Friday night."

"Who's Mike?"

"The bartender. Said Sal was sitting alone at the bar, putting down quite a few boiler makers. Left about eight."

"Oh shit. How did he know it was eight?"

"They close the kitchen then. He thought Sal might want some food, but Sal said he wasn't hungry."

"My God, David." I stood up and paced. "I wish you hadn't asked him."

"I didn't. He came in the store and told me. Said he'd keep quiet, but if the police question him, he said he'd have to talk. Doesn't want to lose his job."

"Goddammit." I smacked my fist into my hand. "Why didn't Sal tell me the truth?"

"I think he's struggling, Julia. You know, mentally."

"What's that mean?"

"All the drinking. And that shit at Woody's. The way he told us about Vietnam. It just wasn't normal."

"Is there a point to this?"

"I guess I'm not sure about Sal anymore."

"What?"

"He lied to you, Julia. He never left town at six."

I sat on the ground, cross-legged, put my head in my hands, spoke loudly: "Don't do this to me, David. I'm already falling apart."

Rachel hurried over. "Are you all right, Julia?"

"I'm a little upset about Sal." I pulled her into my lap.

She glanced up at me. "I'd hate to be in jail."

"If you were, I'd break you out." She was barefoot and I tickled her toes.

She let out a giggle. I stroked her hair for a moment. "Sweetheart, your Dad and I have to talk. Think you can go play with your horses for a little bit longer?"

"Daddy's helping you?"

I tried to hide the sarcasm in my voice. "He thinks he is."

Rachel kissed me on the cheek, then returned to the shade of the maple.

David looked troubled. "Julia, I want to believe Sal, but it's so damn confusing."

"Let the cops think like that. It's our job to prove Sal is innocent. Maybe it was just someone local, just a random robbery and murder?"

"Maybe."

"Maybe someone came with my father from Boston? A drinking buddy. Just an excursion for them, or something like that? Things got out of control?"

"Maybe."

I lay on the grass, looked up at the blue sky, thinking. A minute passed; then, David spoke quietly, as if to himself, "What if it was Sal?"

I stood up. "I don't believe you're saying that, David?"

"But, Julia, it's a—"

I moved closer to him. "Stop talking like that."

There was a long silence, then he said, "Of course. He's your brother."

"Damn right he is. And I know he's not a killer."

"I hear you."

"I want you to do more than that, David. Haven't you figured out that Italians are like Jews when it comes to family? Fiercely loyal."

"Even if they've killed someone?"

I lost it, began pacing in front of him, my voice angry. "Oh, aren't you self-righteous. You're mother's killing me with her disdain. And what are you doing about it? Same as me. You're standing by her even though she's a bitch."

He stood up, raised his hands in protest. "Don't say something you'll regret, Julia."

A long pause. "Sorry, I shouldn't have said that."

He came behind me, put his arms around me.

I pulled away, then turned to him. "I need to hear you say it, David. I need to hear you say Sal is innocent."

He said nothing. I kicked at the ground. "I'm out of here."

He let out a groan. "You're not hearing me right."

I hurried to the car.

He yelled after me. "Call me later, okay?"

Twenty-One

Campbell had phoned me, told me what time the state troopers were returning Sal's pickup truck. I was there in front of his apartment, waiting for them when they arrived. They weren't troopers at all. They were dressed in mechanic's uniforms, and said they worked at the police garage. One guy handed me he keys, then they left in the other car they had brought for the return ride.

Would I find anything of value to prove Sal's innocence? What were the chances? The police said they had already combed the truck for evidence. Well, I'd look anyway.

I climbed up into the back of the pickup truck. It was swept clean. I looked carefully in Sal's large metal chest, then inside his toolbox. Nothing. I went into the cab. Checked everywhere on the dash. Ash tray. Glove compartment. Nothing. I slid the seat forward, looked behind. Nothing. I returned the seat to its forward position. Checked the crease between the seat cushion and back. Nothing. Finally, I looked under the seat. There was a plastic shopping bag with the name: Old Town Groceries, Old Town, Maine. I dumped everything onto the seat. An empty coffee cup. An empty plastic sandwich container. A dirty napkin.

A candy bar wrapper. A few gum wrappers. No receipt, which is what I was looking for. I imagined the cops searched the bag, too.

I took a flashlight from the glove compartment, knelt down, and stuck my head under the seat. There, I saw a small piece of crumbled paper way in the back, inside the metal rail of the seat. Well-hidden. Easy enough to miss. I grabbed it, sat on the seat, unfolded and read it.

"Bingo," I said, using the expression my mother had used when she found something that had escaped her. The receipt said: Old Town Groceries, Old Town, Maine. Date: Day of my father's murder. Amount: $17.64. Last four numbers of the credit card: 8995. Had to be Sal's because he didn't let anyone else drive his pickup. I looked more closely at the receipt for the time—there it was—9:10 pm. *Bingo*, again. Sal couldn't have killed my father. He was at least an hour away from Acadia at the time of the murder.

A day later, I pulled out of the parking lot of the county jail in Ellsworth and headed towards Bar Harbor; then, I turned to Sal, who was sitting in the passenger seat, and asked, "So, how are you feeling?"

"Hasn't hit me yet."

"You look good." He was shaven and in a clean denim shirt and pants.

He ran his hand across his mouth. "Sure could use a drink."

"That's a joke, right? You're lucky you didn't detox in there."

"I wasn't that far gone."

"Come on Sal, you were drunk for days. Skipping work. Wouldn't even talk to me."

"Do you have to lecture me?" He slouched down in his seat.

"Damn right, I do. I hope jail taught you something. You got to mellow out, Sal. You had a crisis with Dad, and what did you do? You drank a lot. Acted just like him. Mean, sarcastic, angry."

He mumbled. "But I never killed him."

"People thought you did. Hello, that's why you were in jail."

"Okay, maybe I should cut back."

"Cut back? Don't you get it, Sal? You got to stop, period. We had a father who was an alcoholic. That means you're at risk, I'm risk. Every day you've got to carry that with you."

He cracked his knuckles, tapped his feet nervously on the car floor. "Think you could lighten up a little, Julia. Been locked up for a week. Feeling kind of low."

I glared at him, my eyes piercing. "Why the hell did you lie to me?"

"What are you talking about?"

"I found out you were at Woody's until eight."

"Who told you?"

"You owe me an explanation."

He reached behind his head, ran his hand along his pony tail, tugged on it. "Thought the cops might use it against me."

"You didn't trust me, did you?"

He shrugged.

"They don't come more loyal than me, Sal."

He let out a deep breath. "I know." He looked out the window, seemed lost in thought.

For me, the worst part of the drive was over, trying to get through to my brother, trying to set him on the right road. He was in many ways still a young kid without a mother, a father. No one to guide him. I didn't like the role, and I wasn't sure I was very good at it.

Now, came the good part of the ride. I took the receipt out of my handbag and gave it to him.

He looked at it, let out an astonished yell. "Goddamn. Where did you find it?"

I told him about his pickup truck, the crumbled paper in the rail underneath the seat. "It's all there, Sal. The date, the time, the town. There's no way you could've been in Bar Harbor at nine."

He let out a holler.

"Give it to Campbell tomorrow, okay? It's your insurance, in case something weird happens with McNamara's confession."

"Right. Things could still get screwed up." He put it in his wallet. "So, McNamara was an ex-con?"

"Breaking and entering. Apparently not a big time criminal."

"Dad didn't know?"

I turned off Route 1 and headed south on Route 3. "What did he care? McNamara was helping him out with errands. They were drinking buddies."

"Why the hell did they come to Bar Harbor?"

I felt my forehead pounding. Bad headache. I'd have to take an ibuprofen when I arrived home. "Might've been Dad's idea. Might've been McNamara's. Maybe Dad wanted to see where we lived? Maybe McNamara thought he would get away with killing him if they were far away from Boston? That was the Boston detective's theory. Maybe McNamara didn't even plan it ahead? Just two drunks in a fight that got out of control. Fact is—we'll never really know what happened. Guess McNamara wasn't smart enough to hide the crime. The bus driver saw him. He lost his lighter. End of story."

When we came into Trenton, I stopped for gas, and we bought some coffee and snacks. Back in the car, I took a long sip of coffee, then said to Sal. "There's more. Keough thinks McNamara wanted Dad's money. Dad never spent his veteran's checks when he was in the hospital. Had about $3,000. He must have told McNamara, must have hid the cash in his room. When McNamara returned to Boston, he took the money and bought a new TV, refrigerator, new clothes. The cops found those things in his studio, plus a lot of cash. McNamara wasn't getting that kind of money on unemployment."

I handed Sal my muffin, asked him to unwrap it. When he gave it back to me, I took a bite. "And McNamara stole a lot of jewelry from Dad's room. Cops said it was just costume jewelry, but Dad must have convinced McNamara it was the real thing, you know, trying to impress him. Keough said the cops are sending the jewelry to us, plus the cash that's left."

Sal let out a short laugh, said sarcastically, "Wow, our inheritance." He took out a pack of gum, offered me one. I shook my head. He took one for himself. "So, how did they get McNamara to confess?"

"Plea bargained. Guess he's hoping he'll get a reduced sentence. Told the cops he was drunk at the time." I felt some tears sliding down my cheeks, and I wiped them with my hands. "I hope he gets life. Nothing less. He killed our father. And for what? A few thousand dollars?" I breathed in and out slowly several times, trying to relax. I reached over, patted Sal's hand. "Right now, I'm just glad you're out."

He let out a loud sigh. "They had enough to send me up for years, didn't they?"

"You bet, but Keough pulled through in the end. So did the Boston cops. Josh said they issued a search warrant for McNamara's apartment as soon as they found out he had done time. Once they had him in jail, they knew he'd crack and give them a confession. He was detoxing and all. Was in awful pain. Wanted medication."

Sal stretched his arms upward, let out a groan. "Thank God."

"Oh, I have something else for you." I reached in my handbag, gave Sal a photocopy of the credit card receipt. "I have one too. Just in case."

Suddenly I felt cold, had goose bumps on my arms, and I rolled up the window. "You know, Sal, I still can't believe it...our father murdered. Doesn't seem possible."

Sal stroked his chin. "All I can say is he died like he lived."

We rode without talking for several minutes. Soon we crossed the bridge to Mt. Desert Island. Sal unbuttoned the top of his shirt, showed me the eagle feather he had strung around his neck. "Like you said, it brought me good luck. Gonna save it." He stuck his head out the window into the wind, his hair blowing wildly. After a minute, he pulled his head back in the car and asked, "Is Deb home today?"

I smiled. "She's waiting for you...And tomorrow, back to eagle duty, okay? They're waiting for you, too."

"Make that two blueberries," David said to the teenager behind the counter.

She scoped the ice cream into sugar cones and handed them to us. Soon we headed out the door onto Main Street. It was early evening, starting to get dark. Bar Harbor glowed yellow from the lantern lamps atop black metal posts. Even though it was a weekday night, there were a lot of tourists out. Why not? It was the perfect, warm summer evening, and many of the shops were still open. We passed Woody's. A bouncer stood at the front door, and the sounds of a rock band drifted into the street. When we came to the town pier, we sat on a wooden bench. Lights on the boats and cruise ships sparkled off the water. In the distance I saw the beacon of the Egg Rock lighthouse, whirling around. Faint evening stars began to emerge.

David tried to put his arm around me, but I pulled back. He said, "I can see you're upset with me."

"No shit. You need to make a big leap, David."

"A leap?"

"You love me, right?"

"Very much."

"And I love you. We're family, right?"

"Sure."

"That means Sal is your brother. That's the big leap."

He scratched the back of his neck, pondering. "I made a terrible mistake. You were right about Sal. I'm sorry."

I put my hands on top of my thighs, sat upright. "I felt like you abandoned Sal and me. Not trusting him, not believing he was innocent. It hurt. How do I know you won't do something like this in the future?"

He put his hand on top of mine. "It won't happen again. I've learned something from this."

"What's that?" I stood up, leaned against the railing on the pier.

"I'm ashamed to admit it."

"I'm listening."

A long pause. "I wasn't seeing Sal as an individual, for who he was. You know, my Dad was a successful businessman. What did I know about the working class? So, I didn't understand Sal, being a carpenter and all. He seemed macho and tough to me. I figured eventually he would screw up big time, especially with his drinking."

I gave him a puzzled look. "And you're embarrassed about that, not understanding him?"

He stood next to me at the railing, but he didn't look at me. "And... well...There weren't a lot of Italians in Portsmouth. Same for UNH. Mostly what I knew about Italian-Americans was from TV and movies. Mafia stuff. I put Sal in that category. I thought he would eventually do something criminal."

He took my hand again. "I'm sorry, Julia. My father taught me not to discriminate, but I was stereotyping Sal. That's why I misjudged him."

I moved away, faced him. "So, how did you figure that out?"

"Had a talk with my Dad. He helped me...I'm not insightful, like you, Julia. People's thoughts, feelings, emotions—they don't come easily for me."

"But you understand Rachel."

"Oh, I'm floundering half the time." He shook his head. "And look at Alice. I missed that by a mile."

I took a brush from my handbag, began brushing my hair. "Well, thanks for telling me. I understand it better, now...And I want to apologize again for calling your mother a bitch. I shouldn't have said that. I do like her, you know, her feistiness, her love for her family. But, as you know, I hate the way she treats me."

"I know," he said.

"Sorry for storming away last week."

"Yeah, Rachel was pretty upset. She thought you were staying the night."

"I'll talk to her." I looked at my watch. It was getting late. "I have to get to sleep soon. I'm exhausted, and I have to work tomorrow." I took David's hand, and we headed back up Main Street.

"Say, you're barely limping."

"It's getting better."

As we headed up the hill, I saw the park and bandstand to the left, the one David and I had retreated to on our first date. I pulled him towards it. We stood at the railing, looking below at the harbor and its lights. I squeezed his hand. "Seems like a century ago we were here."

"It was raining."

I moved closely against his body, gave him a long tender kiss. "And we kissed that day...Who would have guessed then what the future would bring? Not perfect by any means. You know, you get good things in life, but you have to take the bad along with the good. Don't you think?"

"You're asking me?" He held back a laugh. "Do I know how life works?" Then he laughed. "To tell you the truth, Julia, I'm hoping you'll teach me."

We headed back to David's van on Main Street. Along the way, he asked, "So, what's with Sal? He told me he doesn't want Deb to go to the funeral."

I shrugged. "It's a mystery to me."

"Think he's okay?"

I folded my hands, put them to my mouth. "The first night back he took Deb to Woody's. Had to see his old buddies. Told me he didn't drink much. But he doesn't get it. That's not the place for him anymore. I hope he realizes it."

We landed at Logan Airport at seven in the morning, then hurried through the crowded corridors to the car rental place. David and his father, Marc, were dressed in black suits, Sal in a gray one. I wore a purple silk dress and carried a bouquet of lilac flowers that I had picked from David's yard. A half hour later we drove past the last of the Boston skyscrapers and headed west to Milford on the Massachusetts Turnpike. I turned around to Sal in the back seat. “Got anything for the coffin.”

He reached into his backpack and handed me his old baseball glove. “I only have a few good memories of Dad. One of them is playing catch.”

“That’s a great gift, Sal.”

“Where the hell did you get this idea?” Sal asked.

“It’s a Native American custom.”

David steered the car with one hand, and with the other, gave me two toy horses, both chestnut mares. “They’re from me and Rachel. She thinks your father will get there faster on horses.”

We all laughed.

Then Marc handed me a silver chain with a Star of David. “Who knows? Your Dad may need it. God might be Jewish.”

We laughed again.

From my handbag I showed them a half dozen photographs I had gathered for my father. Then I held up his old penknife. “To fend off evil spirits.” Also, I had a pack of cigars and matches. And finally I passed around a small, white statue of the Virgin Mary, one that his mother had given me as a girl. “It glows in the dark.”

“Why don’t you give him a flashlight, too?” Sal asked.

“And the *Boston Herald*,” David said.

Everyone laughed. Was it irreverent? I doubted it. Things had been so hard the last few months; we deserved a few laughs.

As we turned south on Rte. 495, Marc reached his hand forward, put it on my shoulder. “Sorry Harriet didn’t come. Watching Rachel is probably the best thing for her. I hope you understand.”

When we arrived at the funeral home in Milford, I asked the owner, John Sanderson, to open the casket for me. Inside was my father’s body in a thick plastic bag. He wore a dark blue suit and had his hands folded on his chest. I placed the gifts alongside him. “Have a safe trip, Dad.”

Soon we entered the limo and drove a few blocks to St. Paul’s. The church hadn’t changed since I was a child: red brick walls and a wooden steeple, stained glass windows with religious scenes, and evergreen shrubs around the foundation.

Upon entering the church, I dipped my fingers into the marble pedestal filled with holy water, and I made the sign of the cross. I smelled the fresh wax on the wooden pews. I scanned the interior: plaster reliefs of the Stations of the Cross along the side walls, radiators that banged in the winter, and the marble altar in front with its lit candles and large flesh-colored statue of Christ on a wooden cross.

Where was everybody? No old neighbors or friends. Not even my father's sister had come, complaining about her arthritis. It was just like Sal had predicted.

I walked down the church aisle and went directly to the sacristy, a small room off the altar. I knocked. Father McBride answered the door. He had carefully combed gray-hair and wore a purple vestment. I shook his hand. "How was the trip?"

"A lot of traffic on 95, but I got a good night's sleep at the motel." Then, he blessed me, making a sign of the cross: "My deepest sympathy."

I returned to the front pew, where David, Marc and Sal were sitting. Within a few minutes I heard voices in the back. I turned, saw my uncle, Emil, my mother's brother, and his wife Joan with their daughter Rose, and Rose's children, Donna and Joseph. We met halfway down the aisle. Emil kissed me. "My condolences. Too bad he didn't die before he beat the hell out of my sister. I came for you guys, not for him."

Joan poked him. "Be respectful to the dead." She kissed and hugged me. "I'm so sorry. It's horrible the way he went. May his soul rest in peace."

"Thanks for coming." I squeezed her hand.

We returned to the pews. Sanderson rolled the casket down the aisle and rested it a few feet from the altar; then, the Mass began.

During the sermon Father McBride bypassed the pulpit, came directly to us in the front pew, and spoke in an intimate manner. "My dear friends. How are we to understand the paradoxes of life? Look at Francis, struggling with alcohol for so many years, but he just couldn't stay sober. Yet, who are we to judge? We pray that Jesus will understand Francis in a way that we find difficult, that He'll show mercy on his soul, that He'll..."

I glanced quickly around the church to see if anyone else had come. On the other side of the aisle was a bald, elderly man with eyeglasses in a short sleeve shirt. He smiled at me, and I returned the smile, but I didn't know who he was.

Halfway through the Mass, Father McBride came to the casket. Everyone stood up. He circled the coffin and swung a brass censer, spreading whiffs of aromatic smoke above the body. It was a cleansing ritual, one I knew my father would need if he were ever to enter paradise. I closed my eyes and prayed for him.

Later, Father McBride blessed the host and wine. "Take and eat this, all of you, for this is my body. Take and drink this, all of you, for this is the chalice of my blood..." I took David's hand and thought of the *sea of blood* of the six million.

After the Mass ended, we filed outside. The elderly man who had attended Mass approached me and smiled. "You probably don't remember me. My name's Stephen Wawszkiewicz." He shook my hand, then called Sal over and shook his hand, too. "I knew your father in high school. Later your Dad and I were in the same platoon during the war. We saw a lot. Too much. But when we were on leave, we had a lot of fun. I know after the war he caused plenty of problems for you children and Maria. I'm sorry for all the trouble he caused." Tears came into Wawszkiewicz's eyes. He took a piece of paper from his shirt pocket. "Here's my phone number and address. After things have settled, give me a call." Then he shook our hands and left.

At the cemetery I stepped out of the limo, clutching the bouquet of lilac flowers. David and Sal held my arms and walked me to the open grave. Four veterans dressed in tan military uniforms hauled the casket out of the hearse, covered it with an American flag and carried it to the gravesite.

When the service began, we stood near the casket. Father McBride held a crucifix on a pole, and prayed loudly: "Oh Lord, we beg You to free the soul of Your servant, Francis, from every link to sin, then, when raised up from death for the glorious resurrection..."

I whispered to David. "Thanks for being here. I know it's not easy."

Off to the right I saw the lichen-covered gravestone of my grandparents. I prayed to my grandmother: *Don't worry anymore, Grandma. Your son is at peace.*

Father McBride sprinkled the casket with holy water, then gave a thumbs-up sign to the veterans.

"At—ten—tion," the sergeant shouted, and the soldiers lifted their rifles onto their shoulders and saluted. They froze in this position, while another veteran in the distance near a pine tree played "Taps" on a bugle.

When the bugler stopped, the sergeant yelled: "Prepare to fire." The veterans lifted their rifles into the air. "Rea—dy." A pause. "Fire." The shots snapped in the wind. They fired again, and again.

Suddenly, Sal burst into great sobs, his whole body heaving. I began crying too, held onto Sal's arm.

Soon the veterans set their rifles against a gravestone and moved to the casket. Slowly, they folded up the flag. They gave it to me; then, they lowered the coffin into the ground.

I wept openly. After a few moments I divided the bouquet of lilacs and threw half in the grave. *Arrivederci, Dad.* Then, I began moving away from the grave. I was grieving, but I was also feeling something else. I know I wasn't supposed to think it, and I would never say it out loud to anyone, but I realized at that moment that my father's death brought me more relief than pain.

I looked back at the grave. David grabbed a handful of dirt, dropped it on top of the casket. Sal wiped the tears from his eyes and did the same. All at once we trudged towards the cars.

With wide arms Joan gathered everyone together. "We've got food and drinks at our place. I won't take no for an answer."

"Did you say food?" Sal's face lit up.

I took him by the arm. "Say Sal, I was hoping we might visit Mom's grave first."

"But I'm starving."

I raised my eyebrows. "Tough choice. Your mother or your stomach."

"Oh, all right." Sal lowered his head.

I turned to Joan. "We won't be long."

She gave me a hug. "Take your time."

A half hour later Sal, David, Marc and I pulled into St. John's Cemetery on Lake Quinsigamond in Worcester. We milled around my mother's grave, and I pointed out the inscription on the grey tombstone: "A loving mother, a loyal friend and a hard worker. She'll live forever in our hearts."

"That's beautiful." David put his arm around me. "I wish I had known her."

Down on my knees I carefully arranged the other half of the lavender lilac flowers at the base of the stone.

Sal patted me on the back. "They look real pretty. Just like the ones from our old house. I bet Mama's smiling down on us, right now." *Little do you know, Sal, the true story about the lilacs. But who am I to tell you that? We all need some happy memories in our lives, yes?*

For a few minutes we stood silently around the grave, paying our respects. Soon Sal grew restless and drifted away down a gravel road. Marc too wandered off for a little while. David picked up a pebble and put it on top of my mother's marker. I knew this was a Jewish custom, so I searched for a small rock and set it next to his.

Then, I kissed the top of my mother's gravestone, took David's hand, and walked towards the lake. Along the way I noticed a cluster of purple and pink asters in a grassy meadow near the edge of the cemetery. We moved towards them, and as we came closer, I saw orange monarchs gliding from aster to aster.

I knelt among the flowers. I watched the butterflies drink nectar. I heard my mother's voice. I heard the high whistle of an eagle soaring in the sky. And I breathed in the rich odors of summer's ripeness.

Twenty-Two

When I finished typing the report, it was already dark outside. I closed up my office and headed down the hallway. Deb's light was on, and the door was open. I poked my head inside. "Still here?" She glanced up from her desk and lifted up a thick document, tried to smile. "You know how it goes. They want my comments tomorrow. How about you? Going home?"

"Time for tea and a hot bath."

All at once Deb's face grew fearful. "Say Julia, have you got a few minutes? I've been wanting to talk to you about Sal."

I slipped into the chair next to her desk. "Problems?"

"Yes and no. Don't get me wrong. Sal's a wonderful guy. He can be very affectionate and understanding, and when he is, I feel great." Then, she looked at me, her face vulnerable. "But lately he's been real distant, and I think he's pulling away. If we were just friends, it wouldn't matter. But I'm in love with him." She lowered her head. "I don't know what to do."

I touched her hand. "Have you tried to talk to him?"

She crossed her arms, puffed her cheeks. "He gets mad. Says talking just complicates things."

"Come on up," Sal yelled. I found him sitting on the sofa in his living room, eating a sausage sub and watching TV. I sat next to him. "We've got to talk, Sal."

"Something wrong?"

I nodded.

He turned off the TV.

I locked my gaze onto his. "Deb's afraid you're going to leave her."

He squinted at me. "She shouldn't be talking to you about those things."

"Why not?"

"That's personal stuff between her and me."

"Deb's my friend." My face tightened. "I'm worried for her, and for you. Are you thinking about breaking this off?"

He shrugged and looked away; then he took another bite of his sub.

"Would you put that damn thing down for a minute?"

"For Chri...for God's sake, Julia. A guy's got to eat."

"You remembered."

"See, I'm trying."

"You did good." I sat back in the sofa, closed my eyes for a moment. "Let's get back to Deb. Try to understand this, Sal. There's an awful pattern to the way we DeCarloes fall in love. After the fire dims, we usually run." I reached out to him. "Is that what you want to do?"

He seemed unsure for a moment, then shook his head.

"So what are your choices?"

He ran his fingers through his hair. "How come I always feel like I'm suffocating every time I get close to a woman?"

"You tell me."

"It's not Deb." He leaned forward, put his elbows on his knees, his chin in his hands. "She gives me a lot of room. We have great sex. She's been telling me she loves me. I wish I could tell her the same, but I can't." He stood up, moved towards the kitchen area at the other end of the room. "Can I get you something?"

I stood up, pointed my finger at him. "You're not getting a beer."

He smirked. "Coffee. Want one?"

"Oh." I scratched my head. "Well, sure." I moved to the kitchen table.

He poured two cups, put a bowl of chips between us and sat down. "I wish Dad had never came back. He brought nothing but trouble."

"You're right." I took a sip of coffee, looked at him over the top of the cup. "But, you're wrong, too. He forced us to face our past. Look at how much we've learned about ourselves. He showed us who we don't want to be. We have alternatives, Sal. Are you up to it?"

"Sounds like Odette's talking."

"No, it's me."

He lowered his eyes. "Well, maybe you can find something positive about him, but he didn't help me one fucking bit. I feel worse than I have in years."

I reached out across the table. "Is that why you're confused about Deb?"

"I know what you're thinking." He tapped his fingers on the table.

"What?"

"It's my childhood shit getting in the way."

"Is it?"

He rubbed his forehead. "I can see how talking about that stuff in therapy has worked for you, but it ain't for me." His voice was sarcastic. "Maybe it's just my fate to keep screwing up."

"Is that what you want?"

He hesitated, let out a big breath. "No, I want a wife, kids."

"How are you going to do that?

"I don't know." He turned away from me.

I moved my chair closer to him. "You found a good woman in Deb. It's not easy to meet someone who likes you, all of you."

"I hear you." He shifted in his chair, hunched over the table, his hands folded on top of his coffee.

I put my hand on his shoulder. "Odette says she's going to retire soon. Doesn't want to take on any new clients. But I bet she'll see you if I asked her. She's a great therapist."

I felt his body tense up, saw tears in his eyes.

He covered his face. "I'm so goddamn tired of being lonely."

All at once I lifted up my hand and slapped him on the back. He lunged forward, almost knocked over his coffee.

I had never hit Sal before. What was coming over me? Hitting was crossing the line. I knew that. I promised myself I'd never do it again.

He looked at me in stunned amazement. "What the hell."

"Therapy won't kill you."

He spoke through clenched teeth. "You didn't have to hit me."

I put my hand on his shoulder. "I'm sorry. I shouldn't have done that. I'm just trying to get through to you, and I don't know how."

I leaned towards him, my voice gentle. "Don't you see, Sal? You're afraid to ask for help. You think it'll destroy your manhood or something. Sure it's painful to look at yourself in therapy, but in the end it'll make you stronger. Oh Sal, stop acting proud like Dad. For God's sake, ask for some help so you can start living."

He looked like a hurt pup. He lifted his cup and took a sip. He gazed at me. Bit his lip. Stared away. A minute passed like this: a glance, a sip, a look away. Then he spoke, softly. "Maybe you're right. Give Odette a call for me, okay?"

I gave him a huge hug. He wiggled free of me. I rested back in my chair, put my hands to my face and whispered, "At last."

When I woke before dawn, David lay asleep next to me in bed. I kissed his eyes, his lips. He stirred, looked at me, asking, "Leaving?"

I nodded.

He sat up. "You know I'd love to go with you."

"Next year, okay? This time I want to be alone."

"But Sal's going to be there."

"No, he and Deb are going kayaking off Pretty Marsh."

I eased him down and pulled the blanket over his chest. "Bye, sweetheart. I'll see you and Rachel after work."

"No. Wait Julia. I have something for you." His voice sounded sleepy. He rose from the bed, clad only in his underwear, and went to his dresser. He returned with a small box wrapped with an orange ribbon.

I sat on the bed, opened it. "Oh my God." Inside was a topaz gem set in a gold ring.

He knelt before me and looked into my eyes. "Please, marry me."

I was in a state of shock. Yes, I had thought about marrying him, but to answer him at this early hour, in his underwear, just before I went off to work? I didn't know what to say.

He sat next to me on the bed, took my hand. "I know this isn't the best moment. I had a better plan. I wanted to give it to you, later, in the eagle tower. But you want to be alone, and now, I just can't wait any longer. I have to know."

I ran my fingers through his hair, caressed his cheek. I had tears in my eyes. "You're adorable." A pause. "Yes."

"Yes?"

"Yes."

He looked a little stunned. "I wasn't sure what you would say, you know, after I let you and Sal down.

"Yes."

He pushed me down on the bed, climbed on top of me. We were laughing, and I was crying, too. He ran his lips over mine, lingered; then, all at once he sat up. "Try it on."

I put it on, lifted my hand in the air to admire it. Morning sunlight was coming through the window. The ring sparkled reddish-orange. "It's beautiful."

He looked at it closely. "So, why did you want topaz?"

"You remembered, hey?"

"Of course. So why topaz?"

"Love the color, and it was named after an island in the Red Sea."

"Really?"

"Research, you know."

"Do you like it?"

I held it up for both of us to see. "I love it. Thank you." I gave him a long kiss, our mouths wet. He eased me down on the bed. I felt him becoming hard, felt his hands touching my breasts, my thighs.

"David, darling. Slow down." I sat up. "I love you, and I really want to marry you. You're the best. But this will have to wait until later. It's a big day for me, you know. Time to release the eaglets."

He rolled on his back, a dejected look.

"Later. I promise...my house...for lunch, okay?"

He stood up, put his pants on. Then, he gave me a wide grin. "No problem. I can wait." He headed to the kitchen. "Want a coffee?"

I nodded, put my clothes on, but before I went into the kitchen, I stepped quietly into Rachel's room. She was still asleep, her arms wrapped around her panda bear. I held the topaz ring near her face. *See love. This is my commitment to you, too.*

An hour later I climbed the ladder of the eagle tower at Seal Cove and looked through the one-way glass mirror at the two eaglets, Harriet and Francis. I whistled in a high pitch, and they perked up. "No food today. You've got more important things to do."

I pressed my face against the glass and watched them. I tried to memorize every detail about them: the pattern on Harriet's black and yellow beak; Francis's huge tail with extra-large, brown feathers. The eaglets shuffled back and forth on their wooden perches, pecked at one another. Harriet jumped down, paced around the cage, pulled at the bars with her talons.

"I'm coming." I walked towards the front of the cage. The eaglets had never seen me before; they only knew my voice. When they saw me, they retreated, cowered in the corner. I whistled, and they relaxed.

I swept my arms out to the sea and the mountains of Acadia, and spoke softly to them. "There's your new home. Remember to come back someday. Build a nest. Raise your young ones here." The eaglets gazed at me with their yellow-gray eyes. *If only I could speak their language?*

I cautiously stepped forward on the wooden catwalk. It had rained during the night, and now the platform was wet. Suddenly, my foot slid a little. I held onto the bars of the cage and moved slowly to the front. The catwalk was only a foot wide with no railings. I looked down dizzily fifteen feet to the ground.

The eaglets bobbed their heads, watching me with one eye and then the other. I removed a bar of the cage. They looked surprised. After I took out a second bar, I went to the back of the platform.

Harriet and Francis inched to the front. First Harriet, and then Francis stepped onto the catwalk. All at once, without hesitation, one after the other, they leapt off the platform, stretched out their wings, and glided onto a large branch in a nearby maple tree.

I hurried to the front for a better look. In an instant, my foot slipped out from under me. I reached up, grabbed the top of the cage, and felt a sharp jab in my palm. I steadied myself, then looked at my hand. There was a small puncture and blood. A few drops of blood fell onto the floor.

In a flash, it came back to me. The blood in the snow, the pearl handle knife, the steep cliff. I ran my finger along the two white scars on my wrist. It seemed so long ago, like another lifetime. I gave out a little laugh. *You were right, Mama. I'm getting another chance.*

I pressed a handkerchief against the puncture. After a minute, I checked the wound. It had stopped bleeding.

Taking my binoculars, I watched the eaglets in the maple tree. They preened their wing feathers for a while; then, they jumped off the branch in unison, pumped their broad wings, and climbed into the sky. Soon they soared across the water towards Moose Island. I felt my body lift up with them, weightless, free.

About the Author

G. J. Supernovich's short story, "By the Monongahela" was published in *Potato Eyes.* Supernovich's journalistic articles have appeared in the *Boston Globe, Boston Herald, EPA Journal, Tufts Journal, Tufts Criterion, Sanctuary* and *MetroWest Daily News.* Although currently a resident of Vergennes, Vermont, Supernovich always happily vacations each summer on the Atlantic seacoast of Maine, New Hampshire, and Massachusetts.